3 August, 2012

Dear Alex

Live your quest!

Quest, Inc.

Can you buy a new life?

A Novel ☞ W9-BYG-968

Justin Cohen

Happy Birthday

Looking forward to getting to know you.

Justin

TP

TELEMACHUS PRESS

Cover Designed by Karrie Ross and Claire van Niekerk

Cover Art
Copyright © istockphoto/9333114/Vetta Stock Photo

Published by Telemachus Press, LLC
http://www.telemachuspress.com

Visit the author website:
http://www.justinpresents.com

ISBN: 978-1-937387-29-7 (eBook)
ISBN: 978-1-937387-30-3 (Paperback)

Version 2012.03.29

10 9 8 7 6 5 4 3 2 1

Book Reviews

Quest, Inc. isn't a self-help book, yet it is the most useful book on the topic that I have ever read. It contains two vital elements omitted in most self-improvement literature: honesty and balance. Neither extreme optimism, nor extreme pessimism are accurate, when it comes to personal transformation. Positive change is possible, yet hardly ever as simple and linear as it is made out to be. Quest, Inc. takes the reader on a refreshing journey that demonstrates the struggles of those who aim to improve their lives, as well as those who aim to help them. This book should be required reading before you embark on a self-improvement program. It will improve your odds of success.

-Niel Malan, CEO, Leverage Global

Justin Cohen has written a winner! Some of the lines are so well written, I just wanted to highlight them—so that I could look them up again and refer to them. I thoroughly enjoyed the way he incorporated lessons about wealth, self-worth, image, death, spirituality, love, growth, goals, taking action and genuine success into an easy-to-read and enjoyable story. He's certainly found a successful balance between making the reader think, contemplate their life, laugh and well up with emotion. I did not want to put it down!

-Lauren Fleiser, Creator Trutrepreneur™

Besides having over a decade of experience as a human potential practitioner, Justin Cohen knows how to weave his deep insight into a powerful and inspiring story. He skillfully reveals the truth about personal transformation: it's a rocky quest—for everyone, including the experts. This is a compelling read and once you're hooked, almost impossible to put down.

-Paul du Toit, Past President, Professional Speaker's Association, (RSA)

I was captivated. I started reading the book Friday evening and, despite a busy weekend, I finished it on Sunday! If I had to summarize it in one word— fantasticamazingbrilliant! I will be buying this book as a gift to give to my staff, friends and family.
-Paul Kempff, MD, FFG Risk Solutions

I absolutely loved it! I couldn't put it down. My only criticism is I'm getting antsy waiting for the next one. It's innovative and packed full of knowledge, insight and humor. Such a brilliant concept!
-Shira Shakti, Graduate Student, UCT

An absolute blast! A powerful story with nuggets of wisdom on every page. One of the characters has changed my consciousness forever.
-Lusan Cohn, Senior Administrator, Milk South Africa

So much more fascinating than a normal self-help book. I loved the fast-paced, TV drama style and how each story impacted the other. I couldn't stop reading, and finished it in one sitting!
-Hannelie Snow, Communication and Brand Officer

What I absolutely love is the way this book captures the essence of progress: it's a bumpy ride and things don't just happen the instant you change your attitude or approach. I think people are growing tired of quick fixes that promise the world. Quest, Inc, with an emphasis on being truthful and not just telling people what would make them feel better, is what this disenchanted world really needs right now. Justin Cohen has demonstrated a true depth of understanding of transformation and human potential. His insights and life lessons are eye-opening and liberating.
-Lishen Nair, Entrepreneur

Table of Contents

The greatest gift a story has to give
is the lesson of a life we didn't have to live.

Quest, Inc.

Can you buy a new life?

1
Falling Up

BLOG

Can you buy a new life?

Victoria Holt

Investigative Journalist

Over ten billion dollars. That's what the world spends on personal development programs, coaching and self-help books
every year. *The Power of Positive Thinking, Awaken the Giant Within,
The 7 Habits of Highly Effective People*—do any of these books and
programs actually work? Is health, wealth and happiness the
birthright of us all, or is *Think and Grow Rich* really just a way to
make the author rich? I'm Victoria Holt and I believe it's time to
put all that self-help hype on trial. Let's see if the gurus really
can change a life. Or not. With more than a bit of arm-twisting,
I've convinced five leading personal development experts to put
their powers to the test. Sage or snake oil salesman? See for
yourself.

Read Post | Comments (289)

1

FOUR MONTHS AND five days before Victoria's blog appeared in the *Huffington Post* was the worst day of Robert Rivera's life. His wife, Roxanne Stewart—grateful to have kept her own name— walked down a sweeping staircase, her slender frame dragging two big, wheeled bags. Clonk-clonk-clonk, they crashed onto the granite stairs, each collision deepening her determined glare. Halfway down, she and her bags drew to a premature halt. It had not been her intention, but she turned to the wall, letting her eyes wander over a series of gilt-framed photographs. In one, a young man with olive skin raised a massive barbell above his head. In another was the same man, his muscle-ripped torso glistening on the cover of *Men's Health*. There were more photos, all celebration and acclaim. But nothing quite like the one in the middle: five people, including the President of the United States, and him, eyes sparkling with the sudden realization of how far he had come. Underneath the frame, a brass plaque read:

White House Dinner
Acknowledgement of Service

Roxanne wondered what she was doing, staring at the past, a past as flimsy as a fairy tale. It was over, gone. And yet there she stood, staring into the dead snapshot of her husband's eyes . . . She startled. Who knew how many times she had looked at that photograph, but only now, on what would be her last, did it hit her: *That night was the start of the fall.* As if from that lofty height, the only way was down. *What happened?* She shook her head. The time for explanations, for discussions, for interventions, was over. She had tried, God knows she had tried.

Roxanne looked down the twisting stairs. Robert had once said he couldn't live without her. *What if he . . . ?* With a flick of her head, she bounced back a few strands of auburn hair that had fallen into her face and continued the last few clonks downstairs. She couldn't live *with* him. If she didn't leave now he would take her down. As she set down her bags by the door, she took a deep breath, preparing herself, and turned. Through the entrance hall, in the lounge, squeezed and slumped unnaturally low in a brown leather couch, was the man who used to be the man in the photos. His head was drooping, so that his chin nestled in the fat rolls of his neck. Budweiser cans lay scattered around his feet. As he lay there snoring, the vibrations grated through his clogged sinuses into the echo chamber of the hallway. A dark, wet patch had seeped across his crotch. Roxanne thought she might cry; but as she opened the door and dragged out her bags, another feeling came over her: *relief.*

The following morning, Robert awoke to the sun blasting through his eyes into his dehydrated brain. He stumbled upstairs to the bathroom, no easy task, since at least half the weight he used to lift above his head was now hanging around his waist. Walking through the main bedroom, his wife's open wardrobe drew his bleary eyes into focus—the shelves were empty. They'd been robbed. "Roxanne!" He opened *his* wardrobe, but all his things were there. "Roxanne," he called again, with less conviction. He sat down on the bed; the wood groaned under his weight. Robert stared out at her empty wardrobe, feeling like he was going to be sick. Despite her expressions of discontent and her attempts to transform him—a suggested consultation with one of his old colleagues, a weekend at the fat farm—she had never threatened to leave and it never crossed his mind that she would; but like suddenly discovering that a persistent, dull headache was a brain tumor, it all added up. He looked up to see his reflection in the full-length dressing mirror. This was the man who *Cosmopolitan* magazine had once ranked one of the top ten sexiest on the planet. Now, he felt especially oppressed by the misshapen hulk, as if it was sitting on his former self. Before turning away, something scribbled in red lipstick caught his attention. Pressing down on the bed, he raised himself up to get closer. "What happened to the man I married?" it read. He turned to the bathroom. "What happened to unconditional love?"

Having run the water extra hot, Robert lay squeezed into a white porcelain, ball and claw bathtub in the center of a luxuriously large marble bathroom. His fat arms dangled out over the sides like a pair of giant sausages. Any soothing self pity was soon wrung out by one overwhelming question: *How am I going to live without her?*

Her love aside, his life was at stake. She shopped, cooked, organized, managed, administered, *everything* . . . she did it all.

A drop of water plopped into the tub. Silence. He suddenly felt eerily like a little boy who had been abandoned by his mother. They would find him months from now, wild and unkempt, the house chaotic and stinking. Steam floated up over him, a quieting blanket for his anxious thoughts.

The doorbell rang. *She's back!* Robert looked up, feeling like a convicted man who'd gotten a last minute reprieve. Of course she never would have left him. She loved him. She just wanted to make a point. Now, they would talk it through and sort it all out.

He leaned his hands on the side of the bath to lift himself up, but nothing happened. This was the first bath he'd had in over a year; he had taken to showering instead. Now he remembered why. Robert pressed down harder, trying to squeeze his body out—nothing. The doorbell rang again.

"I'm coming!" he shouted. Just now, she'd think he was playing hard to get and leave for good.

He kept pushing, but his fat bulk wouldn't budge. The doorbell rang again. *"Damn it!"* Robert began to panic, as he wriggled and splashed, doing his utmost to get free. After several vain attempts, he finally managed to heave himself onto his side and push up, so that one leg was out. With a grunt and an upward thrust, the rest followed. Slap! Robert lay sprawled on the floor, a beached whale. Leaning on the toilet, he leveraged himself up, wrapped a towel around his waist and shuffled downstairs as fast as his legs could waddle.

"I'm coming!"

He opened the door, dripping with water.

On his doorstep stood the sheriff and a stern looking man in a black suit.

"Are you Mr. Rivera?" the sheriff asked.

"Yes," Robert replied.

"Sir, you were notified of a judgment against this property and ordered to vacate. You have failed to do so. By the law of California, we have come to execute your eviction."

Robert had been aware he was going bankrupt, but he had expected things to somehow sort themselves out. He had his accountant. He had his lawyer. Wasn't that their job? Sorting out the numbers, holding back the pack of wolves baying for their pound of his considerable flesh? Well, they had failed. For a few moments, it was comforting to believe it was their fault. But as he felt himself finally flung from the precipice, it provided little consolation and required too much energy to pretend it was true. They had told him his income was drying up, that he had to cut down his spending, pay off his debts. They'd even bought him time by restructuring his debt—whatever that meant. And now? His overstretched lifeline had finally snapped. Was this why Roxanne had left? For richer or poorer, just not in bankruptcy?

He packed his bags and left the house. Walking anywhere further than the fridge had become an exotic activity. Now, Robert had to do it wheeling two large Louis Vuitton suitcases that kept knocking into his ankles. Like a drowning fish, he had to keep stopping to gasp for air. Unpleasant as it was, drowning on dry land gave him some reprieve from confronting his predicament.

Within an hour, Robert had dragged himself out of the leafy suburbs. Any pang of remorse was dampened by the anticipation of his favorite drug—food. Walking into a cheap diner, with luggage better suited for a five-star hotel, he sat down on a red, vinyl couch at a booth, dug his hand into his pocket and pulled out a couple of crumpled notes and a few coins. An energetic, smiling waitress bounced up.

"Good morning," she sang. "What can I get you?" Her sunny yellow and white uniform was clean and crisp, and her hair was pulled back in a neat ponytail. For a moment, he wondered what it would be like to be her, pretty and carefree. What a paradise that would be.

"I want breakfast. How much can I get for this?" He pushed the money across the table without looking up. Increasing social paranoia had kept him at home for most of the past two years.

"Three fried eggs, bacon, toast, flap jacks in syrup, a couple of sausages, a super-sized double choc muffin and bottomless coffee. Actually, you can have four fried eggs and ..." she fingered the money, working it out, "and four sausages." She flashed him a perky smile, as if she'd come to the end of a showbiz number.

"That's what I'll have," he said.

With Miss Sunshine gone, the specter of what he would do after this meal nibbled on the edge of his consciousness. There were people he could call for help, but he knew he wouldn't. A man had his dignity. He looked out the window, unseeing. Over the past three years, the future had become a dumping ground for everything he knew he had to do. He had surrendered to immediate gratification, a fact he ennobled with the thought that he was living each day as if it was his last. Today, it really felt like it was.

A short while later, the waitress trotted over with his pile of food. He briefly acknowledged her before digging in. Not long after, he was lapping up the final scraps with a faint hint of nausea inching in.

"Excuse me, sir?"

He looked up. A teenager in a red baseball cap stood alongside him, having broken away from his group of friends, who sat looking on. Robert's stomach turned, but he managed to suppress the urge to vomit.

"You're the *Flatten Your Fat* guy?"

Robert didn't reply.

Two of the teenager's friends walked over.

"Told you," he said, turning to them. "You owe me ten bucks."

"No kidding," one of them replied, and then asked Robert, "What happened to flatten your fat?"

"He decided to *fatten* his fat," another boy whispered, more audibly than he'd intended.

"Sorry, bro," the young man, who had first walked over, said, trying to suppress a giggle. "He's our resident comedian, but I got to ask you, what *did* happen?"

"The guy ate half of California is what happened," Joker-Boy said, dropping his halfhearted attempt at discretion.

This was a preview of life without Roxanne—fending for himself. It was already even grimmer than he'd imagined. Robert got up, kept his head down and cut through them.

"Careful," Joker-Boy said, "he might sit on you."

"Don't be an A-hole," the first boy said. And then as they walked out, "You owe me ten bucks."

Robert paid at the counter and turned to go. A young woman who had seen what had happened was standing in front of him. Her small, round face perched upon a plump, round body, resembled a blob of cream on a bun.

"Not so easy," she said in a soft, high voice.

"Huh?" he replied.

"Eat less, exercise more, right?" She had a fixed smile. "I followed your whole low carb, high protein diet for a while and lost a bit and now . . ." She looked down at her body with a little self-deprecating laugh, before looking up again. "I'm heavier than I was before. It's not your fault, just made me feel like a bit of a failure. In a way, it's nice to see that it's not so easy for you, either."

She took his big pudgy hand in her own, and with the same self-deprecating smile, put a folded piece of paper in his hand and walked off.

Robert waited a couple of minutes before leaving the diner. She had written him a note. He opened the first garbage can he came to, dropped it in, and walked off. Nothing she had written could make him feel better; everything about her was a reminder of how far he had fallen. But after a few steps, his curiosity got the better of him. Maybe she was a kindred spirit who, right in his hour of need, had shared something wise. He turned around and went back. Scratching around in the bin like a homeless man—which it occurred to him he

was—he found the note and opened it. There were just three words:
Big Fat Hypocrite.

Life, for most people, was lived forwards and understood backwards.
Every crisis came with a question: *How did it come to this?* One mentally
back-pedaled, trying to find anything that looked vaguely like a cause.
Understand the cause and one could control the effect, in theory.
Sometimes, cause finding became its own morbid entertainment, a
depressive spiral of rumination, leading to blame or self-blame.
Robert had been depressed for years, but not because he was stuck in
the "paralysis of analysis," he seldom thought about his situation. Instead, like an animal stuck in a cage, he had simply existed in a state
of habituated discomfort. Now that he had woken to a full-blown
crisis, despite some initial reflexive blaming, the search for explanations held no allure. If a perfectly functioning appliance stopped
working, one might take it to an electrician to find the cause, so it
could be fixed. If the appliance had been smashed twelve times with
a jackhammer, why bother? Robert felt like he'd been smashed twelve
times with a jackhammer. He wasn't asking why. Soon enough, others would. Certain reasons arouse more sympathy than others. Whatever the reason, getting smashed twelve times with a jackhammer is
never a lot of fun.

Robert walked down a grey street under a grey sky, still wheeling his
incongruously shiny silver bags. He now saw that his wife had done
the right thing to leave him. Love was not unconditional. The condi-
tions had changed, had deteriorated irretrievably. Knowing that
didn't stop the desperate, needy longing he felt for her, gnawing at
his insides like a rabid dog. How could he live without the warmth of
her body coiled into his, or her smell, or her smile that twinkled like
starlight, even through her disappointment? How could he live

without hearing the special name she had for him, murmured in a tone sweeter than music? Without her love, his soul would starve to death. Which brought him to an obvious question: If she couldn't live with him, how could *he* live with him?

Robert passed by a couple of homeless men and offered them his suitcases. They gave him a skeptical look, but didn't refuse the offer. He soon turned into the doorway of a derelict building. The lift had an "Out of Order" sign. Robert took the stairs. Each floor up, he had to stop and rest. He was sweating profusely and had a stitch in his side. Realizing that if he didn't rest, he might have a heart attack, he pushed himself harder. After a few vigorous steps, his body refused. Surrendering to fatigue, he just carried on, plodding up.

At the top, Robert stood before a doorway leading to one of those vast open wastelands in the sky, the undeveloped roof of a building. He found a couple of old Coca-Cola crates, stacked them against the perimeter wall, and climbed up. Peering over the top, he looked down at the road far below. A quick shot of adrenaline helped to smother some of his self-loathing. It helped that he was tall, but it still took some effort to pull himself up and over the wall. Easing out onto a broad ledge on the other side, Robert turned to face the city. A light, cool wind flapped against his face. Without looking down, he sensed the vast space between him and the street. He inched to the edge, as he began a countdown, "Three, two, one . . ."

His body would not obey the command. With no barrier between him and obliteration, he was suddenly gripped by vertigo far more torturous than the self-loathing he had been feeling. *Just dive,* he told himself, like into a cold swimming pool. "Three, two, one . . . Ahg!"

Robert was now even more disgusted with himself. Never mind the courage to live; he didn't have the courage to die. He wanted to be back on the ground. Turning around, he tried to climb back over the wall; but this time, with no crate, he couldn't heave his weight up.

Wasn't that a sign? He had tried to reverse his fate and it was impossible. He was destined to die, like this, today.

Carefully, he sat down on the ledge and leaned against the wall. Even if he wavered in its execution, Robert was clear about what he had chosen to do. It wasn't just the loss of Roxanne. It wasn't just the loss of his home, or his reputation. He had long ago lost himself, or at least the best part of himself. All his passion and purpose, his will and skill, his dogged determination, his generosity of spirit and joy for life were gone, long gone. What would death bring? A new world, or no world? No world was better than this world. Or was it? Was nothing better than something? *Something* still had the seeds of possibility. He shook his head. You had to water those seeds with hope, and that had dried up a long time ago.

It was the muffled noise of people far below that awoke him from his thoughts. A small crowd had assembled. The police were drawing up to the curb. He shifted to the edge of the ledge and peered down.

An officer hollered through a megaphone, "Sir, do not move! We are sending someone up to help you!"

Robert could now add shame to his cocktail of vertigo and self-loathing. He hated the idea of dying in front of all these people; but when his body lay broken on the ground, he wouldn't know the difference.

A slim, striking, dark-skinned woman stepped out of a black, luxury sedan parked just beyond the barricade set up by the police. She strode quickly up to the officer with the megaphone, exchanging a few words before making her way through the front door of the building. Hitching her pencil skirt, she raced up the stairs, two at a time. Following Robert's path, she ran across the roof, stopping briefly to catch her breath.

This was Dr. Carter King's eighth suicide encounter, and still she felt all the trepidation of her first. For her, the sanctity of life meant she was on a holy mission, although she kept that private. She was here as a psychologist, one whose mother had killed herself. Not counting her mother, she had lost one, off the Colorado Street Bridge in Pasadena. He had jumped just as she was making her way across to him. She had learned to manage her remorse, but right now the memory sent a wave of heat up her chest.

Carter pulled her black hair back behind her shoulders and made for the perimeter wall, where Robert had stacked the crates. Climbing up and leaning over, she saw a man huddled against the wall on the other side.

"I know you are desperately upset right now and death seems better than this pain, but I absolutely promise you, if you let me help you . . ."

Robert whipped his head round, "Carter?"

She scrutinized the man's face.

"It's Robert," he said.

"Robert?" Carter didn't know if she was more shocked that it was her old colleague on top of this building or that it was her old colleague inside this blubbery body. He looked like he'd been stretched out into a caricature. His skin had a plump, waxy appearance, like one of the less realistic statues at Madame Tussauds.

On the rare occasion when they had spoken, it had been over the phone, and Robert had implied he was on a sabbatical. Some sabbatical. Realizing her facial muscles had become constricted with fright, she deliberately released them. How could this have happened to Robert Rivera? How could this have happened to her friend? She had to hold her expression from remolding into pity. That was something the Robert she knew would definitely not tolerate.

"What are you doing here?" he asked.

"I'm a volunteer. What are you doing here?"

"Taking in the view."

She looked out at a big, ugly building across the road. "Beauti-ful," she said.

"Can I request a suicide counselor who isn't a co-recipient of a Presidential Service Acknowledgement?"

"Sorry, they're all at lunch."

He turned away.

"Does that mean you're ready to be counseled?" she asked.

He shook his head no.

"So you want to die?"

"You're good," he replied, not looking back.

"Why?"

"Why? Because I'm fat, jilted and bankrupt. If you were me, you'd rather be dead too."

"If I was you, I wouldn't be thrilled—"

"Gosh, no?" he cut in.

"But," she continued, "I would be 100% motivated to change my life, and I'd know that if I really worked at it, I could do it . . . just like *you* can do it." As distressed as Carter was by her old friend's state, her words were no candy-coat. She had staked her reason for being, on her belief in change.

"That's beautiful. You should write self-help books. Oh, I forgot you do."

"So did you."

"And look where that got me." He turned to the city. "Remember those stats from the President's Living Well Campaign? Two thirds of the country is overweight or obese, over 50% will get divorced, and most retire broke. Did we even put a dent in those numbers?"

"Our job was to raise awareness, Robert. We wouldn't have gotten that Presidential Service Acknowledgement if we hadn't made a positive impact."

"You know what I used to think, looking at those stats? What a bunch of losers. Who would do that to themselves? Eat yourself into an early grave, spend yourself into bankruptcy, squabble your way into divorce. How can you ruin the only life you've got?" He shook his head. "I had no idea how easy it is. It's like dropping a vase—no one does that on purpose. It smashes to the floor, you look down and curse yourself for being such a bloody idiot, but it's too late. You've broken yourself."

"It's only too late if you step off that ledge," Carter said.

"I can't put all the pieces back together again."

"The people you helped to lose weight didn't do it on their own. Why didn't you call me, or any of us?"

"Do you know how embarr . . ." He trailed off, dropping his head.

Carter tried to catch his eye. "No one is a loser, Robert. We're all just out there trying to do the best we can, and sometimes, often-times, we get it wrong, *spectacularly* wrong. But the biggest mistake is being too proud to accept a hand." She stretched her hand out toward him. He ignored it. She pulled it back.

"What are you feeling?" she asked.

He shook his head.

"Talk to me," she persisted. "What are you feeling?"

He sighed heavily. "Pain."

"And . . ."

"More pain."

The best suicide counselors listened more than they spoke. Off-loading to a sympathetic, non-judgmental ear was the quickest way to bring relief. Freud called it the "Talking Cure." The mind could be a messy thing with negative thoughts racing at high speed, staging a multipronged, covert assault on the self. Talking slowed the thoughts down, reduced the confusion, simplified and brought the key issue to light. Instead of offering solutions, the listener needed only to be receptive, quietly sympathetic. This brought the added benefit of unconditional positive regard, one thing the suicidal universally lacked. It was just that now, a minute later, Robert was silent, leaving Carter with no choice but to talk.

"Pain," she said, "is a feeling like any other. It comes, it goes. It can be turned up or down. What you're feeling now is temporary. You've felt it before and then you stopped feeling it. Don't make a tragic decision based on a time-limited emotion. You think death is going to give you relief from pain, but relief is a feeling, and only life can give you that feeling. While you are alive, there are ways to turn down the pain, to even turn it off. You turn pain off with coping strategies, tried and tested strategies, strategies to get your life back into order, strategies that work to take away the pain, to bring you peace. Let me share those with you."

Robert said nothing.

Carter was running out of ideas. While she did her best to focus on him, she couldn't help sensing the cost to her own life if he jumped. Failing to save him, she would be culpable—again. Not just her, everyone who loved him, would know they had not been enough or done enough. In their guilt, they would feel they had aided and abetted his death. A self-killer left behind not a suicide, but a homicide.

On impulse, Carter found herself saying, "There's something else, isn't there? I mean, we all mess up, but there's more. Something happened, didn't it?"

Nothing.

"This goes way back, doesn't it?" This time, she let the quiet hang.

For a moment, Robert felt as if she had touched on something deep inside himself. Oddly, it was both comforting and chilling. But as the time passed and he said nothing, she spoke again, perhaps too soon. "Come," she said, stretching out her hand, "let's figure it out."

He shook his head, no, no, no. He didn't deserve her hand, he didn't deserve her help, he didn't deserve to live.

"Robert," she implored, leaning closer.

As he ushered his body away from her, almost immediately the appalling fact hit him. His one buttock had slipped off the ledge, his upper body began to topple, and although he wasn't looking down, he knew that the larger part of his existence was suspended over eight stories of empty space. If he was less focused on his impending annihilation, he may have thought it absurd that he was so shocked. This was what he had come here to do, wasn't it? But intention was no more than a glimpse of reality. This was reality, and it was about to come to a blood-splattering, bone-shattering thud.

As space-time continued its unstoppable turn, it would soon bring the grim consequences set in motion by the various decisions he had made over the past four years. Who could say exactly which of those decisions was the first to put his premature death march in motion? Was it the first day he had decided to swap a workout for a six-pack and a marathon television binge? Or was it after receiving his Presidential Service Acknowledgement, when he had decided none of what he'd achieved was important? There were the multitude of micro-decisions he had made every day, decisions about what to eat, what to do, what to watch, what to read, what to think, where to go, what to say, what not to say and who not to say it to. Every moment of every day had been an opportunity to make a different decision, one that could have turned his life around. Except now. Now, the time of decision-making was over. This was the time of consequence-facing: the horror of a death plunge, tossing down gravity's murderous gullet. The sensation of falling produced a flash reminder of a bungee jump he had done many years before. This, he knew, would end very differently. There was something else he knew with even greater clarity: He didn't want to die.

2

ALL AT ONCE, as if indeed it was a bungee jump, Robert felt his descent cushioned by something elastic, something that soon gave way as he hit the ground.

"Ahh!" It was one of twelve firemen who had been holding a safety net. They had broken his fall, but his weight had thrown the man's back out. Robert looked up, dazed, taking in the faces staring down at him.

"Are you okay?" one of them asked.

Doing a quick internal scan for any pain, he smiled broadly and sat up. "Never felt better."

By the time Carter got down the stairs, Robert's smooth, fat face still had a glassy-eyed, beatific glow. He was hugging each of the firemen, expressing his love and gratitude. Twirling around dramatically, he stretched his arms in the air and screamed to the sky with an incongruent, operatic flourish: "I am alive!" His joy was infectious and, combined with the relief of his survival, some people began to laugh and clap. Carter discretely asked one of the policemen if Robert had hit his head. Equally perplexed, the policeman couldn't say that he had.

After a check-up at Cedars-Sinai Medical Center, Robert was declared injury free and discharged. Driving out of the hospital parking lot, Carter asked if she should take him home.

"I don't have a home," Robert replied calmly, "I'm bankrupt."

She looked for any sign of distress, but the smile on his face still seemed as genuine as ever.

"Robert, are you okay?"

He began to chuckle, calmed himself down with a deep inhalation, and said, "Perfect."

Carter called Mickey Prodi, one of their former team members from the President's Living Well Campaign. While Robert's focus had been on health and wellness, Carter had focused on reversing family breakdown, and Mickey had dealt with personal finance and reducing America's massive levels of personal debt. Although they had all started out as colleagues, they had ended as friends. Yet, like many people who became friends at work, once the job was done, the cement that had bound them, crumbled. They'd lost their joint purpose. That purpose had now been found again.

Carter explained to Mickey what had happened. Without their support, Robert would be destitute. Reluctantly, Mickey agreed to put Robert up. He gave her an address: Cliffside Drive, Point Dumé. They drove in silence down the Pacific Coast Highway, Robert's smile as blissful as ever. Carter felt none of the inner peace she would normally feel after averting a suicide, perhaps because she had done nothing to avert this one. She vaguely recalled a story from her undergraduate studies on the history of mental illness. A king had been struck with melancholia. His doctors tried all the usual cutting-edge treatments, including trephination: drilling a hole into the skull to let out the evil spirits. Amazingly, he survived, but unsurprisingly, was no less depressed. Finally, enthusiasts for experimental medicine that they were, they decided to try something else. Taking the king for his early morning walk across the bridge, his guard was ordered to push him into the river far below. Not being able to swim, the king was struck with horror, believing he was going to die. At the last minute, a boat came to rescue him. Being so close to death, the king's appreciation of life was renewed and his melancholia was cured. Carter couldn't remember how long the cure had lasted.

She withdrew from her wandering thoughts and focused instead on the soothing scenery. The rugged Santa Monica Mountains lined the one side of the road, and broad beaches fringing the big Malibu blue the other. No wonder, Carter thought, this was where the rich and famous had demarcated their "playground." It was exquisite. She opened her window to let the sea air in.

"Ahh!" she exclaimed, closing it immediately.

It was incongruous, that Malibu stink. If the wind was coming from the wrong direction, one's nostrils were invaded by the rich aroma of human excrement. The superstar residents didn't want to build a centralized sewage plant, because it would lead to development. Apparently, a high fecal bacteria count was preferable to sharing your playground.

Robert smiled at her and said, "*Filthy* rich."

Carter had no objections to free enterprise, which made such large accumulations of wealth possible; but he had a point, in Malibu *filthy rich* was a literal truth. She smiled back, wondering how long this post-storm calm would last.

They pulled up to a massive, black, ornate, wrought iron gate and pressed the intercom.

"Please come up," a Mexican accented woman's voice said. "Mr. Prodi will be here soon."

As Carter drove up a long, lavish driveway, she turned to Robert, "Well, you'll certainly be living in comfort."

It was one of those excessive Malibu mansions that hadn't made up its mind about what style it was. The original owner, obviously not used to forgoing one thing over another, chose a Modernistneo-classical-Tuscan fringed colossus ("big" being the only common element). After the architect had gone through the options, you could almost hear the owner demanding, "I want it all!" Circling the center of the driveway was a triple-terraced, stone water fountain, garlanded with lion heads spewing out plumes of water. This drew the eye up to a Roman columned portico, adjoining a double volume, glass facade that curved around the cliff face, fronting the ocean. Given the exquisite natural beauty, all this pomp was entirely unnecessary, but like a first visit to Vegas, undeniably impressive.

Robert's expression didn't change, as if it really didn't matter to him whether he stayed in the Emperor's palace on the hill, or in a homeless shelter. He was simply high on his second life. They got out and walked up the marble stairs. Carter was about to ring the miniature brass church bell, when a silver Bentley convertible pulled up behind them.

Mickey Prodi bounced out in a perfectly-tailored, charcoal suit and a gleaming white, open-neck shirt with solid gold cufflinks. Inconspicuous consumption was still an anathema to the man who had been brought up by a single mother and had depended on food stamps to stay alive. While Mickey had nothing to do with the stock exchange, his brand of brash was pure Wall Street: strident, self-centered and fiercely unapologetic. It wasn't that he was without empathy; but the game of life was played, he believed, like a game. Winner takes all. Losers needed to be washed out of the system; or, as he might have said derisively to a few of his Wall Street banker associates, rescued by a government bailout. Mickey would proudly attest that he had never put a dime into shares or derivatives for the simple reason he had no idea how they worked. He was proud that he had gotten rich without fancy degrees or complex financial knowledge, and had something concrete to show for his wealth—property. Besides, when he had probed any of those Wall Street bankers, he quickly discovered they didn't seem to understand much more about their arcane world of financial contortion than he did. Still, he had spent many a childhood afternoon walking up to Manhattan from the Bronx, so that he could drool over the vestiges of their excess: the exotic cars and gorgeous women, the luxurious hotels and dandy dress. Now that he had it all, despite the warnings of his Catholic education, he was immensely satisfied.

Mickey whipped off his big, black Armani sunglasses and bounded up to them. After kissing Carter on both cheeks, he turned to Robert. Taking in the new proportions of the man whose body he used to eye enviously, he couldn't think of a thing to say. Robert waddled up and gave him a big hug, which made Mickey's short body seem as if it was being eaten by a bear. Mickey's machismo would never have allowed such an admission, but Robert had been the most beautiful man he had ever met. He had reminded him of a more muscular Ricky Martin. Mickey loved success, and Robert—the sporting hero with the chiseled jaw and eight-pack, a sculptured Adonis of muscle, wrapped in naturally tanned skin—had possessed a type of success that, as hard as he tried, Mickey never would. Instead, Mickey had been proud to count him as a friend, to bask in his reflected glory and accept that he would be the man, not of the body, but of the money. He stared at Robert like an onlooker driving by a car accident: low on compassion, high on fascination. Perhaps he felt a vague hint of satisfaction. This was one man to which Mickey would no longer have to feel physically inferior. Robert had lost all power as a mating rival. But the more dominant sense was of the waste. The man had been born with gifts Mickey could only dream of. Commendably, he had made the most of them, but now? He had thrown it all away. It was an appalling act of self-annihilation.

"Shall we go in?" Carter suggested.

"Let's do that," Mickey said, leading them into a double volume entrance, where a sweeping white Onyx staircase led to the upper floor. "The film director, Joe Drummond, put his own money into

Android 2. Big mistake. Never put 100% of your own money into anything. When it tanked, he had to sell the house, the furniture, the works. We got it for a steal."

He took them into the curved, glass-lined living room that bordered a cliff top garden, overlooking an endless expanse of ocean blue.

"One man's loss is another's gain. We've made a few adjustments and put it back on the market, but until it's sold, buddy . . ." He slapped his hand on Robert's shoulder, then flinched as he felt a fat, wet slab of flabby meat through the sweaty cotton of his shirt. ". . . Until then, it's all yours." He looked at his watch, "I need to go."

"You're not staying here?" Carter asked.

A woman in a black pinafore servant's uniform walked in.

"Sofia!" Mickey shouted. "This is Robert. Look after him like a king!"

"Yes, sir," she replied. "Can I get you something to eat, Mr. Robert?"

"This lady and I are going to be firm friends," he said. "Yes, please!"

Carter followed Mickey out of the house. She drew him aside and lowered her voice, "I thought you were staying with him."

"He'll be very happy here," Mickey said, taking out the keys to his Bentley.

"He needs support."

"What's this?" he replied, pointing at the palace.

"*Emotional* support."

"He seems fine to me." Mickey opened the door. "Got the temperament of Winnie the Pooh and the appetite, too."

"He's in some kind of near-death bliss, and he's also bankrupt. He's going to need you to help him sort out his finances."

"I don't do that anymore," Mickey said, opening the car door and getting in. "The Living Well Campaign took it out of me. Since then, I've been focusing on building my property portfolio. I've done my bit for society."

"He's not society," she said, exasperated. "He's a colleague, a friend, and he needs our help."

"Look," he said, starting the engine, "I've got someone waiting for me back home. I need to go."

"Right," said Carter, noticing the lipstick mark on the top of his collar.

"But he can stay as long as he likes, well, until it's sold."

He spun the car around and sped out, the stones of the driveway clickety-clacking under the extensive tread of the Bentley's tires. She watched the car leave, wondering what more she wanted Mickey to do. Maybe just lift the gargantuan burden of their friend from her shoulders. That burden was now, it seemed, hers alone. Robert Rivera would be the test of all her abilities. She felt like she'd just given birth to an utterly helpless, obese, bankrupt, suicidal, thirty-seven-year-old man. Carter breathed through a moment of panic before walking back into the mansion.

"Robert?" she called.

There was a muffled response from the kitchen. She walked in to see him devouring a massive piece of chocolate cake.

"Lemme get you some," he said, jumping up with his mouth full.

"No, thanks," Carter said quickly.

He cut another slice and put it on his plate. "Life's short, Carter," he said, chocolate icing smeared across his chin. "Life is too darn short."

Robert awoke the next morning under silk sheets, his heart still brimming with cheer. Sofia had set up an elaborate breakfast for him in the kitchen, which he quickly devoured. He went upstairs, took off his clothes, wrapped a towel around his extensive waist, came back down and waddled on to the patio. A manicured, green, cliff top garden hung high over a magnificent, dappled, sky-blue ocean. Heading toward a long infinity pool with a waterbed, he was about to drop his towel, when he noticed a figure sitting under a palm tree, in the lotus position, meditating.

He walked around and seeing who it was, shouted, "Jay!"

The man opened his eyes. "Hello, my friend," Jay said, getting up, brushing down his white, Indian-style, cotton pants. Dr. Jay Lazarus was just shy of 40. A shock of grey swooshed through the middle of his curly bush of dark hair.

"What are you doing here?" Robert asked.

"Carter told me you were here. I arrived earlier this morning. I didn't want to wake you."

They hugged.

"You look happy," Jay said.

Robert looked at him puzzled.

"What?" Jay asked.

"Whenever I meet someone I haven't seen for a few years, they get this 'Oh-my-God-what-happened-to-you' look. They usually manage to keep their mouths closed, but they can't stop their eyes from gaping. That didn't happen with you."

Jay laughed. He had a broad baritone laugh that sent smiling lines from the corners of his eyes to the dimples in his cheeks.

"What's so funny?" Robert asked.

"That 'Oh-my-God-what-happened-to-you' look. When I came back from a six-month meditation retreat looking like this," he fingered his wooden beads through his white cotton shirt, "I got that a lot."

"You changed your clothing. Me . . . I mean, this doesn't shock you?" Robert said, looking down at his belly spilling over his towel.

"Bodies, like everything else, are transient."

Robert gave him another puzzled look.

Jay led him into the shade of an overhanging oak tree. "On my Bar Mitzvah," he began, "my mother gave me my dead grandfather's Omega watch. I loved the old world, black leather strap, the elegant pearl face and manual winder. When I put it on, I felt my grandfather's intelligence and charm rub off on me. One Saturday, after taking it off for a long swim in the sea with my friends, I returned to my towel and it was gone. I felt like I was going to be sick. But perhaps, I had unconsciously prepared for that day, because I also realized I had a choice. I could continue to feel devastated. I could feel as if I had lost my connection to my grandfather, lost all the good parts of myself, or I could do something else. I could accept. I had already lost not just things, but people, and later, like my grandfather, maybe I would lose my bodily functions and sanity. Life is inseparable from loss. Whenever I resisted loss, I had felt pain. And so right there and then, I decided to be okay with what I'd lost. I'd loved that watch, because it had reminded me of my grandfather's charm and intelligence. Now, I would have to find those qualities in myself, rather than on my wrist. As I walked home from the beach, I felt strangely calm. This was my first lesson in impermanence: resistance brought pain; acceptance brought peace. It would lead to my research and writing on meditation and mysticism. I guess it also means that when I look at you, I'm less interested in what you've lost and more in what you've found. You look really happy."

"I am, I really am. I guess when I nearly died, I realized how great it is to be alive."

Jay nodded. "A man never loves life as much as when he's led to the gallows."

"Where've you been all these years?" Robert asked.

"Well," Jay began, "once I had created the National Happiness Index for the President's Living Well Campaign and discovered that all these wonderful things we build for ourselves"— he waved at the temple-like building on the other side of the pool—"don't make us much happier, I decided to go stay in the mountains, grow my own vegetables and focus on where happiness lives." He put his hand on his chest. "In here."

"I want to come out there with you."

"You're welcome. Drop your ego-based existence and come live in the here and now."

"I'll go get dressed."

"You want to go now?" Jay asked, a little put out.

"Now is all we have, right?" Robert turned and headed for the house.

"I thought we'd have a cocktail, maybe watch a DVD . . ." Jay said forlornly to no one.

Ten minutes later, Robert came down the marble staircase dressed in the clothing he had worn the day before. Jay was in the lounge, browsing through a collection of Steven Segal DVD's.

"I guess we'll eat when we get there," Robert said.

"I'll make us some lentil soup," Jay replied absently.

"And perhaps a couple of burgers."

"I'm a vegan, so it's pretty much just vegetables."

A sudden look of terror crossed Robert's face. "You know what? Maybe I should stay here. Mickey might take it the wrong way if I just left."

"Yeah, maybe you're right," Jay said, relieved not to have to leave. "What about kicking back with those cocktails and watching this?" He held up *The Karate Kid,* adding with a guilty smile, "I guess I miss not having a TV."

"Great!"

Jay switched on the TV. A Channel 9 News reporter with model looks was animatedly sounding forth: "There were no clear reasons for the suicide attempt, but speculation revolves around his dramatic transformation from one of America's top weight loss experts . . ."

Realizing she was talking about Robert, Jay quickly changed the channel.

"Turn that back," Robert said.

Jay reluctantly complied.

The insert had gone on-site to where Robert had fallen. An old woman wearing a yellow sun hat was explaining what she had seen: "You didn't want to be anywhere nearby. It looked like a whale was falling out of the sky."

The insert went back to studio, where the newsreader was interviewing a pundit. "Greg Callahan, thanks for joining us. Robert Rivera, weight loss guru, tries to kill himself. Why?"

Greg launched in, "This is a man who made millions off the weight loss industry and was now obese. He couldn't live with his own lie. But what really disturbs me, Jane, is that he must have realized that, with his sheer size, he was going to kill other people in the process. Does the phrase 'suicide bomber' come to mind?" He left a dramatic pause. "I think the authorities may just have an attempted murder case."

"Wow! Robert Rivera falls from hero to zero—literally. Thank you, Greg. In other news . . ."

Jay turned off the TV.

Robert was giggling. "Suicide bomber," he muttered. The giggle turned into a belly laugh, until he suddenly stopped and deadpanned, "I wish I'd died."

3

ROBERT CLIMBED THE stairs to his room. Jay called after him, but he didn't respond. He got into bed and pulled the covers over his head. Slipping through the vortex of death had awoken his love of life. Yet the mental state was fleeting; like a particularly talented character actor, it could switch mid-scene into one of its many other forms. Watching himself being scorned on national television, Robert instantly slipped from elation to humiliation. Humiliation—a suffocating assault on the self, at least a painful notch above what his sidewalk-splattered body would have had to endure.

"Robert," Jay said from the doorway.

"Hmm." Robert's voice was barely audible.

"I'm going to let you sleep, but I need to know you're not going to do anything stupid."

"Too late for that," he muttered.

"You know what I mean."

He pulled the duvet further over his head.

"Robert?" Jay called.

"I won't off myself," he grunted from under the blanket. "Life's just too gorgeous."

A few hours into the night, Jay woke to a terrible, guttural sound coming from Robert's room, like an animal being slaughtered, like a man murdering himself. Jay darted out of bed and ran in. Robert had flipped over onto his back, head up, mouth open. He was snoring in a tone Jay previously would have thought impossible for a pair of sinuses to make.

The following morning when Robert turned down a tray of eggs, bacon and pancakes made by Sofia's deft hand, it became even clearer how critical the situation was.

Jay pulled up a chair to Robert's bed. "Robert." Nothing. Louder: "Robert!"

Nothing.

"Robeeeeert!!!" another voice shouted from behind.

Both Jay and Robert flipped their heads back to the door from where the scream was coming. It was Mickey, decked out in black pinstripe. "How are you today, big guy?"

Robert re-immersed himself under the duvet, as if he'd only been briefly roused by a bad dream.

Jay got up and led Mickey outside the room. "'Big guy?'" Jay said, looking at Mickey incredulously.

"We don't have time for this," Mickey said. "Looks like we've got a buyer for the house."

Just then, a voice sounded from below: "Hello."

They looked over the balustrade, down on to the marble hallway. It was Carter. Instantly, Jay's heart began to flutter. Before she'd called yesterday to tell him about Robert, he hadn't seen or heard from her for at least three years. Yet there she was, like some exotic deity who had miraculously descended in her glory, to charm and torment. Many years earlier, he had dedicated his life to emotional state management. It was that pristine state of equanimity he was after, where no matter what happened, one remained beautifully unruffled. Be the event good or bad, it lost its power to overwhelm. Long bouts of meditation were supposed to provide the mental cleansing necessary for this state to flourish. So, why then, he wondered, after all those hours of cross-legged solitude, was he feeling so distinctly ruffled? How could the mere sight of a woman demolish in a second the mental sanctuary he had so painstakingly built on the architecture of centuries of ancient wisdom? Did all that disciplined focus and contemplation mean nothing? This was why the monks confined themselves to their monasteries, the nuns, to their nunneries, to be free of the tumult of one another.

"We'll meet you down in the dining room," Mickey replied, making for the stairs.

Jay lingered, watching as Carter walked to the big glass sliding doors to look out at the garden. She was as splendid as ever. He had never met a woman with skin as thoroughly flawless as hers, yet also animated with an alert intelligence, a determined passion that made her far more significant than merely beautiful. Perhaps, after all, he was willing to forgo the hallowed state of equanimity for the gorgeous butterflies playing havoc in his belly.

The three of them sat down at a long, mahogany table in the wood paneled dining room downstairs.

"We need to do an intervention," Carter said, pulling her chair closer to the table.

"An intervention?" Mickey asked.

"We've got to find out as much as we can about how he got himself to this point, sit him at this table and hold up a mirror to his soul. Something happened, I don't know what. It's something that he did or something that happened to him; but we need to find out what it is. Then we've got to facilitate a recovery."

Jay shook his head, "I don't believe in interventions."

She looked at him wearily.

"They're too intrusive," he said, "in his current state, he'll feel put upon."

Jay had a gift, she would give him that; but quite frankly, his dainty, New Age approach irritated her. Perhaps 'New Age' wasn't entirely fair. You couldn't call him flaky, even if all those beads and white cotton made him look like he was playacting Gandhi for his local Am Dram Society. Jay was smart; that was what had attracted her to him. Maybe there was something else irritating her.

She took in a deep breath. "The man is drowning, and you're worried about him feeling 'put upon'?"

"Anyway," Jay said, "I'm not the right guy for this. I haven't done therapy for years, and at this point, I don't seem to be getting through to him."

"This isn't for me, either," Mickey said.

Carter slapped her hand on the table. "Now look, I'm sorry if the two of you have better things to do," she said. "But our friend is checking out, so I'm going to ask you only once: Will you help to save his life?"

Silence.

She continued, "We were brought together for the President's Living Well Campaign to help the nation. Now we have to step up to help one of our own. As soon as we're done, Mickey, you can go back to your property empire and dancing girls. Jay, you can go back to your mountain bliss bath. This is it, okay? The last time any of us will have to be graced by one another's company. For Robert."

Jay and Mickey glanced over at each other.

"Carter." Jay had caught up with her as she was getting into her car. "We're on board."

"I know," she replied, inserting the key into the ignition.

"Listen," he said, "it's great what you've done, bringing us together to help him." He put his hand through his hair. "It's good to see you."

She looked up into his blue eyes, and in that moment, she made a decision. She decided that this time around she would not be drawn by their sky-like luminosity. They were just eyes, right? A product of low melanin content in the iris.

"Look," she said, "we're here for a specific purpose. Let's focus on the mission. Okay?" She started the car.

Jay hesitated. There was not much he could do with that. "Okay," he conceded, feeling nothing of the sort.

She drove off, smothering any of her own faint yearnings by commending herself for clearing things up so efficiently.

That night, something beautiful and unexpected happened to Robert. Roxanne phoned. The sound of her voice suffused his body with warmth like liquid gold, like a stiff drink after weeks of abstinence. In an instant, the steel vice of his impossible life unwound and he could breathe.

"Ro-ee," she sang softly into the receiver.

He could almost feel the rose of her lips brushing his ear. Nobody called him that. Only her. Each syllable played its own part in her distinctive cadence. The "Ro" hung on an upper note, tapering down to a lower "ee." Praise be to God, how that sweet vibration flowed from her mouth into a digital wave that whooshed to him across the heavens at the speed of light, falling back down to earth, into the song that soared through the speaker, into his ear canal, pummeling to its final destination—the addiction center of his brain.

"Roxie," he replied, trying to hold back his ecstasy.

There was a pause.

"Roxie," he repeated.

The pause protracted into a silence.

"Roxie?" Nothing.

"Roxie!" His torso snapped upright, as he screamed himself awake.

Robert sat there, wide-eyed, his breathing shuddering in and out like a hand-pushed pump. What sadistic corner of his brain had concocted such an apparition? A dream that turned to a nightmare on realizing that it was nothing but a dream. Jay had once told him that, to Freud, dreams were wish fulfillments: the mind's secret shortcut to instant gratification. Now he felt shortchanged. Was that all he was getting, the sound of his name on her lips? No wonder all he wanted to do was sleep. He should live the rest of his life asleep, coaxing dreams of her.

Over the next few days, like investigators on the trail of a crime scene, Carter, Jay, and Mickey set out to find out whatever they could about how Robert had hit ground zero. While Sofia was put on suicide watch, they went off to speak to his family and associates.

After emerging from a meeting with Robert's accountant, Mickey walked to his car in a daze. Robert wasn't just down to zero; he was in the red to nearly a million dollars. It was true he hadn't worked in three years, but he shouldn't have had to. He still had royalties coming in from two books. Of course, now that word was out the weight-loss guru had flown his 267-pound bulk off a building, there might be fewer of those books flying off the shelves; but up until now, he'd had a substantial passive income. Mickey had seen it many times before. You could earn a fortune; it didn't matter. Earnings didn't equal wealth. Earnings minus expenditure equaled wealth, and Robert had been spending like a Kardashian in Barneys New York. Just last week, he'd spent six thousand dollars on a vintage gnome.

Mickey, Carter and Jay came back to Mickey's to discuss their findings and formulate a plan.

"Once the Living Well Campaign came to an end," Carter began, "and we all went our separate ways, he took a holiday, virtually the first proper holiday of his adult life. Robert achieved everything he wanted and then he rewarded himself with some time out. He just never went back to 'time in.' He had no reason, his part of the campaign reduced national obesity levels. His mission was accomplished. The drive was gone."

"But how did he let himself become the very thing he's fought against?" Mickey asked.

"The messenger is attracted to the message he needs most himself," Carter replied. "Robert always struggled with his weight. He only got it under control during about a twelve-year period. By breaking his routine, he reverted to his default habits. You stop maintaining a house, it doesn't take long for the rot to set in; and then it's a much bigger mission to get it back to where it was. People say, 'It's no big deal if I miss a few days.' Soon, a few days has become a few months, and the fat guy in the mirror has crept up so slowly, he's become the new normal."

Jay shook his head. "There's something else going on here, something we're not seeing. Nobody destroys themselves like this without a skeleton in the closet."

"I'm not sure we have to page Dr. Freud," Carter said. "Sometimes, what it looks like is what it is. Every day people decide to let themselves go."

"Why has he had no contact with his father for nearly four years?" Jay asked.

Carter nodded. That still required some exploration.

"What's this?"

They turned to the door to see Robert on the threshold, his bulk filling up the thoroughfare.

"An episode of *CSI?*"

For a moment, no one said anything.

Carter got up. "We've been talking to some of your family and associates, so we can understand how to help you."

"I don't remember asking for your help," Robert replied, "and I don't remember asking you to go snooping around my life."

"We felt the situation was critical enough to warrant that," Carter said.

Without another word, Robert stormed out of the room. They stared at each other, the helpers feeling decidedly helpless.

"That went well," Mickey said.

Robert marched up to his room to pack his bags. Indignation had clawed back his self-esteem from the jaws of shame. He would not be condescended to; he would not be patronized. But once in his room, he quickly remembered that he had no bags to pack and nowhere to go. He stood a while, contemplating his predicament, swallowed hard, and sat down on the bed, feeling the mattress conk in under his bulk. Anger turned in on itself, transformed into that languid beast called depression. He stared ahead. They couldn't help him; he was beyond help. He didn't even know how to commit suicide properly. He could always try again—hanging, perhaps. His weight would make it quick; but the thought of strangulation made him wince. A gunshot to the head would be the quickest; but he didn't have money for bus fare, never mind a revolver. He tensed his body, scrunching his face in steely concentration, willing himself to have a heart attack . . . before punching the bed with both fists, as the immense stupidity of it hit him.

He walked out of the room and back down the stairs. The three of them were just getting up. They stopped, as they saw him enter.

"I don't think there's anything you can do for me," he said, "but if you want to try . . ."

Beaming, Carter walked briskly toward him, "That's all we can do—try."

"Four weeks," Robert said.

"Twelve," Carter countered. "Twelve weeks is what we'll need to help you turn your life around."

Robert didn't have the energy to resist.

"We'll start at 9 a.m. tomorrow," she said.

The following morning, when they led Robert into the dining room to do his consult, he felt like a geriatric in a hospital gown being led in for a procedure, with little sense of his own free will. When you reached rock bottom, what more was there to do other than surrender to the specialists?

"Anyone seen him?" Carter asked, annoyed.

As if on cue, Mickey stumbled in, slightly pale, rings under his eyes. "Sorry," he said, stifling a yawn. "Big night last night, had the twins over."

"Your nieces?" Jay asked.

Mickey looked aghast. "I don't do pedophilia, pal, or incest, for that matter."

Carter's lip curled in distaste. "I wonder if you could leave the sordid details of your life at the door."

"Relax," Mickey said, sitting down. "Casey and Romey aren't actual twins, it's just their thing—identical dresses, pigtails . . ."

Carter slammed her fist onto the table. "Stop!"

Mickey flashed a mischievous look at her. "Do I not know that my body is a temple of the Lord?"

She could have told him the verse: 1 Corinthians 6:19. What was stunningly clear was that very soon they would have to do an intervention on *him*. She made no attempt to demonstrate a sense of humor.

Jay bit his lip, painfully reminded that anger added a flush of passion to Carter's features, making her even more compelling—like an Old Testament prophet reconfigured for *Vogue* magazine. He really would have to recondition himself to end this futile attraction.

"Before we begin," Carter said, turning to Robert as she took a deep, steadying breath, "I have some good news. The authorities have accepted that you didn't jump—you fell—and the ludicrous suggestion that you could face an attempted murder charge has been dismissed."

Robert nodded joylessly.

"Okay," she continued, "on to your life analysis. We've researched your history. We've spoken to everyone close to you—"

"You spoke to Roxanne?" Robert asked, unable to conceal his hope.

"Yes," Carter replied.

"How is she?"

"She's okay."

Robert just managed to resist the desire to ask for more.

"What we're about to do may seem daunting—"

"Daunting," Robert broke in, "is losing your wife, going bankrupt, falling off a building."

"Then this should be much more manageable," Carter said.

They spent the next twenty minutes giving Robert their analyses. Nothing seemed to be particularly illuminating, and he didn't say anything.

"Tell us about your father," Jay asked.

Robert became instantly alert, as if a firecracker had gone off in the other room. "My father?"

"We haven't been able to get a hold of him," Carter added.

"He's a good man," Robert said quickly, "salt-of-the-earth. No pretences." He tried to think of more things to say, but nothing came. So, he just nodded to reaffirm what he'd already said. If, at that moment, he'd been asked to dig deeper, he wouldn't have been able to. Like a shovel hitting rock, it didn't mean that there was nothing lower down.

"I got to ask you, bro," Mickey said, changing the subject, "you knew you were nearly a bar in the red, right?"

Robert shrugged.

"Yet, just last week," Mickey continued, "you dropped six grand on a garden gnome, vintage admittedly, but what was going on in your head?"

"I love gnomes." he said, "They're cute, they smile, they don't judge you."

"Okay, fine, knock yourself out. Buy a set of Smurfs for a hundred bucks. But why spend six grand? Six grand that you don't have!" Mickey looked at him incredulously. "That's just dumb."

"Easy there," Jay cautioned.

But Mickey was on a roll. "That's like, you-couldn't-be-more-stupid-if-you-chopped-off-your-head dumb."

"Mickey!" Jay called, uncharacteristically raising his voice.

"No," Robert said, "he's right. I don't know why, but eBay and the fridge became my two best buddies."

Mickey shook his head.

"Dumb," said Carter to Mickey, "is just a dumb way of saying, 'I don't understand why you did that.'"

"Look, I don't want to be a hypocrite," Mickey said. "I've been known to drop a bit of dough, but I've got it to drop. And, no, I may not have burnt six grand on a troll, but I've burned more on an overpriced trinket from Tiffany's. At least 30% of the price is the blue box, whose real cost can't be more than a dollar—that is dumb—but hey, if that's what floats the lady's boat, and she floats my boat, maybe it's not so dumb. But spending more than you've got? That's suicide."

"Money means different things to different people," Carter said. "Besides servicing your feral libido, money is survival for you. That's why you accumulate and hoard. Each dollar spent brings you closer, however miniscule, to a childhood where you had to decide to walk six miles and eat, or take the bus and go hungry. Right?"

Mickey didn't respond.

"So you're obsessed with opportunity cost—every dollar spent is an opportunity lost, the opportunity to invest that money and make more, building a bigger wall between you and destitution. And so there's only one thing that truly relaxes you, and it's not those boxes from Tiffany's—you'll buy them as a means to an end—but they actually make you nervous, because they put cracks, however little, in your wall. The thing that sedates you is the mounting numbers in your bank account."

Carter turned away from Mickey. "Now, to Robert, money means something else entirely. The numbers in *his* bank account are abstract, so he can ignore them. To confront them would be to confront the wreck of his life. Besides, he *has* to ignore them, because his sedative is spending. Spending and getting, those are some heady drugs. Most people get off on a little retail therapy, but given his spiraling descent, Robert was going for a retail lobotomy. Each thing bought was an attempt to sever his consciousness from the reality of his demise."

Mickey and Robert both looked at her, and almost in unison said, "She's good."

"I'm just curious," she said, "about what lies behind the word 'dumb.'"

"But why throw your life away?" Mickey asked.

Robert shrugged. "I don't know. Takes a lot of effort to keep the Success Train running. Haven't you ever wanted to just . . ."

". . . Give it all up and go live in the mountains?" Jay filled in with a smile.

"Didn't you all love what you were doing on the President's Living Well Campaign?" Carter asked. "Promoting personal development, helping people, seeing change . . . Isn't that the purpose of life? Realizing our potential, nurturing it in others, watching them blossom?"

Mickey smiled. "That's touching."

Robert leaned forward toward Carter, "Don't you ever want to just kick back with a cocktail and veg out in front of the TV?"

"Who said it had to be one or the other?" Carter replied.

"Or get naughty, Carter," Mickey threw in. "Let down that coif and throw yourself a naughty, selfish, decadent *debauchereeery*?" Mickey drew out the extra syllables, as if the word debauchery just wasn't long enough to capture the extent of his excess.

"Does that never grow boring?" she asked wearily.

"Uh . . ." Mickey looked up thoughtfully, and then back at her, "no."

Getting back to business, she turned to Robert. "You'll be starting therapy with Jay."

Robert looked at Jay. "No offense, but I'm not sure what's going to come of that."

Carter continued, "Mickey will get you back on your financial feet."

Robert shrugged dubiously.

"I'll do the counseling session with you and your wife," she said.

"Roxanne agreed to that?" Robert asked with a flicker of hope.

"We're working on it."

He put his head down. "I can't really see it happening."

"Don't be so sure," she replied. "And then your health and weight . . . We thought the best guy to handle that would be . . . Robert Rivera."

"Yes, check out the fruits of his good work," Robert said, patting his extensive belly.

"You know what to do," she said. "You just haven't been doing it. I'll help you put the plan together, and we'll all be here to monitor your progress."

Robert shook his head. He couldn't sense anything beyond the present, and the present stank—he was a fat, bankrupt, jilted hypocrite. Could they not see the elephant in the room? That elephant was reality. Everything else was a naive fantasy. "I don't know," he said wearily.

"Listen," Mickey snapped, "you want to know the truth? I can think of a few things I'd prefer to be doing right now. I'm here because I don't want to go to your funeral." He shrugged. "I'm not good with death. But if you're not going to get up and help yourself, I may as well head back to my . . ." he looked at Carter, "'property empire and dancing girls,' because we can't do this without you. I will just say this: Compared to the mountains that men have conquered, what you have to do right now is not high up on the ladder of human possibility. The question is do you want to do it or not?"

Robert sat on his bed. If they believed he could do this, who was he to argue? Even if they were wrong, they were all he had. He wasn't sure if they were his lifeline, but they were his "loveline." If he felt any better at all, it was only because of their love; and he didn't want to disappoint them. Besides, he knew what he had to do. Move. Pull on the pair of running shoes and shorts that Carter had bought him, and put one foot in front of the other. Shortly after their last meeting, he had written up an exercise program. That had been easier than he expected. He'd actually enjoyed it, felt a twinge of excitement as he planned the route to a new body. That was because his brain had its own anticipation-of-reward neurotransmitter called dopamine. It could be stimulated by the thought of any pleasure, like food or drugs. Anticipating the reward of a new life also stimulated dopamine. Hence, the self-help addicts whom Robert had encountered in his health and wellness programs, who had read every book, and attended every seminar, with little to show for it. Anticipating was easier than doing.

So right now, all Robert could do was sit, with the inertia of a boulder at the bottom of Latigo Canyon. He had not taken into account the activation energy required to set the plan in motion. Like the immense energy required to launch a rocket, it seemed beyond his resources. Briefly, he let his mind wander into a perfect future, imagining what his new body would look like, trying to use the rocket fuel of dopamine to propel him forward. Roxanne was there, full of love, marveling at his transformation. He got up. That was good. Just move. "Move, move!" he yelled at himself like a boot camp captain.

Walking outside, he stood on the sidewalk, squinting up at the sky, his stomach straining at the elastic waistband of his ludicrously skimpy shorts. He took a few steps, and smiled weakly at his mini triumph. The rocket had launched. But launching wasn't enough to keep this rocket airborne. His feet stuttered to a halt. He caught his breath and limped on. The strain on his body felt unnatural, like he was in the grip of some sort of extended pre-death event. Panting, Robert marveled at the irony that choosing to live might kill him.

But he did live, and each day he would go a little further and faster. He had gone back to his pre-obesity diet, which left his 267-pound bulk feeling like it was on a hunger strike.

Over the next couple of weeks, despite his progress, there were slip-ups. Whether it was stuffing a Krispy Kreme doughnut into his mouth, or skipping a work-out, each time he heard Carter's words, "Failure is only terminal if you don't get up."

After slipping up on his runs on two consecutive occasions, producing what Carter called a "slip down," Robert figured something out. He needed to lower the barriers of entry. Getting dressed in his running clothes was a barrier. As quick as it took, it was easy to procrastinate, to con himself that he'd run later. Now, if he was already in his running clothes at the start of the day, he would remove that barrier to entry. There would be no internal debate. He'd create a barrier to not running, as he'd have to get out of those clothes. The solution was simple, if not entirely elegant: Sleep in his running clothes. So that was what Robert began doing; and when he woke up, there was only one thing to do—run. It was the last time he missed a workout.

One morning, he found himself running toward a group of teen-agers. They had all the super cool and swagger of the rap artists they thought ruled the world. He saw them, seeing him, his gait lopsided and awkward, his hulk of fat slipping out from under his t-shirt, bouncing against gravity's merciless heft. They turned to one another, eager to be the first to point out the hilarious, cartoon-like charac-ter—Humpty Dumpty—bounding toward them.

The gates of a nearby home were open, and on an impulse he slipped in, ran up the driveway to the front door and rang the bell. He looked over his shoulder and saw the teenagers peering in as they passed by. No one was home, saving him from a story. He waited a while and then tentatively walked back down to the street, vigilant, like a man on the run, looking from side to side, in case they'd come back around the block. They were gone. He sat down, his feet in the gutter, and let the familiar balm of self-pity wash over him.

Just then, a bicycle wheel screeched up in front of his face. He lurched back and wobbled to his feet. Was there no peace? Looking ahead, he breathed a sigh of relief; it was Jay.

"No slacking allowed," he said.

"You're just in time to kick my butt," Robert replied.

Jay dismounted his bicycle. "You never needed anyone to kick your butt." He leaned the bicycle against the perimeter wall of the house. "You were the most disciplined guy I'd ever met. You had the focus of the Hubble telescope. You knew what you wanted, where you were going."

Robert sat back down on the sidewalk, where Jay joined him.

"You ever get a ding in your car," Robert began, "and say to yourself, 'I've really got to get that fixed,' but you put it off. Then, you get another one and now you've got the two of them to sort out. 'I'll get to it,' you tell yourself, but you don't. Then, there's a third one and something new happens. You don't lie to yourself, you're not going to get it fixed. Why bother? The damn car's full of dings! You'll just drive it into the ground. That's me—so full of damage, I stopped bothering. Besides, once I married Roxie, it didn't seem as important. I'd won her with my best self. I guess I thought I could keep her with my worst."

Jay nodded, making a mental note. "You win them with your best self; you think you can keep them with your worst." He could definitely find a use for that little gem, if he ever went back to doing seminars.

"The thing is," Robert continued, "I was a fat kid, and losing weight was like draining a swamp with a straw. Even at my peak, I hated it—the boiled vegetables, the running."

"So don't eat boiled vegetables," Jay said, "and stop running."

"I don't think that's what you're supposed to be telling me."

"I'm with you. Running is a pain in the neck."

"What happened to 'No pain, no gain?'" Robert asked

"I don't mean to argue with the fitness guru."

"You mean the *fatness* guru? Please, argue away."

"Well, the way I see it," Jay said, "the way it really works is 'no pleasure, no push on.' If I hated cycling, I would have given up long ago and today I'd probably look like you. Although," he quickly added, "you've definitely lost some weight in your . . . neck. Find some pleasure, exercise with uplifting music, play tennis, go back to basketball, take Salsa classes."

Robert looked at him skeptically.

"Whatever . . . if you don't find something you enjoy, you won't stick with it."

"I've got to get back," Robert said, heaving himself up from the sidewalk, "I've got a session with Mickey. I'll catch you later."

"Robert," Jay called after him. He turned around. "You've started panel beating, all you need to do is knock out those dings, one at a time."

A little later, Mickey was helping Robert negotiate the labyrinth of his financial ruin. They were sitting at a Victorian writing table in a small study on the upper floor. Robert stared ahead with his hands on his lap, like a penitent schoolboy waiting for the verdict on what was sure to be an appalling report card.

Mickey looked up from a pile of papers. "You know, I'm not one to put lipstick on a pig. You've lost everything."

Robert nodded. This wasn't a surprise.

"If you'd only declared bankruptcy earlier, you could have kept your house and your retirement fund." Robert looked confused. "Bankruptcy is designed to give you a clean start," Mickey explained. "That's why it lets you hold on to the essentials for survival. You were squeezing your home and your retirement fund to pay the interest and penalties on your credit cards. In bankruptcy, credit card debt gets cleared."

"Cleared?"

"Game over."

"That doesn't seem fair."

Mickey laughed. "That's beautiful! You're up to your eyeballs in code brown and you're worried about fair." Mickey leaned forward, "Let's talk about fair. You know what the biggest cause of bankruptcy in this country is?"

Robert shook his head.

"Medical expenses. Illness kills people twice—first, financially. The second reason is getting laid off. Don't those people deserve a chance to get back up on their feet?"

"I wasn't ill and I wasn't downsized."

"True," Mickey replied, sitting back. "With no less than fourteen credit cards, you were stocking up on the essentials, like vintage garden gnomes. But those credit card companies shouldn't have kept offering you more money at increasingly exorbitant rates of interest."

"They didn't hold a gun to my head."

"Yes, my friend, you screwed up, but the law gives you another chance. What do Abraham Lincoln, Walt Disney, Henry Ford, Larry King and Donald Trump have in common? They all filed for bankruptcy. They couldn't have gone on to make a contribution to society, if they'd been thrown into debtor's prison. Now, you have a responsibility to get back up on your feet and give something back."

Robert nodded.

"The only problem is, unlike most people who declare bankruptcy early enough, you don't have the essentials for survival. You have nothing, zip, zero."

Mickey used truth like a defibrillator, to shock the financial flatliner into new behavior. What he wouldn't have guessed, was that Robert felt strangely liberated by zero. It was a single, smooth circle. Clean and neat. Open to new possibilities. So unlike the negative numbers he had been wading through for so long.

"Tell me something," Mickey said, "how much did you spend last year?"

Robert looked blank.

"How much did you earn?"

Robert shrugged.

"You don't know what you earned and you don't know what you spent?!"

He shook his head.

Mickey pushed a document toward him. "That's how much more you spent than you earned." It was a balance sheet.

Robert looked down. On the bottom, in red lettering, it read $382.543.00. He flinched.

"Ignorance isn't a legal defense, my friend."

"I didn't know it was that bad," he said, shaking his head.

Mickey slapped his hand on the table. "You weren't drowning in debt! You were drowning in a river called denial!" He got up and walked over to Robert's side of the table. "What's the secret to weight loss?"

Robert gave him a blank stare.

Mickey bent down and prodded the side of Robert's head with his finger. "Is this thing on? It was your slogan!"

Perhaps to dispel the drumbeat of Mickey's finger on his temple, Robert's brain seemed to quicken. "More out, less in."

"Exactly, put out more calories than you put in."

Mickey sat down on the table in front of him. "It's the exact reverse with money: *More in, less out.* Your problem is that you got them turned around, like half the people in this country. Just reverse your strategy. Calories: put out more than you put in. Money: put in more than you put out. It's not $E = mc^2$!"

Robert felt a tiny drop of Mickey's saliva shoot onto his chin. He didn't want to embarrass him by immediately wiping it off, but it was interfering with his concentration.

"Sorry." Mickey rubbed the droplet off with his thumb. "You once told me about a study that showed the single most common strategy used by people who lose weight. What was it?"

At the risk of having his head prodded again, Robert began to warm to Mickey's Socratic approach. "They all kept a daily record of what they ate and how much they exercised," he replied.

"Right! In personal finance, we call it a budget. They kept a *body budget*. While you're staring at the numbers, you can't take a swim in denial. So Rule #1 . . ." Mickey slapped his hand on the sheet in front of Robert, "you can't manage what you can't measure. If you don't know what you earn and you don't know what you spend, you can't be sure you aren't heading for debt and destruction. *Capiche?*"

Robert nodded.

"Two thirds of millionaires know exactly how much their families spend on shelter, clothing and food. Jay always likes to say: 'Know thyself.' What do I always say?"

Robert felt dangerously close to having his head jabbed again, but really had no idea what Mickey always said.

"Jay says: 'Know thyself' I say: 'Know thy wealth'! What's true of weight is true of money: You can't manage what you can't measure. From now on you're going to keep a budget. I'm going to give you a small monthly allowance."

"I can't accept . . ."

"Relax, I'm not that generous. You'll repay me when you get back on your feet. I'm going to give you a spreadsheet. You're going to keep track of every last cent that comes in and every last cent that goes out. Okay?"

Robert nodded.

"Now, as I ultimately expect the money back, I need to know how you're going to earn a living."

Robert shrugged. "I could offer weight gain solutions to sumo wrestlers."

"Nice."

"I don't know, everything I've ever done has been in sports and health. That's gone down the drain, along with my credibility."

"What does the pastor do after being caught with his pants down?" Mickey asked.

Robert shook his head.

"Confess," Mickey said. "Repent, brother. When you get back into shape, you're going to have a killer story to tell. You know what those   I-survived-cancer-and-climbed-Mount-Everest-on-crutches speakers get paid? That's going to be you: *Fat Man Falls, Phoenix Rises*. You're going to sweep up the speaking circuit."

Robert shuddered at Mickey's delusional optimism, but thought better than to contradict him. He wasn't going to be shouted at for being a defeatist. Of course, that didn't erase the question: How *was* he going to earn a living? Getting into physical shape may have been necessary for his health, but getting into financial shape was necessary for his survival.

Carter had suggested that Robert meet with the significant people in his life. On the road to recovery, it could be helpful to deal with unresolved issues. That was why, he told himself, he was sitting opposite his parents in a downtown LA diner. For some reason, he hadn't told Carter about this meeting.

His father was about the same size as him. The tan skin of his shaved head shone under the fluorescent lights. His mother, a smaller version, sported a puffed-up, red, thinning perm. A waiter had just deposited three large pizzas and three large cokes. They were all pleasantly ignoring the fact that Robert and his father hadn't spoken in nearly four years.

"You look good," his father said.

He was still terribly overweight, but it felt good, really good, to hear his father say something positive to him.

"Doesn't he?" he repeated to his wife.

"He always was *el bebé más bonito*," she said, smile beaming.

"Come home," his father insisted. "I'll get you a job on the construction site."

Robert hesitated. There was a part of him that wanted to just say, *Yes, let's go, now, I'll do whatever you want*; but instead, he said, "I must get better first."

His father turned away and then looked back at him. "Just don't let them make you loco." He whirled his finger at the side of his head. "No funny ideas. Get better and come home." He stuck his big thick fingers into the pizza, "Let's eat."

Robert ate half his pizza and experienced a strange sensation: he didn't particularly want any more. Yet, the thought of leaving the rest behind filled him with discomfort. He didn't want to waste food or insult his parents. He put another slice in his mouth.

Not long after, Robert discovered an unlikely redemption from the dereliction of his life—swimming. There was a 15-meter infinity pool on the side of the cliff top garden overlooking the ocean. The buoyancy afforded by the water gave him relief from the uncomfortable mass he lugged around on land. He found himself more agile than he expected. Each, smooth meditative stroke hypnotized him into a deeper state of calm, and he often kept going much longer than his designated time. Here, there were no gawkers, ogling in self-satisfied scorn. It was just him and the quiet solitude of the water, broken only by the gentle lapping of his limbs against the surface.

He got stronger, swam further, but was rewarded with little more. Every few days when he stood on the cold, mottled surface of the scale, the digits seemed to have moved down—if at all—with the speed of a glacier's thaw. It was disappointing, but not defeating. He now swam for the joy of submerging himself in liquid, stretching his limbs, clearing his head, and the deep relaxation that he carried around for hours afterwards. A few weeks in, he found himself making a bizarre observation—exercise had become the best part of his day, even if it wasn't going to radically change his body.

One day, as Robert walked by one of the ground rooms, he heard some grunting interspersed with the ting of metal on metal. With the door slightly ajar, he peered in. Mickey was working out on the bench press. He dropped the barbell on the stand.

"Sorry," Robert said, closing the door.

"No, come in!" Mickey shouted. As Robert walked in, he saw it was a fully-fledged gym room, filled with weights of every size.

"Come pump some iron," Mickey said.

"I can barely lift one leg in front of the other."

"Get over here!" Mickey commanded.

From that day on, Mickey and Robert began lifting weights together, three times a week. Robert found himself looking forward to the camaraderie of the shared challenge. The cheering encouragement to push harder, the way the one would prop up the other's arms on a particularly grueling final rep. They would fall into conversation about everything from the social conservative domination of the Republican Party to the unending length of Carter's legs. Building muscle had become a social event. There was something else that happened, of which neither of them realized the importance. Occasionally, Mickey would stop, look Robert in the eye and give him the gift of five words: *You're going to make it.*

Then there was the workout itself. Despite what Jay had said about avoiding pain, Robert found that he actually liked the ache of the weight pushing down on his muscles. As he heaved the metal against its downward inclination, he felt as if he was attacking a much deeper struggle. Each time he pushed the bastard with a grunt and sometimes an expletive, he conquered, inch-by-inch. He may have been bankrupt, his wife may have left him, the rest of his life may have collapsed; but each bench press was a single point where he was in control, where he had the power—and that power began to give him the confidence to face off against the rest of his life.

Carter sat behind an antique Georgian mahogany partners desk, in a lavish, wood paneled study on the upper floor. There was a knock on the door.

"Come in," she said. Robert entered. "Take a seat, she should be here any minute." Robert fiddled with a button on his shirt. He hadn't seen Roxanne since she had left.

"You okay?" Carter asked.

He nodded.

"You really love her."

He nodded again.

"You realize that she may not be ready to just fall back into this relationship."

He looked up. "I want to look her in the eyes, you know? Feel her support."

"As long as you realize that only you can change your life."

He looked away. "I just miss her . . . so much."

After a few moments, Carter asked, "How's your father?" She noticed his face stiffening.

"Fine."

"Have you spoken to him since all this happened?"

"Shouldn't she be here?"

Carter looked at her watch. "Any minute. Excuse me for a moment." She stepped outside into the passageway to make a call.

"Hello, Roxanne," Carter spoke quietly into the phone.

"I'm sorry. I should have called," Roxanne replied. "I can't do this."

"You're not coming?" Carter asked.

"No."

Carter let out a raspy breath. "What should I tell Robert?"

"I can't go back," she said. "I need to move on."

"Are you ending the relationship?"

"I want the very best for him. Please tell him that. I just . . . I can't."

"Is there someone else?"

"I'll always love Robert."

"Is there someone else?" Carter repeated.

After finishing the call, Carter walked back into the room. Robert was paging through a psychology textbook. He looked up at her, as she walked toward him.

"I'm sorry. She's not coming."

"She can't make it?" he asked.

"She's not coming . . . ever."

Robert looked as if he'd lost his breath. "She's divorcing me?"

She sat down next to him. "Yes."

4

CARTER, JAY AND Mickey stood in the atrium under the expansive, ring-glass domed ceiling.

"This is bad, very, very bad," Carter said.

"What a bitch," Mickey said, looking away.

"Excuse me?" Carter said affronted.

"To leave him now," he continued, "at a time like this. At least pretend. Get your rocks off with the guy next door, but have a bit of compassion. Your husband just smacked himself off a building."

"She's entitled to her decisions," Jay said, "as is he."

"Does he look like he's in any position to make rational decisions?" Mickey asked.

"Ahhhhhh!"

They jumped as they heard a scream. Robert had rushed in and thrown himself on the floor. Water dripped off his outstretched body onto the marble. Before they could dash to him, he jumped up.

"Yes!" he screamed, and then grabbed Mickey's face with both hands and kissed his forehead.

"Are you okay?" Carter asked.

"150 lengths! I want to thank you for helping me *believe*," he said before running upstairs, screaming, "Yes! I! Can!" as he pumped his fists in the air, punctuating each word.

Carter shook her head. "It looks like some kind of manic phase."

"Let's hope it lasts," Mickey said.

"Manic phases never do."

Yet weeks went by and Robert kept up the fierce pace. He swam, pushed weights, cooked himself tastier, healthy food, followed a strict budget and drew up plans for the future. There were moments of weakness—when attacked by the urge to sleep in or eat up the fridge—he would doubt his staying power and hover on the edge, ready to dive into temptation. That was when Roxanne would come to save him. He would see her turning away, taking her belief in him, her respect, her love. An indignant rage would rise up. Whispering a wild expletive and, resolving to "show her," he would pull back from defeat. It was infantile, he knew; but if proving to her—and the world—that he was a man of conviction, a man who had fallen, yes, but a man who would rise up on sheer guts and determination, if proving this fact was what kept him on the path, he was happy to keep the rage burning.

Of course, without any progress, rage could easily turn into despair; and one Monday morning, about seven weeks in, it almost did. After a session of weight training, followed by a long, hot shower, Robert walked to his bedroom, wrapped in a towel. Preparing to get dressed, he dropped the towel and caught his reflection. There was no denying it; he was still a fat man. Barely restraining himself from smashing his fist into the mirror, he wondered for the umpteenth time if this was all a colossal waste of time; until something he used to tell his clients occurred to him.

While the decision to turn one's life around could happen in an instant, the actual transformation was like the earth's orbit, almost imperceptible. The earth may have been spinning at over a thousand miles an hour, but nobody was doing a NASCAR commentary. Like personal transformation, there was an illusion of stagnation. The illusion stood, whether you were moving forward or backward. In the spiral of decline, Robert never woke up one day and noticed that yesterday he was thin and today he was fat. The reverse also wasn't going to happen, unless he could deliberately create that perceptual shift.

Carter had given Robert a laptop to document his journey. He sat down and typed in his name under Google Images. The pictures began to cascade—images of his books, raising a barbell above his head, shaking hands with the president . . . and there, in the middle of the page, was the photo he was looking for: Robert was sitting on the road, having just been caught by the firemen after his fall. His face had its near-death glow. He looked like a sumo wrestling cherub, the blubber dispersed out the sides of his shirt like excess cookie dough.

Robert went back to the mirror. With the Inflatable Cookie Dough Man fresh in mind, he saw just how much he *had* changed. He may have been far from his best; but for the first time, he saw how far he was from his worst. This was his tipping point. If he could come this far, he knew he could go the rest of the way. Up until now, he was lured by a fantasy; now, he would be lured by reality. This was how success bred success. For the first time, he knew absolutely that he could complete the mission.

While this feeling of mastery over flesh was satisfying, there was something else gnawing at his guts, a nagging feeling in the pit of his stomach, some nameless worry, like when one woke up from an unpleasant dream, but couldn't remember its contents.

Over the next six weeks Robert's progress almost doubled. Nutrients usurped calories, muscle displaced fat, depleted cells were reenergized, and the encroachment of disease was turned back with the force of a life in reverse. His blood pressure and cholesterol dropped, while his lung capacity shot up. Each step of progress boosted his motivation. Robert calculated that, due to the regimen he'd diligently followed, he had lost about ten years of biological age. It was like a physical rebirth.

Mickey and Carter stood on the patio, watching Robert do push-ups on the wooden decking alongside the pool. His face had begun to reveal its original chiseled contours.

"Beautiful," Carter said, "human alchemy."

Robert got up and walked over to them.

"Hey, Comeback Kid," Mickey called out, as Robert approached.

"You're right," Robert said, "I've got to confess."

"You ready to preach the Word again, brother?" Mickey asked.

"I don't know about that, but I've started writing my book, *Thin to Fat and Back Again*. I'm finding it really cathartic."

"We should all be getting back on the circuit," Carter said. "The world needs us."

"Been there, done that," Mickey replied.

"I agree, we need to do more than speak and campaign," Carter said. "We need to do what we've been doing with Robert. We need to change lives, one at a time."

Carter had floated the idea of a personal development agency a few times. Mickey would be responsible for personal finance and vocation. Robert would manage health and wellness, and Jay, emotional state management. She would take charge of relationships and general transformation. With their work on the President's Living Well Campaign, it would be the premier firm of its kind. She felt certain that this was their destiny, even if they weren't. Never one to let a lack of enthusiasm get in her way, she had simply pressed forward.

"We may have thrown Robert a life buoy," Mickey said, "but if there's one thing I've come to realize, it's that we each save ourselves."

"You achieved all your success on your own?" Carter asked, ironically.

"I didn't have a coach pull me out of the Bronx, no. I mean did Einstein have a goddamned—"

"Please!" Carter interjected.

"—coach? What about Bill Gates, Spielberg?"

"Nobody gets where they want to go purely by pulling themselves up," she said. "They get there because somebody bent down and gave them a hand."

"Right, I had my Nonna, and I didn't pay her a consulting fee."

"Good for you, but not everyone has your grandmother."

"If you're hungry enough," Mickey said, "if the greatness is there, you'll go get what you need to make it happen. Sure, I didn't just build my property portfolio without good advice. I heard about what people like Trump, Kiyosaki and de Roos were doing, and they certainly weren't going to be my coach. So I went on Amazon, bought their books for $16 apiece, and—"

"You know the story about Roger Bannister?" Robert interrupted.

"First man to break the four-minute mile," Mickey replied.

Robert nodded. "Most people call Bannister the hero, but I'm not so sure. See, before it happened, people thought a four-minute mile was an impossible barrier. The closest anyone had gotten was four minutes, one second, and that was nearly a decade before. There were doctors who said pushing the body below four minutes would kill you. Not even Bannister thought it was possible; but one day, before a race, his coach, Fritz Stampfl, said something that changed his mind. He said, 'You can do a 3:56 mile.' A good coach sees you not as you are, but as you can be. When you trust that person and internalize their belief in you, miracles can happen. Bannister said everything changed after he heard his coach say those words. That comment broke him through the real barrier, the *mental* barrier. Not only did he beat four minutes that day, now that people knew it was possible, not long after, ten other runners did it too! Way I see it, the real hero of the four-minute mile is Fritz Stampfl, who made one man see that the impossible was possible." Robert looked at Mickey, "You know how you used to say to me: 'You're going to make it?'" Mickey looked uncertain. Robert laughed. "You don't even remember. Anyway, thank you." And then to everyone, "You all are my Fritz Stampfl. Without you, I wouldn't be here. I'd probably be dead."

Mickey was about to give Robert a hug, when he noticed a tall, dark-haired woman walking toward them, with Jay.

"Here's the lady you're looking for," Jay said, indicating Carter.

"Hello," the woman said, as she approached with a broad, confident smile, stretching out her hand.

Carter took it, "Alexia, welcome."

Mickey had only ever seen Alexia Redmond on TV, so he hadn't realized how tall she was, nearly 5' 11". Besides the almond eyes and shoulder length, brown hair, she had the suspiciously unlined, tanned, toned skin of a 20 year-old. She was 29. Mickey wasn't sure if her nose was a little long, her face a little too angular, or whether that just added to her regal air.

"Alexia is the author of the international bestseller, *Make Yourself Over,*" Carter said, by way of introduction. "I thought she would be a perfect addition to our agency."

"I have great respect for what you all did on the President's Living Well Campaign," Alexia replied warmly with a faint Southern lilt, a remnant from her childhood in Atlanta. "You changed lives."

"Alexia focuses on clothing, cosmetics, voice and body language," Carter said.

"I'm very superficial." Alexia flashed an ironic smile.

"Me, too," Mickey threw in, with less irony.

"It's an outside-in approach to change and it certainly has its place," Carter added.

"I couldn't agree more," said Mickey.

"Excellent," Carter replied. "So we're all on board."

"Sounds like another series of *The Swan*," Jay cut in. "Not to ruin the party, but have you thought about what this business tells the world? 'You're not good enough as you are.' That's not a very uplifting message—it also happens to be a lie."

Carter took in a deep breath, trying hard not to roll her eyes. "Fourteen weeks ago, was Robert good enough as he was?"

"It's one thing to help someone out of the abyss," Jay replied, "but it's another to sow seeds of discontent. Bliss springs from acceptance, not by prodding the dog of desire."

"We need you on board," Robert implored.

"Thank you, but . . ." Jay shook his head, "my bags are packed."

Carter sighed. "You better get out of here or you're going to miss the bus to Nirvana." She turned to Alexia, "Come, let me show you around." They walked back into the house.

Mickey looked at Jay. "Don't you want to touch people's lives?"

Jay smiled. "Not as much as you want to touch Alexia Redmond."

Mickey performed a mock display of indignation before conceding, "Insightful analysis, Doctor."

Robert stood on the scale. It had been nearly four months since he had started conquering his personal Everest; and if he'd done his calculations correctly, he'd lost 69 pounds of body fat and added ten pounds of muscle. It had been tough, but way less tough than living in a 267 pound mound of lard. Looking in the mirror filled him with quiet satisfaction. He had summited the mountain of himself. Looking down at his abdomen, he winced. There was still a flap of excess skin on the bottom of his belly. If he kept working out and gaining muscle, his skin would hopefully recover its elasticity. Until then, he had a memento of what would happen if he slipped back.

Later that afternoon, Robert was on the beach having publicity photos taken. Wearing a tight white T-shirt that accentuated his chest and biceps, he had just about emerged into the man they remembered. Mickey and Carter looked on like proud parents; Alexia stood by their side with admiration of a less familial kind.

After the final photo, Robert walked over. He was no longer smiling. "Four years," he almost shouted, "four years of my life *lost*, because I was too damn proud to ask for a hand. If I ever slip up again, just remind me of that."

"Deal," said Carter. "Now it's time to pay it forward."

"Do you really think," he said hesitantly, "I'll have any authority out there?"

"If I was going to choose someone to show me the way," she replied, "I'd want them to know how to get out of the wilderness. You've done what so many people want to do. You're no longer just a teacher; you're a role model."

A little over a week later, Robert stood outside on the patio with the portable phone in his hand. He was about to make a call. His heart was racing and his hands were sweaty. It felt like he was twelve again and about to ask a girl on a date. Even knowing there was a good chance the call would go badly, he couldn't resist. He needed to hear that voice; he needed to feel that approval. Robert pressed the numbers. After a few rings, a woman answered.

"*Hola mamá,*" he said.

"Roberto!"

"I'm better, Mamá."

"I know, I know. We heard."

"I left a message for Papi last week."

"He's been very busy, my boy."

Robert could hear the muffled voice of a man in the background. "Can I talk to him?"

She put her hand over the receiver and, after a few moments, uncovered it and said, "He's not here."

Robert didn't say anything for a while, and then finally, "He knows I'm better?"

"Yes."

Robert nodded. "Okay, Mamá, *te quiero.*" He hung up.

That night, Robert sat at the kitchen table. It was laden with food he had bought and snuck in during the afternoon: hot dogs, fried chicken, chips, coke, muffins, Hershey's, M&M's, all his favorites. He was the only one living in the mansion; but they all had keys, and he couldn't be sure that someone wouldn't come in and catch him. Maybe that was what he wanted. They'd find out anyway, sooner or later. He wolfed down a hotdog and was about to put a second one in his mouth, when Mickey walked in. Robert looked at him a little surprised, but without guilt.

"What the hell are you doing?" Mickey nearly screamed.

It took a while for Robert to swallow enough of the food in his mouth to reply. "Saving us all from a lot of disappointment," he finally managed to answer. "Let's just short-circuit this thing. This is who I am."

Mickey shook his head. "You are seriously pissing me off." He pulled up a chair, deliberately scraping it aggressively on the floor. "What the hell happened?"

"Nothing. I just know, now, that not everybody has to be thin, rich and successful. Don't worry, I'm not suicidal. You guys have really helped me. I just figured it out, like that thing Jay used to say: 'Love what is.' I'm going to love who I am, rather than chase something I'm not. I'm already feeling better."

"You're not going to feel better when you're half a clogged artery away from a heart attack, and girls go back to thinking you're a set of Siamese twins."

"Whatever, I might get hit by a bus first. It's up to God."

"No, it's up to you," Carter said, as she entered the room.

Robert looked over at her, still guilt free.

"But I get it," she continued, "success never really made you happy, did it?" She sat down next to Mickey.

Robert looked over at her. "I just don't think it's worth the trouble."

"No," Carter said, "it's more than that. You really don't *want* it."

He shrugged.

"You were a fat kid, right?"

He nodded.

"Right up until your late teens. When did you turn that around?"

He breathed in deeply, thinking about it. "Georgia Riley," he said. "She told my friend Dan that she would never date me, because I was fat. Those were her exact words. Or maybe Dan just told me that, but it did the trick. I lost all that weight in a year and pretty soon, I was entering weightlifting competitions. I didn't get Georgia Riley, but I did start getting girls. Enough is enough, I'm not living my life for anyone else anymore."

Carter nodded. "And then?"

"And then I married Roxanne and dropped the charade. She couldn't love me for who I was, but that's fine. I'll find somebody who does."

Mickey was incredulous. "You're going to throw away everything you've created over the past four months, just like that?"

"I'm not living for anyone else anymore," he repeated.

"But you *are* living for someone else," Carter interjected. "Or rather, destroying yourself for someone else. Your father."

Robert took in a short, sharp breath.

"He hated everything you had become, right? *'Rich people are bloodsucking misers,'* isn't that what he always said? Isn't that partly why you spent yourself into poverty? And bodybuilders are *maricons*, right? *Faggots*. To top it off, in his world, a son is supposed to know his place, not go around trying to be better than his father. You went after success to win a girl; you went after failure to win your father."

"Who told you about him?" Robert asked quietly.

"Your mother's sister. I knew there was more going on. It just took me a while to find someone who was prepared to talk about it." Robert pushed his chair back from the table. "Quite a double-bind you were in. Fit and rich, you lose your father's love. Fat and poor, you lose your wife."

Robert looked out ahead, over the table. For a long while, he said nothing. Finally, without shifting his glassy-eyed gaze, he spoke. *"No todo lo que brilla es oro.* That's what he said to me after I received the President's Acknowledgement of Service. That's all he said. No *'Well done,'* no *'Congratulations,'* just those words: *'Not all that shines is gold.'"* Robert chuckled. "He had a point, didn't he? He was right to deny my achievement."

"It had nothing to do with what you achieved or didn't," Carter replied. "He couldn't deal with you shining. Instead of being proud, he felt threatened. Now, you think that if you polish the food off this table, and get a job in construction, like Papi, he'll finally love you."

"Is she right?" Mickey asked.

Robert shrugged.

"Listen to me. Listen to me!" Mickey repeated. Robert looked at him. "If he only loves you broken, he doesn't love you, okay? That's not love. So here, I'm going to say it. This is probably not what they teach you in therapy school, and Carter's probably going to bust my balls, but I'm going to say it: *Your father doesn't love you.* Okay? Get used to it. Nothing you do is going to change that. You're going to kill yourself for nothing! *Do you get it? Your father doesn't love you.* He can't! He doesn't have it to give it. Yeah? I'm sorry, man." Mickey breathed in deeply to hold back a surprising torrent of emotion he felt welling up inside him for his friend, but it didn't help—his eyes filled with water, making the next words difficult. "I wish I could tell you that your old man loved you. I really wish I could. You don't know how much I'd love to tell you that. But I can't. Okay? I can't. *Because he doesn't.*" He caught his breath; let the emotion subside a little. "But it's alright, because *I* love you. And Carter loves you, and Jay loves you, and the way I've seen Alexia look at you, I think she might love you, maybe in another kind of way, which pisses me off a bit, but I'll get over it." He wiped his cheek with the back of his hand. "*We love you.* Okay? I'm sorry he doesn't, but *we* do. Let that be enough. Please, Jesus, Mary and Joseph, let that be enough!"

Robert turned from Mickey and looked ahead over the table. After a few moments, he stood up. Very quietly, he said, "Please stand back."

Carter and Mickey looked at each other.

"Just stand up and step aside, please."

They pulled their chairs back, got up wearily and took a few steps back.

Robert picked up his end of the table and jerked it forward with such violence that all the food went flying across the kitchen and smashed into the wall. He stood there looking at the carnage, and then he turned to Carter and Mickey. "My father doesn't love me. It's okay."

5

MICKEY TOOK THE property off the market. With a few alterations, it would become their professional home. There was nothing subtle about the Emperor's Palace on Point Dume. But that was the point in an industry where many life coaches' personal success extended no further than the certificate they were awarded after a weekend life-coaching program. The mansion would stand as a beacon, a temple—if somewhat garish—to the magic of manifestation. *Look what's possible*, it shouted, *when you pick the right team.*

Robert wrote his book at a feverish pace. Exploring his relationship with his father helped him understand his self-sabotage. It was one of those bizarre notions from the psychological literature that only now, when he saw that it applied to him, did he understand. A person could destroy themselves to serve some hidden, unconscious need. It wasn't that he hated success; he had just been forced to trade it for paternal approval. This bargain had taken place in the dark recesses of his mind, like a corrupt back room deal between city officials that would have grave repercussions for the citizenry. *He* was that citizenry—badly affected, yet ignorant to the cause and so unable to do anything about it. By bringing the rotten deal to the light of consciousness, Carter and Mickey had helped him resume governance of himself. No longer would he sacrifice his potential on the altar of his father's approval. Yet, as he put the last word down on the chapter, "An Unholy Exchange for a Dad's Love," there were vague murmurs on the edge of his consciousness, like the muffled voices of some other backroom deal behind a locked door.

Carter, Robert and Alexia sat in silence around what was now the boardroom table. Carter's brow was furrowed. They all turned as Mickey walked in noisily, bringing in a whiff of smoke and perfume. Again, he had the unmistakable look of someone who'd pulled an all-nighter.

"Sorry, sorry," he said, pulling up a chair.

Carter looked him up and down. "You haven't been to bed."

"Sure, I have," he replied with a roguish smile, "just not to *sleep*."

She shook her head. "I can't work like this. You're going to have clients soon. You're going to be their role model. You're going to have to demonstrate discipline, punctuality . . ."

"Hey, I'm human, right? We're all human. Let's get off our sky-scraping stallions, shall we? These hypothetical clients of ours are going to want someone real, someone they can relate to."

"Exactly, and I'm not sure how many people relate to Hugh Hefner."

"That's a very generous comparison," he said, smiling. "Hugh would be flattered."

This was the sort of thing that Alexia had definitely not expected from what was supposed to become the world's number one per-sonal transformation agency.

"Besides," Mickey added, "I didn't help elect Bill Clinton, or Newt Gingrich, for that matter, because I wanted to see what James Dobson's perfect family looked like. I wanted someone who could do the job. What too many people in this country forget is that if being devout and monogamous was a prerequisite for office, there would have been no President George Washington. No one is coming to me to role-model my private life; they're coming to emulate my wealth-creation strategies. If they're looking for moral guidance, they can go to a priest."

"If you're immoral in your private life," Carter said, "how can anyone be sure you're not immoral in your wealth strategies?"

"Immoral? You call a consensual act between two adults immoral?"

"Just two?" Robert teased. "When did you become a social conservative?"

Mickey looked at Alexia. "Just so you know, I'm actually a regular guy, just looking for my true love."

"That's right," Robert threw in, "and when he finds her, he's going to sweep her off to Little House on the Prairie, have eight kids, teach Sunday school, and make James Dobson's perfect family look like the Osborne's."

"Laugh, if you will. I don't apologize for the life I choose to live, but I also know this isn't it forever."

"And all I know," Carter said, "is that your lifestyle is affecting this operation. This morning you were late, again."

"Right," Mickey replied, "those four minutes without me, and the agency nearly slid into catastrophic collapse."

Carter drew her hand over her hair impatiently. "How can we expect our clients to be disciplined about their money, their eating, their relationships? How can we expect them to respect our time, if we can't do the same?"

"Okay," Mickey said with a touch of adolescent petulance, "*relax.*"

Relax? If there was one word that could immediately achieve its opposite, it was the word "relax." Carter consciously slowed her breathing; not because she'd heard the word "relax," but because she knew if she didn't, she would explode.

After a few moments, she spoke. "My mother could have been CEO. What am I saying? My mother was the CEO of her own *crack den.* When you start using and sleeping around at age fourteen, that's the pinnacle of success. I was destined to take over the family business. I was just lucky enough to have someone point out another way. The day my mother shot her brains out, I felt . . . relief. Relief that the drug-fueled rages were over, the street fights with her latest boyfriend, the disappearances, it was all over. She couldn't screw up her life any more. Pretty quickly, the relief gave way to something else that visits me every day. The ghost of what could have been, if only I'd done a better job of helping her. I failed."

"That's not . . ." Robert began.

"I failed," she repeated. "My sister's heading the same way and there doesn't seem to be a damn thing I can do about it—as much as I've tried. But," she said looking at Robert, "we didn't fail with you, and that gives me hope." She swallowed and turned to Mickey. "If I sometimes seem like a Salem witch burner, it's because when I see anything that threatens our mission, I see people dying, their potential dying. I don't know that this thing is going to work, but on my deathbed, I need to know that I gave it my best, that *we* gave it our best."

They sat in silence for a few moments.

"Look, Carter," Mickey said finally, "I get that this is some kind of personal redemption for you and I respect that, I really do, but the truth is, I just don't know if I need this in my life like you do. I feel like I've done my bit."

"What sort of impact do you think we had through the President's Living Well Campaign?" she asked.

"Huge!" he said. "A lot of lives got revamped. I'm proud of that and maybe that's what's going on here. We've proved ourselves, and now we're going to put it all on the line again with this agency. What if it doesn't work? What if no one changes?" He stood up. "I've just convinced myself. I'm out."

Alexia Redmond started to reflect forlornly on her career options. Her TV show was over. When Carter interviewed her for the job, Alexia made it sound as if she'd chosen to leave the show. Actually, after a season of declining ratings, the channel failed to renew. She, too, had discovered that success was a waypoint, rather than a permanent destination. As much as she'd professed to Carter her passion for helping people, what she really hoped was that being a part of one of the world's top personal development agencies might revive her career. Not that she was against helping people, but that had largely been a nice by-product to helping herself.

Alexia was a model for the power of good grooming. Her socialite mother had been largely absent from her childhood. Obsessed with preserving her reputation as one of Atlanta's great beauties, she had little interest in facing competition from her flowering daughter, and so subtly encouraged Alexia's dowdy, bespectacled image. Going off to study microbiology at Cornell had been her great awakening. She had roomed with Tanya, a girl who had seen it as her duty to upgrade her roommate's appearance, partly because they had become good friends, and partly because, unlike Alexia's mother, Tanya saw her friend's potential assets as an enhancement to her own. The right haircut, skincare, make-up and clothing had changed Alexia's life. Almost overnight, she went from wallflower to central exhibit. No boy had ever given her the slightest bit of romantic attention. Now, men looked at her, brushed passed her, and even stuttered in front of her. She couldn't have felt more powerful if she'd discovered she was Superwoman.

Of course, deep down she knew she was the same Alexia; and so she developed a disdain for men, for their dumb enslavement to prettiness, even as she continued to do her utmost to enslave, and taught others to do the same. Her career success was important because it proved that she was more than pretty. Now, she saw her latest career prospect receding. Maybe she should just throw it all in, do an *Eat, Pray, Love,* and head to India for a year. She just wasn't very good with flies, or heat, or poor people.

"Sit down for a second," Carter said to Mickey.

Mickey remained standing. "You're not going to persuade me."

She held up a thick, white document. "This," she said, "is the final report on the President's Living Well Campaign. It came out a few days ago. This is the verdict on all our messaging, our beautifully constructed billboards, advertisements, websites and blogs."

Mickey sat down. He and Robert waited to hear the judgment on what was supposed to be the most important accomplishment of their lives.

"They took a few years before doing the final assessment, to see if there were any delayed results," she said. Turning to the last page of the document, she read aloud: "'In conclusion, we find that there has, indeed, been a statistically significant difference in obesity, divorce and personal debt levels. Each has increased.'"

"Increased!?" Mickey shouted.

"'Therefore,'" Carter continued, "'the campaign did not achieve its objectives.'" She gave them a few moments to take it in, before closing the folder and adding, "There are already rumblings that we should never have received the President's Acknowledgement of Service."

After a period of dazed silence, Robert spoke, "Those rumblings have probably got more to do with me than anything else."

Mickey slapped the table. "What a waste of time!"

"It's not you," Carter said to Robert. "What we've definitively seen is that you can't just beat a drum and expect people to follow. You have to get involved in their lives. This agency gives us one last chance to prove that real change *is* possible. If we can produce enough positive case studies, we can create franchises to replicate our methods and really make a difference out there. If we don't pull this off, we'll go down as a bunch of charlatans who wasted tax dollars. So," she said turning to Mickey, "our mission is very far from accomplished. We've got a lot of work to do."

Mickey put his head in his hands, rubbing his temples, before looking up. "I don't really have a choice."

"You always have a choice," Carter said.

"Not if I want to save an ounce of my reputation."

"That's not the reason to do it."

He slapped the table again. "How can people be so apathetic about their own lives? How can they just watch themselves fall apart, in the face of good advice?"

"I might have an idea," Robert said.

Mickey looked at him, remembering where Robert had been four short months earlier.

"They need tools, support, coaching, insight. You lit a fuse under my butt. That's what we need to do for them."

"Start a bloody revolution," Mickey said.

". . . One life at a time," Carter added.

Seeing that things were getting back on track, Alexia felt particular relief that she could "eat, pray, love" right there in California without the threat of dysentery.

"So?" Carter said.

"It better work," Mickey replied. "If it doesn't . . ."

"What are we going to call ourselves?" Carter said, cutting him off, as she looked down at her Moleskin notebook. "Change Makers?"

"*Change Makers?*" Robert repeated dubiously.

Silence.

"What about *Zero to Hero*?" Mickey piped up.

For a moment they wondered if he was joking.

"*Quest.*" The voice came from the doorway. They turned around to see Jay. "You still got place for one more?" he asked.

"Always," Robert said, standing.

"Quest, I like that," Alexia added.

"What happened to being 'good enough as you are'?" Carter asked.

"They were discussing the ineffectiveness of the Living Well Campaign on National Public Radio," Jay replied.

"Great!" Mickey said. "Let the lynching begin."

"They did say my Gross Domestic Happiness Index was still being used to measure the national mood, even if the national mood continues to be far from euphoric."

"So that's why you're back?" Carter asked.

"Partly," he said, sitting down, "although it's probably more selfish than that. See, when I got back to the mountains, I meditated like a demon, six hours a day. There were moments of bliss, but . . ." He looked up searchingly and then back at them. "Nirvana is just another kind of ambition, only more painful, because it's an illusion."

"Whoa, bro," Mickey cut in. "Easy, there. Some of us are only getting by on a high school education."

"I missed what we've had over the past few weeks: friendship, service—*quest*. That's what's made me happy. I thought about you," Jay said, looking at Robert, "how you did this turnaround, not on a mountaintop, but right here in the messy sandpit of the city. Not through Zen incantations, but through swimming, eating right, getting your financial affairs in order, dealing with the end of your relationship, confronting the issues with your father. It's a dirty business, but I'm ready to roll up my sleeves. Let's help the world on its quest, and let's help ourselves along the way."

"Why do I feel like starting a slow clap?" Mickey asked.

Carter had been looking away thoughtfully, but she now turned to Jay, "We've mapped out everyone's responsibility, and I just don't think there's any place for you."

"Like I said," Robert cut in, "I couldn't have done it without *any* of you."

A little later Jay found Carter in her office.

"Do you want me to go?" he asked.

She looked up from her laptop.

"I don't need to be part of this, if you don't want me to," he added.

"I won't pretend this is easy for me."

Jay moved in closer. "Because, there's still something between us."

"No, Jay, no." Carter shook her head. "There's nothing between us."

"Look, I can't erase the past . . ."

"No, you can't."

". . . But we *could* move forward."

She stood up. "This is how we're going to move forward. I apologize for letting my personal feelings get in the way. You are needed here, you are. But for this to work," she paused, "you need to back off. Can you do that?"

"Is that what you want?"

"There is nothing between us anymore."

"You want to throw it all a—"

"Yes," she cut him off.

He let out a deep sigh. "Alright."

"Thank you," she said, sitting down. Then she went back to her laptop.

If there was one thing Jay knew, it was that the key to peace was acceptance. He just couldn't help thinking that if he was graceful enough in defeat, she might realize what she was losing and change her mind, which wasn't really acceptance at all.

"Alright," he said again.

Even before the conversion to Quest, Inc., Mickey's mansion had its own top-of-the-line cinema room. With five raked rows of six chairs, the screen was a wall-to-wall, floor-to-ceiling behemoth. The team sat together in the middle, hearts revved up, as they watched a late-night infomercial:

Over forlorn chords of music, a collection of unsubtly overweight, drab and poor looking people enter a building through a large revolving door. A Hollywood-trailer-style voice rumbles earnestly.

Voice
Ever wished you could totally overhaul your life? Maybe it's your body you want to transform, your financial situation or your relationship? Or is it that you've just had enough of your nine-to-five job? You want to take the leap, but you just don't know how.

Music key change to rousing/uplifting. Monochrome, black and white to dazzling multicolor, as people exit the revolving door, well-dressed, thin and beautiful.

Voice
The answer is at Quest, Inc.: America's Number One personal development agency.

As each team member is introduced, they appear.

Voice

Dr. Carter King, psychotherapist, author of *Life Plan* and *Life Plan for Two,* has spent the past 12 years helping people and couples realize their potential.

Mickey Prodi, self-made property mogul and the man behind the *Master Your Money and Grow Rich* program, which has financially empowered hundreds of thousands of young adults, is now on hand to give you the secrets of the super rich.

Dr. Jay Lazarus, the man who invented and measured our GDH—Gross Domestic Happiness, and author of *Natural Ecstasy,* will help you figure out what you need to do to set free a fountain of joy in your life.

People make up their mind about you in the first ten seconds. Alexia Redmond, author of the international bestseller *Make Yourself Over,* will help you to transform yourself, outside in.

And finally, he's credited with reducing the rise in obesity, Robert Rivera: A man who has had to rebuild his own body from scratch in twelve weeks . . .

Before and after images of Robert.

Voice

. . . he will give you everything you need, to do the same.

Revolving door with Quest, Inc. inscribed on top.

Voice

Seminars, books, one-on-one coaching. Call 555-QUEST for the life you've been waiting for.

The screen fades to black.

Carter stood and clapped. "Ladies and gentlemen, we just launched Quest, Inc. to the world."

"More like the dead screens of a sleeping America," Jay said. "Does anybody actually watch television at 4 in the morning?"

"We did," Mickey said.

"That was a recording," Jay replied. "It's nine o'clock."

"Oh, yeah," said Mickey, yawning. "Big night last night."

"It was the only affordable time slot," Carter said, sitting down. "By the way, I've given our publicist all your numbers, so we can try to secure interviews."

"Yeah, I've been meaning to tell you," Robert said, "Oprah called."

Carter nearly yelled, "Why didn't you tell us? That's fantastic!"

"When are you going on her channel?" Alexia asked.

"I'm not," Robert replied.

"Jackpot!" Mickey said, until the words made it to his brain. "Huh?"

"You're not?" Carter asked.

"She was very supportive," Robert said, "loved the interviews I did when I was working on national obesity, but she felt that I'd . . . betrayed the public trust."

Mickey got up in a huff. "We don't need Oprah!" They looked at him skeptically.

"There's always *Jerry Springer*," Robert said in an unsuccessful attempt at levity.

"The good news is that we have our first client today," Carter said.

"We do?" Alexia asked.

"She's coming with a journalist from *The Huffington Post*. The site is going to document her journey."

"Great!" said Alexia.

Carter nodded. "She called to interview us about the Living Well Campaign. No doubt to lambaste us for its failure. I told her about our agency. Now, she wants to do a feature article on the multi-billion dollar personal development industry. The big question: 'Does it work, or doesn't it?' If we succeed with the client they're bringing us, we'll help vindicate not just ourselves, but the industry."

"And if we don't?" Jay asked.

Carter thought about it. "A withering critique of our exaggerated claims followed perhaps by an expose on *60 Minutes* of the false hopes and dreams peddled by the self-help industry."

"Hmm," he replied, "all that should at least give us as much exposure as *Oprah*."

Their newly-appointed receptionist, Doreen, a neat, well-groomed lady in her mid-fifties, with a dark brown perm and a smile that made her eyes twinkle, came through to tell them that a writer from *The Huffington Post*, Victoria Holt, along with Laura Cobb, had arrived for her introductory appointment. The team went out to meet them. Perhaps it was the contrast with their grandiose marble-floored atrium; but as they saw what they saw, almost in unison, their smiles flickered off like they'd been struck by a momentary power failure.

Determined not to reveal any more of her disbelief, Carter switched her smile back on, lurched forward and stretched out her hand. "Hello, Laura! Welcome to Quest, Inc." And then turning to the severe-looking woman next to her, "And you must be Victoria Holt from *The Huffington Post?*"

As the team did their smiling introductions, their brains quietly took in the horror before them. Laura Cobb looked like the resident of a homeless shelter. This was not just a failing of her appearance; she had, in fact, been homeless for five years. Long strands of straggly hair were oiled to her face. Over a floral dress that looked like it hadn't been washed in weeks, she wore an asparagus green jersey that stretched past her knees. More disconcerting was the alcohol infused, days-without-a-bath stench that emanated from her. She looked up and gave them a big, open smile. If at that point any of them softened, the high-pitched, nasal noise that screeched out of her broken toothed mouth, like a train coming into station, made the train seem as if it had slipped off the rails and crashed right there in their beautiful lobby.

"Ready to turn me into a princess?!" Laura shrieked.

Alexia was the last to step forward to greet Victoria and Laura, her standard powerful-first-impression routine delayed by a momentary mental collapse at the scale of the job before her.

"What if we don't pull this off?" Mickey whispered to Carter.

"Failure is not an option," she said under her breath.

Mickey steered Carter away from the spectacle of Laura Cobb, and whispered, "You know as well as I do, long-term homeless people don't change."

"Says who?"

"Look at your sister. Wait until little Ms. Victoria Nosy Parker discovers that."

2

Makeover

BLOG

You too can be president

Victoria Holt
Investigative Journalist

Some of you have asked who these five self-help guru superheroes are. Suffice to say, you know them and you've heard them promise you the sky. Patience! All will be revealed when I release my feature article. What I can tell you is that they remind me of an old aunt of mine who used to say to every kid she met: "Anyone can be president, even you!" Really? There are 312 million people in this country—did she imagine that we'd all share the title simultaneously? Of course, she was just parroting the great self-help anthem: "You can be anything you want to be!" Get ready to find out.

Read Post | Comments (467)

1

DR. CARTER KING stood in front of the floor-to-ceiling cinema screen facing the rest of the team. Looming out was a giant-sized image of Laura Cobb. Big, toothy smile, disheveled hair, a blackened scab above her left eye, hand on hip to complete a picture of street-living chic. The same alarm rang through all their heads: *This isn't going to work.*

Thwack! A sharp, slapping sound woke them from their reverie.

"What *is* that?" Carter asked, irritated.

Jay raised his left wrist, pulling the rubber band around it—thwack! "Negative thoughts," he said proudly. "This is how I change them. The moment I hear my monkey-mind sounding off, 'I can't do this. It's futile. I'm going to fail . . .' I pull the band. The sting breaks the association, stopping my negative response. All change starts with a change of mind."

Carter just about rolled her eyes. "This is going to require a lot more than positive thinking."

"More like a frontal lobotomy?" Mickey deadpanned.

"Look what you did with me," Robert said. "If you could take me from broke, obese and suicidal to here, you can do this. *We* can do this."

Thwack!

They looked at Jay.

"No, we can't. My monkey mind, again. Sorry." Jay pulled his white cotton sleeve over the black band on his wrist and sat rigid, like a Tourettes syndrome patient straining against the impulse.

Carter took in a sharp breath, determined to continue with no further interruptions. "You're about to see the interviews with Laura's friends and family. You're about to get inside her life. Here she is, our first client, the test of our powers, the one to make or break us in *The Huffington Post*: Laura Cobb." Carter clicked the remote control, the lights dimmed and the screen flickered to life.

A well-dressed, elderly woman sits in the middle of a heavy, dark wood couch. A tagline on the bottom of the screen reads: *Marlene Landon, Laura's Grandmother.*

"Laura had the world at her feet," she begins, "and tripped over it." Her hands lie neatly folded on her lap. Only her mouth moves, a thin-lipped, down-crescent slit. "She had everything the others had: good schools, church, neighborhood. The family wasn't rich, but Jonathan and I would always help, if necessary. She could have done anything, been anyone. Well, look at Greg, he's an auditor at a marvelous firm. June is married with three beautiful children, she has a lovely home in Santa Monica. And Laura?" She closes her eyes and shakes her head. "Don't talk to me about Laura." Opening her eyes, she adds, "No family should have to deal with that. I do hope they will be able to snap her into shape."

Cut to: A woman standing in a park. The tagline: *Laura's sister, June Roberts.*

June turns to the jungle gym behind her.
"Kelsey, pull your dress down." She turns back
to the camera and pats the side of her hair.
"Okay?"

"We're still rolling," the cameraman says.

"Laura came top of her class at secretarial
school. She got a great job. In her third
year, she was promoted to office manager, and
a month later, she resigned. Six months later,
she was living on the streets. Don't ask me
why she left, but times are tough and she obviously couldn't get another job, and that was
that. We're praying that this is going to get
her back on track."

The film cuts to a small woman sitting at a
kitchen table, fidgeting with a soup ladle.
The tagline reads: *Laura's mother, Gina Cobb.*

"She was with this . . . *man,*" she begins,
before quickly adding, "this isn't getting
shown on TV, is it?"

A voice from behind the camera: "It's just
for the Quest team."

She breathes in deeply. "I think it was
. . ." struggling to say the word, "*sex,* if
you really want to know. He was handsome in a
devilish sort of way. He died in an assault.
That's what happens on the streets . . ." She
shook her head in despair. "Anyways, a few
weeks ago, I was looking in on her at the
homeless shelter, where she sometimes goes for
a meal, and to help out, and I saw this message on the notice board offering a free,
twelve-week, life-changing program with all
these experts, and I just knew this was it! I
called right there and then and spoke to a
very nice lady, Victoria, who told me that out
of everyone who applied, they were only taking
one person, and they were going to be picked,

you know, like a lottery, out of a hat. And that's when I started praying. I don't think I really stopped until I got the call that Laura's name had been picked." She smiled brightly. "That was God's hand. Then, when I told Laura, she . . . ah, she was very surprised . . ."

There is the sound of a door opening. Gina looks to the side, worried. The camera follows her gaze to a man in a white shirt and tie, carrying a briefcase.

"What's this all about?" he asks, his brow furrowed.

"It's for Laura," she replies, "so the people at the agency can understand how to help her."

He walks up to the camera and looks into the lens. "Here's how to help her: Don't take any of her nonsense, you hear me? Be firm with her. You tell her this is the end of the road. Her last chance!"

Cut to: Two people sitting on the pavement under a highway bridge, their belongings piled up in plastic bags. Caption: *Laura's street friends, Tom and Liz.*

The woman, her plump, wrinkled midriff exposed below a hauled-up dirty white vest, turns to the man. "Laura has been on the streets for . . . how long now, Tom?"

"Dunno," he says, drawing on and then removing the joint from his mouth, holding in the smoke as he squeezes out the words, "longer than me. I been here 'bout four years." He lets out a billow of smoke.

Liz continues, "When the road's your home that long, you don't go back. Not possible. Like trying to tame a wild dog—he'll bite your hand off. Like Laura bit that cop, remember,

Tom?" She laughs uproariously, until the laugh
turns into a phlegmy, hacking cough.
  "Lau went in the slammer for that," he says.
  Choking out the last of the cough, Liz adds,
"I missed her then and I miss her now."
  "Remember that time I got the flu that
nearly turned to pneumonia?" he says to her,
before looking back at the camera. "She gave
me an extra blanket, got me medicine. When is
she coming back?"
  "I'm not sure," the muffled voice of the
cameraman replies.
  "Whose going to bite the cops for us now?!"
Liz asks, letting out another raucous cackle.

Carter flicked a remote control that brought up the lights.

Alexia looked dazed. "And Victoria Holt has given us *how* long on Eliza Doolittle?"

"Sixty days," Carter replied.

"Since when did we say we were going to take on homeless people?" Mickey asked.

"Why shouldn't we?" Carter said.

"Because," he replied, "we're here to help normal people realize their potential, not bang our heads trying to rehabilitate crazies and junkies."

Carter winced. Political correctness had never been a hallmark of Mickey's vocabulary. "Laura Cobb has neither mental health nor substance abuse problems. Besides, what's normal?"

Mickey folded his arms. "Being homeless isn't."

"Then I guess I'm not normal." Robert smiled. "If you guys hadn't helped me, I would be sleeping on the streets. I was evicted, I had nowhere else to go. One thing I learned is that each homeless person comes from a home and each has the chance to go back to one. At least one previously homeless person, Liz Murray, has gone on to graduate from Harvard University. I don't know if that will be Laura Cobb, but I'm willing to give it a try."

Mickey looked doubtful.

"You went from food stamps to a multimillion-dollar fortune," Carter said. "Is that not possible for anyone else?"

"Sure," Mickey said, "but I don't see this woman rolling up her sleeves. Because God knows that's what I did."

"And when you nearly lost it all a few years ago?" Carter asked.

He shrugged. "The economy nose-dived. That wasn't my fault, but I got it back together. That's what built this country into the world's greatest—the spirit of self-reliance."

Carter smiled. "I'm all for self-reliance, but sometimes it gets confused with self-congratulation."

Mickey screwed up his eyes.

"There's a tendency that we have to take responsibility for our successes and blame external circumstances for our failures. Yet, with no irony whatsoever, we're quick to put other people's success down to external circumstances, while blaming their failures on their own shortcomings. It's called the 'self-serving bias' and it's a neat trick that enables many of us, here in the richest country in the world, to turn our backs on the more than half a million people who will sleep on the streets or in a shelter tonight."

"Look," Mickey said, "you know how moved I am by bleeding heart liberalism, but don't ever forget that when the Republicans introduced welfare reform in the 1990s, forcing people off grants, it was a huge success, which led many of those getting handouts to get jobs."

"Laura Cobb is not on welfare," replied Carter, "and that's exactly why we're trying to help her get a job—so she doesn't have to sleep under a rainy sky tonight."

"Well," Mickey said, "she just doesn't strike me as someone who's taking responsibility."

"We've signed up to do this, now *we* have to take responsibility." She glanced at her watch. "We have our first paying client with whom I need to meet." She stood up. "Robert, you're going to be showing Victoria Holt from *The Huffington Post* around. Mickey, you've got the first session with Laura. Try this: Imagine she was your daughter."

Frank Brogan, 66, was sitting in the center of a long, white, curved couch in the atrium. He had piercing blue eyes with a jaw that was finally losing its hard edge to age. Looking up at the circular ceiling high above, he gazed down the massive sheets of glass looking out to the terrace and cliff-top garden. The spherical shape of the space reminded him of a planetarium. Maybe that was the intention: *Reach for the stars!* Frank fiddled nervously with his sleeve. He would be reaching for something much less lofty. Looking over at the globular, red, wood-paneled reception desk, he was reminded of an opulent hotel. Sitting behind it was Doreen, Quest, Inc.'s receptionist.

"Quiet day," he said.

Doreen was daydreaming.

Louder: "Quiet day!" His voice echoed through the marble-floored lobby.

"Hmm," Doreen's head wobbled at the interruption. "Um, yes, no. Busy . . ." She looked at the silent phone. ". . . ish." Actually, she couldn't remember the phone ringing once in the past two days. Doreen shuffled some papers, and shone her beaming smile at him.

"So these guys are the best?" Frank got up and walked to her.

"You're going to leave here a new man," Doreen said, eyes twinkling.

"I hope so."

She looked over Frank's shoulder. "Here she comes."

Frank turned and found himself looking at Carter, her hand stretched out to greet him. He took a step back and started coughing.

Carter moved in, "Can I get you some water, Mr. Brogan?"

"No, that's okay, just ..." He coughed some more, stepping back.

"Doreen, please get a glass of water," Carter asked.

"Of course." Doreen ran off.

Frank's cough settled.

"Let's go up," she said. "Doreen will bring it up to my office."

Frank kept his hand in front of his mouth. "Are you taking me to Dr. King?"

"I am Dr. King, Dr. Carter King."

"You are?"

"Pleased to meet you." She stuck out her hand again.

Frank drew his hand to his mouth and started coughing again. "Excuse me ... to be honest ... I'm not really sure about this whole thing."

"Well, you came here, so you must be more sure than you think. Let's go." Carter made for the stairs.

"No." Frank stood frozen, a look of extreme discomfort lining his face.

Carter turned around. "What?"

"I can't do this."

"You've already paid for your initial consultation, Mr. Brogan. Why not just see how that goes?" Carter walked back toward him, lifting her hand to put it on his shoulder.

He took a step back. "Excuse me, I ... ah, have this thing about being touched."

She looked into his eyes sympathetically. "Is that why you're here?"

"Sort of."

"Okay, not a problem. There are many people with wide proximity boundaries. We'll address that in our session. Follow me up."

Carter proceeded before realizing that Frank was not coming. She turned around.

"Is there anyone else I could . . . ?" He trailed off, realizing that he was about to give the game away.

"Anyone else you could . . . ?"

They looked at each other. Carter began to register. Frank registered her registering.

"I don't want to be like this, I just didn't know you were . . ."

"Black," she filled in.

He looked down, closing his eyes. "Is there anyone else?"

She gave him an icy stare. "You could try the Ku Klux Klan."

Victoria Holt was in her early 40s. She had the clenched, severe expression of a journalist with a radar for rot. In one of her rare poetic moments, after a glass of red wine or two, she would have told you she was a truth seer. For some reason that she never stopped to question, the truth invariably stank.

Robert was taking her on a tour of Quest, Inc.

"So how long do you work with each client?" she asked, notebook and pen in hand.

"It's not one-size-fits-all, but for a body transformation, you're looking at about twelve weeks."

"What do you charge?"

He hesitated. Like most businesses, they had struggled to come up with a price. They could never charge for one-on-one coaching what they charged for an hour's speech. Besides, coaching was more of a way to prove their effectiveness, provide material for their books and seminars, and give back. Still, it had to be a profitable business. So what to charge? Price signified value. What was the price of fixing a broken marriage or extending longevity? How did you price a method for happiness, or a key to achieving a dream? Or in a world where models could get paid more than surgeons, did price really signify value at all? Economists had a simple equation: high demand plus low supply equals high price. That was why one man, Michael Jordan, could get paid more by Nike than all their Malaysian factory workers combined. There were millions of people available to do factory work (high supply), but only one Michael Jordan (low supply). In the same vein, while you could pay under a hundred dollars for a life coach, there was only one Quest, Inc. So, why was Robert struggling to tell Victoria Holt the price of an hour of their time? Maybe because it meant putting a value on himself, and after everything that had happened, he still wasn't sure he was worth it.

"Well, as you know we're not charging for Laura," he began, "and we do take financial need into consideration. We expect to do a lot of pro bono work."

"What do you charge?" she repeated.

Robert tried to say the words without altering his expression: "Fifteen hundred dollars per forty-five minute session."

Victoria smiled incongruously, but didn't flinch. She made a note.

Robert led her into a room with the words "Body Temple" emblazoned above the grand, double wooden doors. Victoria looked out at the high-tech exercise equipment. "So this is your gym?"

"Do you like going to the gym?"

"Not particularly." She scribbled something down.

"You're not alone. 90% of gym contracts are bought and not used. We call this room our 'Body Temple.' The name inspires our clients to come and honor, through activity, the only home they've got."

"Right," she replied, "and my dog's name is Einstein, but he still can't do calculus."

"You know better than anyone, Ms. Holt, that a good headline draws readers." He led her across the high-gloss wooden floor. "But it's more than a name—our training is based on the pleasure principle. Through music, affirmations and identifying the correct program for the individual, our clients are taught to love the process of getting and maintaining a beautiful, healthy body. You won't continue with something you hate. Our motto is: No pain, no pain."

"Sounds great," she finished scribbling. "Why didn't it work for you?"

Robert knew this was coming, he just didn't expect it so soon. "I was dealing with a bunch of personal problems."

"Surely this—your *Body Temple*—should have been your savior, not your Achilles' heel."

He turned to her. "Is this story about me or Laura Cobb?"

"Both, if she fails. I know, terribly unlikely, but if she does, I need to be able to explain to the world why the peddlers of instant transformation are unable to take their own medicine."

Robert felt the anger rising. "None of us ever said we were perfect." It sounded petulant, even to his ears.

"No, you said it was easy. So easy, that by the end of your national campaign, obesity, personal debt and divorce had increased." She shook her head. "That's quite a result you bled the public purse to get."

"None of us got paid. It was all voluntary."

"And the twenty-four million dollars spent on the awareness campaign, on your recommendation, who stumped up that? I'll tell you who. We did, the American people, who are fatter and more indebted than before."

"Things might have been even worse without the campaign," Robert managed to splutter. "We can't say for sure that it didn't help."

She laughed. "Of course, look how well it helped you to—what was that snappy phrase of yours? *Flatten your fat.* Helped you so much that you didn't just pack on a few pounds, you became obese. Or are you saying that without the campaign you would have been . . . worse?"

Robert didn't reply.

Victoria Holt stood poised with her pen on the page. "No comment?"

Robert felt like he was swimming inside his own brain, a microscopic avatar sloshing about in the lake of chemicals that filled a single bouton, the bulbous end of one of his ten billion neurons. The particular neuron, in which Robert saw himself splashing about, was frantic. Along with its own tribe of hundreds of thousands more, it had been stimulated by the stress of Victoria Holt's implied accusation that Robert Rivera was a fake and a fraud. Robert sensed that the more he thrashed, the more he would kick up the turbulence of those nervous chemicals. Then he knew what would happen. A neurotransmitter would burst through the bouton, firing up the nerve in front, setting off a chain reaction that, in microseconds, would lead him to make a very bad decision. He had not wanted to ask his colleagues to hide away any high fat food; he didn't want them to know how much he was still haunted by the allure of big number calories.

As he leaned on the open fridge door, his ravenous eye immediately radared in on the sugar and fat-packed double chocolate cheese and cream cake. He knew one slice would never be enough—that when he polished off that plate, he would still want more, and more, and more. If he could just hold on, calm down, float on those chemicals instead of flail, the craving would subside. He needed to divert his attention, close the fridge, and choose something else—an hour of weight training. The relief that came from exercise would not come as instantly as the swirl of sweet fat coating his mouth, sliding down his gullet and gently padding the empty interior of his belly; but from experience he knew it *would* come, and when it did, that tribe of warmongering nerves that urged him to eat himself into a stupor would be quelled. Could he wait? Did he really control those chemicals or did they control him? He stuck his face into the fridge—all he needed was a smell, the smell of coco-infused cream on a biscuit base. Like a ghost, his hand glided in.

"Robert."

He shot up turning his back to the fridge, as he shut it behind him.

It was Alexia. "You okay? You look pale."

"Great! Just getting a quick snack," he said, holding up a celery stick and walking out.

If opposites attract, looking at Laura Cobb and Mickey Prodi, one would have thought them soul mates. Him: a thin pinstripe, tailored suit with the white, open-collared shirt standing high at a perfect, flop-proof angle. Her: a dirty white bra protruding from a stretched green sweater pulled over her knees. Her oily hair and smudged complexion was the perfect foil to his smooth, clean, tanned features.

They sat next to one another on an antique black and white damask upholstered couch in the Freedom Room, the place where money matters were discussed—freedom, according to Mickey, being the ultimate goal of wealth creation. Other than the couch and a desk and chair, the Freedom Room was a blank canvas—literally. The walls were lined with white canvas, and projectors were installed in the ceiling.

Mickey was not comfortable sitting next to Laura Cobb. It was less about the unwashed tang wafting off her and more about growing up two blocks down from a Bronx shelter. Mickey's family was seldom more than a paycheck away from homelessness themselves. Laura was everything he had spent his life avoiding.

"Depending on who you talk to around here," Mickey faced Laura, "you'll get a range of colorful explanations about why you find yourself . . ." he searched for a diplomatic term, "habitat-less. Early childhood deprivation, self-sabotage, lack of affordable housing, compassion fatigue—you've probably got a few explanations yourself; but I'll tell you how you landed on the streets, and it also happens to be the only way you're ever going to get off the streets—money!"

Mickey didn't think that Laura looked sufficiently enlightened by his simple, yet profound revelation. Clicking on a discrete remote control in his hand, he stood up. The projectors whirred into action, animating the empty, white canvas lining the walls. For him, the proverbial "blank canvas" was a perfect symbol for money—it could become anything. Mickey went into showman mode for his audience of one—a puzzled-looking homeless woman—having re-entered the high-end, professional speaking circuit, where he commanded five-figure sums. He had always believed the impact of a communication was directly proportional to the size of the show.

"I know it's not fashionable to say so," he began, "but money is *everything*. It's survival: food, shelter, medical care . . . all this comes at a price." The walls filled up with images of various items in each category with a *ka-ching* sound accompanying pop-up price tags. "But that's just the beginning: travel, education, status, leisure and luxuries, all cost. With enough money, you can have virtually anything. Want a meeting with the Pope? Show me the money. What about love? Love stands above money, right? Wrong. Disputes over money are the second leading cause of divorce. People say we focus too much on money; I say we don't focus enough! Most people spend a third of their day working at a job they hate. Why? Money. When you have enough, you go to the Caribbean or work because you want to. Money is freedom."

He sat down next to her, delighted to be guiding this lost soul out of financial purgatory. "So, we need to find a way for you to leverage your talents into some cold, hard cash. Let's consider your job options . . ."

Laura tilted her head. "I've got a job."

"Yeah?"

"I collect recyclable trash."

"Right, but you do that because you *have* to. That's a horrible job."

Laura frowned.

"How much do you make?"

"A few dollars a day."

"There you go, that's why you're on the streets. No one can survive on that. But if you *really* believe in what you're doing, perhaps in an Al Gore, save-the-planet kind of way, we've got to look at how you can expand the economies of scale—maybe build a team of recyclable trash collectors, maybe get in a venture capitalist and see how we can get your own recycling factory, or write a book on recycling, put together a presentation and hit the speaking circuit. Do you have any idea the fortune Gore has made out of that? We both spoke at a banquet in New York last month, and there was at least one more zero on his check than mine." He took a moment to reflect on this with a mixture of perplexity and admiration. "It's a good gig, the whole global . . . greening thing." Mickey looked back at Laura. "What about bringing in the government and getting Third World countries to take the trash in exchange for debt relief?" He looked away, musing to himself. "I know guys who'd put big Benjamin into that." He narrowed his eyes. "I wonder if that would be kosher?" And then after a nanosecond, "Sure, win-win! The world's your silver plate of a dozen A-grade oysters. What do you want to do? We've got to find a way to get you off the streets, ASAP."

Laura opened her mouth.

"Yes . . ." Mickey prompted.

"I'd like to get my hair done with Alexia Redmond."

2

CARTER FELT UNDERSTANDABLY depressed that their first paying client was resistant to the pigment in her skin. But she was certainly not going to let business trample principle.

"Haydon!" A uniformed guard walked toward them. "Please escort Mr. Brogan off the premises."

"Wait!" Frank took a little step toward her. "I want to do this."

"This organization is not in the business of helping racists."

"Isn't that a little prejudiced?" he asked.

"Are you trying to be funny?"

"I didn't choose to be a racist," Frank said, "anymore than you chose to be black."

Carter folded her arms. "You're going to tell me it's the way you were brought up?"

"Yes."

"Well, now, you're a big boy. You can choose."

"I would never call you a girl. Why are you calling me a boy? Isn't that derogatory?"

Carter motioned to Haydon and turned to go.

"You are as allergic to me as I am to you!" he shouted after her. "The difference is that *I* want to change."

Haydon put his big hands on Frank's shoulders.

Carter stopped and turned round. "You want to stop being a racist?"

"That's why I'm here. I want to have this thing cut out of me."

"Let me get this right. You're a racist, but you don't want to be a racist?"

He nodded.

Carter looked at Haydon. "You can let him go." She turned to Frank. "If we do this, you'll be doing it with *me*."

He screwed up his face. "I don't know if I can."

She motioned to Haydon.

"Okay!" Frank shot back, resisting the big man's grip, "I'll do it with you."

Victoria Holt needed a cigarette, not because she was anxious or worried, on the contrary, she was feeling the thrill of it all coming together. Years before, she'd done an article on homelessness. She'd seen how tough the problem was. You didn't get people off the street with a motivational speech and a facial, particularly not a long-term homeless, no-hoper like Laura Cobb. It was incredible how quickly Carter had agreed to the random selection of a candidate. Her only condition was that they be free of mental illness or substance abuse, as if nothing more was necessary for the salvation of a chronically homeless person than the divine touch of Quest, Inc.

Victoria stood in the garden looking out from a grassy cliff, which sloped down dramatically into a tanzanite ocean. She pulled out a cigarette, lit up and inhaled deeply. The place was exquisite; she'd give them that. Of course, "exquisite" was affordable when you shamelessly collected indulgences by promising heaven-on-earth deliverance from a shitty life. She watched the afternoon light flicker across the ocean. That was good, she thought, comparing the overpriced fees of the self-help guru (some of these empty heads earned twenty thousand dollars a speech!) to indulgences, the medieval practice of paying for salvation. Her editor would love that. Of course, she'd have to find another word for "shitty." Besides, she didn't want to rub it into the faces of readers who saw themselves reflected. Her blog posts could afford to be more cynical, they were personal. The feature article would be positive. It would liberate those with the delusion that any of this stuff actually worked, and others from the guilt they felt for not turning their lives around after reading Carter King's, *Live Your Best Life: The thirty day program to a happier, healthier, wealthier you.* Jesus! Where did they get these titles? After she knocked them off their pedestals, they could go back to selling soap powder.

"There are worse places to get your fix."

She turned to see Mickey Prodi behind her, lighting up a cigar.

"You smoke?" she asked.

He looked out at the view. "No, I just want to impress you with my rebellious spirit."

The hypocrite wasn't even trying to hide it. These clowns were making this the easiest article she'd ever written.

"You don't think smoking puts out the wrong message?" she asked.

He looked at her skeptically. "Have you looked in the mirror lately?"

"I'm not selling people the promise of a perfect life."

He looked up, rounding his lips as he let out a plume of smoke. "Life without a cigar would be a life half-lived."

You had to give him a certain brazen candor.

"Besides, I'm not in the health business," he continued, "I'm in wealth. My clients expect a little excess. Not that I encourage anyone to smoke. I'm here to offer financial guidance, that's it. What drugs get put into my body is my business."

"Drugs, plural?" she asked, eyebrow raised.

For a moment, Mickey felt like he'd stepped into sinking sand.

"Yes, Victoria, nicotine is a drug . . . caffeine, alcohol. I guess that will be the title of your article: 'Wealth Creation Expert is Raging Drug Addict.'"

She gave him a wry smile. "No, not the title."

When Mickey was a little boy, he was almost constantly in trouble. He wasn't willfully naughty; he was way too timid to court adult outrage. Poverty spurred some to revolutionary action. To a small, skinny child like Mickey, it was a rope around his neck, reminding him to preserve the little he had. So, when a bouncing ball went crashing through a school window, a library book was lost, or a friend's toy broken, it wasn't deviance; it was clumsiness, forgetfulness, a general incompetence. But to the nuns at Holy Cross Elementary, motive was nothing; consequence was everything. Never known to spare the rod, judgment would fall with a butt-thumping whack. This happened with such regularity, that the moment Mickey realized he had infringed their moral code, like one of Pavlov's dogs, he would feel the cheeks of his buttocks begin to tremble. Mickey was furious to feel his buttocks doing that now.

He walked into Carter's office to find her standing behind her desk, packing up a slim, burgundy laptop bag.

"Laura Cobb doesn't seem very motivated," he said.

"Is it her who's not motivated, or you?"

He ignored the question. "There's something else."

"Yeah?"

"I'm worried about Victoria Holt."

She looked up.

"It's her line of questioning. She's looking for dirt."

Carter clicked her bag closed. "Well then, you better keep yourself clean."

"Me?"

"I'm sorry," Carter said, "did I stand on your petticoat, bump your frilly bonnet? Yes, you. I've said it before that your lifestyle is a risk to this business."

"I'm careful."

"Everyone always is. That's why no one ever gets caught and the papers are empty of scandal."

"This is not about me."

"You're right. It affects all of us." She made for the door. "I'm doing a keynote presentation at the chamber of commerce. I'm going to be late."

"Let's hope it's not the last any of us will be doing for the chamber, because if she finds out about your sister—"

The moment Carter turned and locked his eyes, he knew he had said too much.

Her words came out slow and steady, "Why don't you start with the man in the mirror."

Jay's office could have been a storeroom for theatrical props. There was an elaborate gold throne with a crown and scepter, a white couch in the shape of a cloud, and a toilet without any connecting plumbing, but complete with cistern and bowl. This was where Laura sat looking quizzically ahead. Jay followed her gaze to the four rustic wooden framed pictures on the wall.

"Each picture," he said, "represents the four principles of a successful life."

The first picture on the left was a watercolor of Moses leading the Jews out of Egypt, staff raised in the air.

"Freedom," he said, by way of explanation.

Her gaze shifted to the next picture: Jesus, with too-blue eyes, smiling beatifically.

"Love," he said. "My rabbi's not thrilled about that one. I said to him, 'What, you don't like Jews?'" He laughed; but receiving no response, he coughed and carried on. The next picture was of Buddha, fat and round, in the lotus position. "That's equanimity," he said. The last picture was a blurred photo of a cyclist from behind. "Lance Armstrong," he said proudly. He mistook her blankness for skepticism. "Really. I was there. 1999, 7th stage, Tour de France. I took the picture, he was just so fast. Practice, he represents practice. Four principles of a successful life: freedom, love, equanimity, practice."

Laura didn't respond, but continued to look confused. Jay realized that he still hadn't explained why he had asked her to sit on the disconnected lavatory.

"The toilet," he said, "is the place that we go to flush away the waste, the stuff that's no longer useful to us. What do you need to flush away?"

"You want me to . . ." She made as if too lift up her dress.

"No, no." Jay waved his hands in front of his eyes. "It's a symbol to help you think of what's holding you back, so you can let it go. To get you off the streets, we need to resolve your underlying issues. What's making you unhappy?"

She shrugged her shoulders.

To a hungry therapist, this was opening a bare fridge. No matter, Jay was not one to walk away on an empty stomach. "Everybody's got something."

Her face clouded over. "Well, I guess my family . . ."

"What about them?" he prompted.

"They're embarrassed by me."

Jay bobbed his head up and down, sad and sympathetic, but with the therapist's secret thrill of having found something to chew on. "Go on."

"That's it."

He clenched his brow, failing to conceal his disappointment. She had him on a diet of crumbs. "Too painful?"

She shrugged.

They sat quietly for a few moments, Jay hoping for something to emerge from the therapeutic silence. Attuned to every flicker of her face, he caught her eyeing the gold throne. "You want to step up?"

"Huh?" she replied, confused.

"You want to step up," he repeated, "and claim your rightful place in the world, but you're scared of another misstep and disappointing them some more." Jay motioned in the direction of the throne. "You want to sit there? See what it feels like to be the queen of your life?"

"I'm okay."

"Okay in the pain that you know, unwilling to face the pain of the unknown?" Hearing his own linguistic contortion, Jay suddenly felt like a sitcom parody of a therapist.

Laura seemed to think about it and then frowned. "Actually . . ."

Finally! He had been too quick to judge, the process was working. "Yes . . ." Jay coaxed gently. She had just been laying the table; she was now ready to dish up.

Laura stood. "I need to use the bathroom."

Jay looked away, in more pain than her.

Alexia had her first session with Laura Cobb in an hour. She was on her way to the Makeover room, when she was stopped in her tracks by a beating sound, followed by a muffled yelp. She pricked up her ears. There it was again. She turned to the source, looking up at the bronze, engraved plate on the door: *Dr. Jay Lazarus.*

She knocked discretely. "Jay?"

"Come in."

She opened the door.

He peered over his laptop. "Hello, Alexia."

Everything seemed fine. "Sorry," she said, "I thought I heard a scream. I must have been mistaken."

"Oh, don't worry about that, I've just had to up the ante." She looked at him confused. "The rubber band wasn't extinguishing my negative thoughts, so I've started using a stick." He pulled a long broom from under the table.

"You're beating yourself."

"I'm beating out the pessimism, teaching my monkey-mind to cease its oracle of defeat."

Self-flagellation was another thing that Alexia had failed to envisage when she'd been hired by what was supposed to become the nation's number one personal development agency.

"Our thoughts are not true or false." He put the stick on the floor next to him. "They're just an interpretation of reality. We need to lead them as one might a stubborn mule."

"How's it working for you?" She looked at him dubiously.

Jay steepled his fingers under his chin, contemplating the question. "Aha, another one." He bent down, picked up the broom and smacked his back. "Ow!"

She winced.

He put the stick down. "Too early to tell."

"Is it a good idea to be hurting yourself?" she asked.

"Oh, it won't leave any lasting scars, and it's a really great way to break a negative association. You can't think, 'I'm an idiot and this is never going to work and experience a sharp, stinging sensation at the same time.' Once you've broken the association, it's easier to replace the thought with a more positive and resourceful one. Do you want to try it?"

"I don't think so."

"Come on." He got up and walked toward her, raising the broom.

Alexia backed away with fear in her eyes. "I'd prefer not to."

He closed in on her. "Think of something that's bothering you."

She put her hands up, "This, *this* is bothering me, that you are about to hit me."

"Okay, good. So, I'm going to hit you, and at that point, use the opportunity to shift to a more resourceful thought, such as: 'I am learning a new strategy to escape the captivity of negativity.'"

"No, no, I don't want to do this." The stick came down on her back. "Ow!" she howled.

Hearing the commotion, Carter opened the door. "What's going on here?!"

"We're practicing thought control," Jay said casually.

Alexia was relieved to realize she hadn't been hit very hard. "I don't think it's working very well," she said.

"That's a negative thought." Jay raised the stick to hit her again.

Carter grabbed his arm. "Have you gone out of your mind?"

"It doesn't leave any bruising," Jay said.

"You *have* gone out of your mind," Carter insisted.

"Precisely, we need to get outside our mind to change it."

"Put it down!" Carter commanded.

Jay put the stick under his arm.

"I hope you're not going to try these ludicrous techniques on our clients, and if you are, I hope you have multi-million dollar liability insurance." She took Alexia's arm, "Let's go."

Jay shouted after them, "Laura Cobb is not going to move forward! She has insufficient motivation!"

Carter turned back. "Clearly, it's not working. Maybe you should try hitting yourself harder."

Carter walked back into her office, where Frank was sitting, waiting for her return. Having heard the commotion, he looked at her with an unspoken question.

"It was, ah, nothing," Carter said. "Just a psychological process my colleague was experimenting with."

Frank looked wide-eyed. "A beating?"

"Just pretend it was white on black." She sat down. "So, what is it, Mr. Brogan? Do you think I have a smaller brain, or that I haven't discovered the hygienic properties of soap, or is it an innate disposition to rape, pillage and plunder?"

He shuffled in his seat. "Black people are more likely to be convicted of violent crimes."

"In that case, you must be terrified of white men."

He looked confused.

"World War I and II led to the deaths of over one hundred million people, those wars were largely started and executed by European males." She got up and walked to his side of the table and sat down on it. "Let me tell you what 'primitive' looks like. When my grandmother was fourteen years old, she was walking home a little later than she should have been, when a group of white men stopped their pick-up truck to ask her why she was 'walking white.' If you looked a little too confident, if you didn't seem quite certain of your inferior status, you might be asked such a question in rural Alabama. My grandmother may have looked confident, but it was most likely vigilance. When a pick-up truck full of white men drove by, fear could make you forget yourself and you might lift your head wide-eyed, and wonder if you were going to make it home. She didn't. Not that night. She was raped so badly, she didn't get out of the hospital for three weeks. She was lucky, I guess, that she survived, even if she never was the same."

Frank shook his head. "Those men were evil."

"Were they? If you don't believe someone is human, you treat them inhumanely. Sick beliefs, sick behavior." She stood up. "Most racists believe they're right. At least you know you are wrong."

He looked up at her. "I'm far from the savages who did that to your grandmother, but if I believed I was wrong, I would believe something else. I'm no 'some-of-my-best-friends-are-black racist.' I don't like black people."

Six months since Robert had nearly killed himself, he put down the last sentence of his book. "We never arrive," he wrote, "we just visit." He looked up before adding, "If we want to extend our stay, we need to keep on keeping on." It was an honest reminder that success was not a destination, but an ongoing journey, one he had struggled with, one he *was* struggling with.

Robert felt far from certain his story would be accepted, but he told himself he was writing it for himself. If it got panned, he'd say goodbye to his public life. He'd leave quietly, saving Quest, Inc. from his deadweight. That would be unfortunate, but tolerable. There was another possibility that would *not* be tolerable. It would be devastating. He could barely express it to himself. It scratched on the edge of his consciousness, like a ghost in the shadows. If it could have spoken, it would have said this: "If you publish this book, America will forgive you for your hypocrisy, the public will relate to your fall and embrace your rise. Your book will be an even bigger success than your others. The talk shows will love you, because you won't just have weight loss tips, you'll have a story. There will be clients lining up at your door, because you'll have the ultimate weight loss sales tool—your own 'before and after' pictures. And that's where the truth lies. Nice to blame Papi for your downfall, but deep down you're still a slave to sloth and high-cal snacks. The *real* you is in that 'before' picture, and it's only a matter of time before that's what you become again. And then America will hate you for fooling her not once, but twice, and she will cast you out for good. And you will wish that when you fell off that building, there had been no net to catch you."

3

IN AN UPPER floor lounge of Quest, Inc., there was a spiral staircase that led to a roof garden. Above the roof garden, there was a flat, white, cement roof to protect the stairs and provide some shelter from the Californian sun. Against the supporting wall of the roof was a metal ladder. Victoria's journalistic curiosity, or just the allure of a spectacular view, had got the better of her. She climbed up the ladder and once she reached the top, saw Jay closed-eyed and cross-legged, facing the ocean. Hearing her, he turned.

"Sorry," she said, backing down.

"It's okay." He got up and walked over, giving her a hand up. They stood together on top of the world, a 360° view stretching forward to the ocean, backward to the Santa Monica Mountains, and on either side the lush, winding Malibu coastline.

She scanned from one side to the other. "Wow!" Her lips remained in a fly-in-the-mouth "O."

He looked at it afresh with her. "It's a good place to reflect."

She turned to him. "I haven't told you how much I respect your work."

Now the fly flew in Jay's mouth. "Your Gross Domestic Happiness Index was illuminating. I appreciated your rigor, the nationwide interviews across every demographic. How did that bring you here?"

"I wanted to apply what we learned."

"Money, beauty, material things were surprisingly low on the happiness ranking," she said. "This agency tells people that without those things, they can't hold their heads up."

"We aren't here to dictate," he replied. "If you're okay being obese, but want to deal with a broken relationship, we'll focus on that."

"You fuel their discontent. You tell them, 'This is where you are, but look where you could be!'"

"Without discontent, we'd still be living in caves. I've realized you can want more and still be happy wanting more."

"And it's all possible, right?" She gave him an ironic stare. "Whatever the mind can conceive and believe . . ."

He reflected for a moment. "If there was a sure-fire way to the pot of gold at the end of the rainbow, we'd all be there. It's trial-and-error. You try something out—if it works, great, if it doesn't, you try something else. You can't just be willing to change your life, you have to be willing to change your strategy." He fingered the black band on his wrist. "For weeks, this little band was helping me control my negativity. Then it stopped working. I don't know why. Maybe it's like a song you've heard too many times, you grow immune to it. That doesn't mean you should give up on music. Nothing is guaranteed to work or work forever. You've just got to keep on trying."

"Pity you don't sell it like that."

Jay turned to her. "All marketing focuses on the best-case scenario. Think they'd sell any Ferraris if the advert said, 'Not having back seats can be inconvenient, but at least you'll always get there in style . . . as long as you don't burn to death in a high speed crash?'"

She smiled. "So, is Laura going to get there?"

He looked back at the ocean. "Certainly won't kill her, but I don't know. Maybe not."

"I appreciate your honesty." Making for the ladder, she added, "You're right though, it probably won't win you more clients."

Carter found Robert doing bench presses in the Body Temple. He dropped the dumbbell back on the holding bar with a clang.

"I can come back," she said.

He sat up. "I was just finishing."

She took a seat on the bench opposite him, while he patted his skin with a short towel.

"How's your book going?" she asked.

"Yeah, good."

"Still not finished?"

"Ah, no," he lied.

"We need to start planning the release. The publicity is going to be crucial for the agency."

"It's not quite there, yet."

"Don't let perfection be the enemy of completion."

He nodded.

"So, tell me," she said, changing the subject, "as a Latino, have you ever pretended to be white?"

Robert looked at her quizzically.

She continued, "To pay my way through college, I did some freelance editing and typing through this agency based in Atlanta. My contact there was a woman, Loraine. We only ever met on the phone. I was efficient and she was always happy with my work. I got to know a bit about her family. She had a severely autistic son. She'd set up a non-profit daycare for other autistic kids whose parents couldn't afford private care. When I was having difficulties of my own, she was really supportive, a great listener. Then one day in passing, she mentioned she'd just had to fire one of her editors. 'Right from the start,' she said, 'he was unreliable and lazy'—and then she slipped in, as if this would explain it all—'. . . black,' before moving on to ask how things were going at college. And what did I say? 'Fine, Loraine, just fine.' I worked with her for about another year, never brought it up. Never quite forgave myself, either. Later, I made a commitment that if ever anyone made the slightest racist/anti-Semitic/anti-Muslim remark, I would come down on them like a ton of bricks. 'That is racist, ignorant rubbish,' I would say, in those exact words. I rehearsed them, so I would never feel tongue-tied, so I would never seem to be supporting them, so I would never again be a traitor."

"How did they respond?" Robert asked.

"Ended the conversation."

Robert got up and started his post-workout stretch. "My grandfather still can't refer to whites as anything other than 'anglos, gringos, desabridos.'"

"How do you respond?"

"'*Abuelito,* you didn't get the memo? They're you and I, just a little paler.' He's pretty stuck in his ways, but with some people it gets a conversation going. That gives me the chance to maybe sow a new seed. First year I played high school basketball on an all-white team, every now and again one of my teammates sidled up to me and told me how we had to take out the nigger point guard on the other side, as if I might appreciate getting included on the right side of the racial divide for a change. 'Hey, bro,' I'd say with a smile, 'you should be in a museum. I didn't know there were white people who still used that term.' Sometimes it would lead to a discussion—they weren't always interested—but pretty soon that language was gone from the team."

Robert put on his tracksuit top and zipped up. "You need to invite Frank over for a little home-cooked meal, let him meet some of your friends, so he can see there aren't any horns growing out of anyone's head."

Carter got up shaking her head. "He repulses me. They all do. The small-minded stupidity of their Nazi beliefs."

"Wh—" Robert tried to get a word in but Carter was on a roll.

". . . The demented vanity of it, that he's better, not because of anything he's done, but because he was born susceptible to skin cancer. What the hell do these people think? That 67 million people elected a black president out of some guilt-ridden, bleeding heart liberal, affirmative action—"

"Where's your compassion?" Robert broke in.

The question silenced her.

"Racism is delusional, it's a mental disability. Help him. Unless you're too clouded by indignation. In that case, maybe *you* need to work something through."

Mickey stuck his head through the door. "Have you seen Laura?"

They shook their heads.

"We're supposed to be doing a job search and interview skills session and she hasn't turned up!"

Mickey walked past the Makeover room. With Laura not pitching, he had an hour to kill. The door was open. He glanced in and saw Alexia working on her laptop in an armchair by the open window. Her smooth, dark hair was pulled back into a high ponytail. Her brow was furrowed, a little crevice of concentration. He wasn't quite sure yet where he'd place her. A 7.9, maybe an 8. He would never have admitted to anyone that he placed women on a 'babe scale.' Even he realized there was something distasteful about converting a human being into a number, like tattooing a quality grade on a cow. But actually, it was a good reflection of how he saw himself—not as an aesthetic number—he was no Brad Pitt, he had long since come to terms with that—but as a financial number. His self-worth was directly linked to his financial worth, and the greater the number on his income statement, the greater he expected the number on his girl-friend. As a gawky teenager, girls had almost uniformly spurned him. Even now, with his extensive plume of greenback feathers, getting women wasn't effortless, but it was way easier. Because, he reflected in his more cynical moments, to them, he too was nothing more than a number, the number on his bank statement.

Still, here was Alexia, throwing the whole damn scale out the window—no more than an 8—and yet there was something about her. He hovered at the door. *Go talk to her,* he told himself, but he couldn't move. Inside the big man, there was still the gawky teenager, and that gawky teenager couldn't move. He headed for the restroom.

Above the two gender symbols on the bathroom door, indicat-ing a unisex restroom, there was the word "Gratitude," a reminder to use the time not just for bodily relief, but also for private thanksgiv-ing. Mickey entered and immediately began scanning under the doors of the stalls. Confident he was alone, he faced a silver framed mirror over one of the porcelain basins. He straightened the lapels of his tailored suit jacket, took a deep breath, smirked, and whispered something to the mirror. He shook his head, it didn't sound right. Putting on a winning smile, he whispered the words again, this time concluding by kissing his bunched up fingertips. Better. He fiddled with his hair and headed for the door. Before he could get there, it opened of its own accord. Alexia walked in.

Taken by surprise, he launched in, "Hey, tonight sushi and sun-downers at Zuma's." He smooched his fingers tips. *"Delizioso."* It was one of four Italian words he knew.

"Cool," she said walking through. "I'll meet you all there."

This took him by surprise. "I don't know . . . about the others. I mean it's just . . . me."

She turned back to him slowly, allowing her brain to process a revised interpretation of the invitation. Ordinarily, receiving a proposition from a shameless womanizer like Mickey Prodi would have elicited a verbal slicing of the balls. "I'm such an idiot," she said breezily. "I forgot, I've got a family thing tonight." So why, instead, was she going for Miss Congeniality?

"Okay," Mickey said. "Tomorrow?"

"Tomorrow?" she repeated, trying to buy a bit more time, for yet another congenial lie. Was he going to force her to manufacture a third one after this?

"Tomorrow, I've got . . . another thing." Congenial lies were not her specialty.

"Oh," Mickey said, the subtext finally breaking through the layer of ego insulating his brain.

"Yoga . . . I've got yoga on Thursdays. Thanks, though. Enjoy!" she said, running off before he asked her about the night after that. She scolded herself for trying to think up a lie. It was true, she did have yoga on Thursdays. Then she scolded herself for pandering to a womanizer. Why did she do that? Why not just tell him the truth: She would sooner tattoo a tramp stamp on her face than go on a date with him. Why the tact? Well, there was the obvious: Empowered woman that she was, he was a senior partner, to whose power she was still subject. Then, there was the less obvious, the thing she didn't quite articulate to herself: It was pleasing to have an adoring dog, an adoring Top Dog, running after you.

Having waited for her to beat a merciful distance between them, Mickey walked out of the bathroom. He wouldn't have felt more winded if she had shoved her elbow into his stomach. He'd just been rejected by a 7.9. And that was why that 7.9 had just become a 10.

Laura thought she would make it back in time for her session with Mickey, but on the street, time was a less pressing issue. Besides, she was checking up on Billy. He had been hit by a car last summer. She was relieved to see him panhandling at his usual intersection, his green and yellow beanie glowing in the sun.

"Florence!" he called out when he saw her, his face lighting up through a big graying beard that rested over his expansive chest. He had come up with the nickname after her Florence Nightingale exploits, one of which was resuscitating him after his accident.

"Billy Potter," she said admonishingly, "should you be up on your feet?"

He grabbed her by the waist. "Happy for you to take me off my feet!" He put his hand on her lustrous hair, taking in her new complexion and fixed-up teeth. "Look at you—beautiful! I hope you're not going to get all la-dee-da on us."

She brushed his hand off her hair. "Hands off the goods," she said with mock superiority.

"Hey," he said, laughing, "did I ever thank you for saving my life?"

"Only a hundred times."

"Thank you for saving my life. There, now it's a hundred and one."

She had probably saved many lives. The clinic had even put her through a first aid course. She was their early warning system. If someone was in trouble, she would do what she could and call in the medics for the rest.

She looked at him, her brow a crevice of concern. "Should you really be up on your feet?"

"Doc has given me a clean bill of health. 'Cept my liver, I'm the healthiest man alive."

"How's Casey, Tom, Sarah, Dennis . . . ?"

"Casey's back on the White Sugar. She says she's just freebasing, but you can see the drill marks."

Laura gave him a pained look.

"Dennis is as loopy as ever, but you think we can get him admitted to Universal Psychiatric? So, all in all, we're the same old, happy family. Tom and Sarah are good. Just . . ." He pulled a big, sad face. "We miss you."

She smiled.

"You're coming back, right?"

No reply.

"We need you here," he said pleadingly.

"Where're the others?"

"Under the bridge."

"Come," she said, grabbing his hand. "Let's go find them."

Sitting opposite Frank Brogan, Carter felt the disgust coil in the back of her throat. Of course, Robert was right, her judgment was clouded. A good therapist was impartial. A good Christian would face hate with compassion. She knew this, and yet she could summon neither impartiality nor compassion. The deep faith in her expertise that she had developed over years of practice had now given way to the doubt of a beginner. Was this her lesson? To be reminded that she wasn't as great as she thought? It was so infuriating knowing what she needed to feel, yet being unable to feel it. Was that Frank? Wanting to feel something else, yet not being able? And if so, how could she help him, when she couldn't even help herself?

She leaned her elbows on the table, cupping her chin in the palms of her hands, and then shook her head from side to side. "I don't know if I can do this."

Frank sat far back in his chair. "You don't like me."

Carter put her hands on the table. "I guess it's mutual, except you dislike me because of something I have no control over."

"And you dislike me because of how I was brought up. I was never allowed near . . . African Americans."

"You've never had contact with black people?"

"You're the first I've ever had a conversation with."

She screwed up her eyes, incredulous.

"My father was a founding member of Aryan Nations. I've lived most of my life amongst white supremacists."

Carter couldn't quite believe who she had sitting in her office. "I didn't realize that organization was still around."

"There're only a few hundred members left. I was never a card-carrying member, but I was part of its segregated community." He shifted uncomfortably. "We never hurt black people."

"Your beliefs hurt."

He pulled his wallet from the inside pocket of his jacket, took out a small dog-eared photo, and placed it on the table in front of her. Carter picked it up. The picture was of a smiling black boy, about five years old. He was looking up at something, perhaps a kite or an airplane, delighted, unconscious of the camera's lens.

Frank leaned forward, "That's my grandson."

She looked up at him.

"He's twelve now, I've never met him. Six weeks ago, my wife died. I found it in her drawer. When our daughter married a black man, I cut her off. When I saw this picture . . ." He swallowed stiffly. "I want to meet my grandson."

"The great promise of the self-help movement: *Follow this formula and success is guaranteed.* Is it true? Sure, if you happen to be the self-proclaimed guru with your name on the book, selling millions."

Victoria was puffing hard on a cigarette, composing the opening lines of her blog, as she paced the cliff top garden overlooking Point Dume beach. Turning around, she nearly bumped into Jay, who had run out to meet her.

He stepped back, a little breathless, but undeterred.

"You know, people *do* change. It can take a long time and it can happen in an instant," he snapped his fingers. "We give them a rough map and we give them hope. Sometimes, we oversell it—we make it sound easier than it is—and sometimes it just doesn't work, but often it does."

Victoria inhaled and blew out the smoke through the side of her mouth. "I've been smoking this muck since I was fourteen," she began. "I wanted to give it up for almost as long, but I couldn't. It wasn't because I didn't believe enough. Up until I started trying, I would have told you I could have given up any day I decided. But I couldn't. It wasn't because I didn't try hard enough. I've been on the pill, the patch, smoke-enders. So why can't I stop? Well, the fact that my grandparents and parents were smokers and my grandmother and father were alcoholics may give you a clue—addiction runs in our genes. Having started as a teenager, when the conditioned response kicks in harder and faster, is another factor. Then, there's the fact that I'm prone to anxiety, and nicotine is a form of self-medication— it calms me and helps me to focus. My point? Many people, like me, are not going to change. The weight of nature is just too heavy. You're going to get us high on the dream of a new life, and we're going to wake up the next morning hung over as we scramble for a cigarette, feeling even more of a failure."

Jay nodded. "You're right. You won't change."

She looked at him, surprised. "What happened to all that: *From quest to success* talk? But once again, I do appreciate that someone in this agency has a little honesty."

"The reason you won't change," he continued, "is you've given up on the possibility. You're like a boxer who's hung up his gloves. You can't win the match, if you don't get in the ring."

"Okay . . . *Coach*," she said with a sardonic smile. "I'll get back in the ring. Get me to stop smoking and you'll have something at least as good as changing Laura, maybe better—you'll have changed the cynical journalist writing the piece. I like you, so I'm going to make this easy for you: You don't have to take on the challenge. If you decline, I won't report on this, but if you do agree and you don't succeed . . . Think about it." She started walking off.

"Victoria!" he called. She turned back. "You have a deal."

She smiled. This was getting fun.

Laura had made it back in time for her exercise session with Robert. They sat on deck chairs alongside the outdoor pool. She was in a bathing suit with a towel wrapped around her.

"You know when my mother told me she'd submitted my name for this program," Laura began, "and I'd been chosen, I almost turned it down. I'm glad I didn't." Voice work with Alexia had taken out her shrill nasal tone.

"You've missed appointments."

She scrunched up her face like a naughty schoolgirl. "I know."

"You were top of your class at secretarial school?"

She nodded.

"That must have taken a lot of discipline. Within three years, you got promoted beyond your qualification."

"I thought the raise they gave me would make me hate my job a little less. It didn't. When I resigned, my father lost it. We only started talking again when I agreed to do this program."

"This is your chance to get back up again, find something you love."

"What about you?" she turned to him. "How'd you turn your life around?"

He looked away. "I was dying. Through the cracks in my destruction, I saw life and I decided I wanted it." Looking back at her, he added, "And there were all these great people to help me."

She looked up at the sky and closed her eyes.

"Whenever it gets too tough," he said, "just think about what you're escaping from—the dirt, the druggies, the harassment."

"I don't know," she mused, "for lots of people, the street is better than what they're getting at home—like being forced to be their father's girlfriend. Sure, there're the crazies who'd be better off in a mental ward, but until they stop chucking them out to fend for themselves . . ." She shook her head. "Wish we could do more for the druggies. Lots of people would be better off elsewhere."

"Surely *everyone* would be better off elsewhere?" Robert asked. "Isn't it dangerous?"

"In the early days, I was robbed, nearly raped, but then you figure out where to go, where not to, who to hang with. I first hung with a crazy guy. We broke up ages ago. I hadn't even seen him for about three years, but . . ." She pursed her lips and looked up. "He was killed earlier this year. He was drunk, got into a fight, fell off the curb and got hit by a car." She looked back at Robert. "This life isn't for most people, but . . ." Laura smiled. "Ever been on Venice Beach at sunrise? Tucked into your sleeping bag, you got a buddy next to you boiling an early morning cup of tea. If I want a night in a bed, I can go to one of the shelters, or stay in my brother's garden cottage—his wife isn't over the moon about that, but I keep to myself. There's a free clinic. The Evangelicals provide food handouts, but I don't take that, I make enough on my recyclables, but I sometimes help them at the soup kitchen."

She looked at the pool and whipped off her towel. "Time for a swim!" Running over, she jumped into the air with a scream of delight and water-bombed, sending up a cascading fountain.

Victoria came down the stairs leading to the pool. "Someone's having fun," she said.

Robert turned to her, "She's sticking to her workouts."

"I can see."

It wasn't much, but it was the first inkling of something positive he'd heard from Victoria Holt.

"Everyone wants to be more," he said. "They just need a chance."

She nodded, watching Laura swim.

Robert should have felt pleased, but instead he found himself wondering if everybody *did* want to be more.

The Quest, Inc. team convened in the Think Tank, the renamed dining room. Mickey finished off a chocolate donut, as he stared at Alexia, thinking that she was the most beautiful woman he had ever seen in his entire life. Alexia turned to look at him. He averted his gaze. The last thing he wanted was for her to think she was the most beautiful woman he had ever seen in his entire life. But unless he was seeing things, out the corner of his eye, he sensed her still looking at him. He looked back—she was! Staring at him, intently, and now, caressing her lips. Holy mother and child, the woman had succumbed. He gave her a flirtatious smile, almost regretting how easy it had become. She drew her fingers across her lips more rapidly. It was irritating to be interrupted in this beautiful moment—their first *real* moment—by Robert leaning in and handing him something. He looked down. It was a tissue.

"You've got chocolate icing on your lip," he said.

Carter swung her laptop around, so that the screen faced the team. "We picked up these hearty blog posts from Victoria Holt. Nothing about us yet, but her tone . . ."

They leaned in, taking a few minutes to get the gist.

"The good news," Robert said, "is that we've turned a corner on the health front and Victoria seems to have acknowledged that."

"Wonderful," Carter replied, "except . . ." She threw a book on the table, it spun toward Jay, its red and yellow cover glared: *SCAM: How the Self-help Movement Deceived America.*

Jay picked it up. "Well, maybe the industry should be looking at itself a bit more critically. Flush out the charlatans."

"According to the authors," Carter clenched her brow, "we are all charlatans."

"Free speech," Jay said, opening the book. "I don't see the problem. Anyway," he said, checking the date, "this book has been out for years."

"The problem is," Carter replied, "the researcher on the book is a woman named Victoria Holt."

Silence.

"She's going to fry us," Alexia said, a stray line of worry marring her otherwise smooth brow.

Mickey pointed at Carter. "You let the fox into the coop."

Carter remained calm. "We all agreed to this."

He stood. "It was your call, Madame Leader."

She looked up at him. "Is that what you tell your clients? There's a simple solution to your problem—find someone to blame."

Mickey paced the room. "We're finished, do you realize that? When she's done with us, we will never be able to step foot on a stage again. I'm going to spend the rest of my life in a back room managing my property portfolio." He looked around the table. "That is, if we don't get sued for malpractice first. In that case, let's hope Laura Cobb can show us the ropes on Main Street."

Jay shook his head. "Hold on, it's not so bad."

They looked at him.

"I made a deal with Victoria today. If I can help her to stop smoking, we're going to get something really positive out of her, even if things don't totally work out with Laura."

Alexia turned pale. "And if you don't get her to stop?"

"Even if she wants to stop," Carter added with a grimace, "do you really think she's going to let any of us be the catalyst?"

Mickey picked up the book. The letters "S-C-A-M" glistened in the light. "This is the woman's bible. She's here to make sure the charlatans are sent to hell."

4

FRANK HAD HAD five sessions with Carter, two more since he'd revealed his grandson. At their last session, she'd made an appeal to science: "Do you know that I could be genetically closer to you than I am to another black person? There are bigger differences within racial groups as there are between them. I have also run from that fact, deciding that if you think I'm worse than you, I will make you worse than me." But as he had got up to leave, it was her final question that stopped him in his tracks: "Frank, do you really believe that God made a terrible mistake when he brought an entire group of people into the world?"

Tonight, at her home, would be his last session. It was to be part treatment and part test. Dressed in a brown corduroy jacket with a knitted tie, he smelled of Old Spice cologne. He rang her bell. When she opened the door, a stream of party sound—music, chatter and laughter—flowed through the gap, until she closed it behind her and stood with him outside.

"This is not easy for me . . ." Carter began, "or you, I suppose."

He nodded.

"If you make any racist remark, if you cause offense in any way, I will ask you to leave."

He nodded again.

Carter shifted nervously, still unwilling to let him in. She took in a deep breath and put her hand on the door.

He hesitated, "Um . . ."

She turned back to him.

"Do they know . . . about me?"

"I don't want them to have any assumptions about you. Maybe you can return the favor."

He nodded and walked in behind her.

It wasn't that Frank had a swastika tattooed on his forehead, but ever since Carter had suggested that he join her for a social gathering, he was concerned that they would figure him out and he would be ridiculed and perhaps violently ejected. For the first time in his life, he knew a black person—Carter. He wasn't sure he liked her, but he respected her. Then there was his grandson—with those angelic eyes—how could he be anything but good? Of course, his grandson was partly white. In the worst-case scenario, there probably wouldn't be violence. Besides, Frank knew how to hold his own, but what if he said the wrong thing and embarrassed Carter? It wasn't in Frank's nature to pretend.

Walking in behind her, he looked around for other white people. There were none. He felt a powerful urge to just turn around and leave until, despite his own nervous aloofness, a woman greeted him smilingly. Frank nodded, holding a respectful smile up as best he could. Not everyone was super-friendly—some were wrapped up in their own conversations, while others seemed less outgoing. As he wandered through the lounge, on to the porch, overlooking the back garden, he hovered around people talking about things he wasn't interested in, or didn't understand, or occasionally drew him in. It was strangely ordinary. He soon found himself being greeted by a couple of men with whom he fell into conversation.

A few yards away, also on the porch, a psychologist was talking to Carter about a patient. Carter was attempting to listen, while unsuccessfully trying to hear what Frank and her two cousins were talking about. The conversation seemed amicable enough and she let down her guard. At least half an hour passed and they were still at it. But that's when Carter noticed things getting heated. Marvin was raising his arms above Frank's head in a forceful motion.

Carter excused herself and ran over. "What's going on?"

Wrapped up in the moment, they ignored her.

Marvin raised his arms higher, "You lift the rod right up, but when you come down, it's all in the wrist—"

"But you got to think like a fish," the other man cut in.

"That's exactly it," Frank agreed, "you got to lure them in with what they understand. If you take a bit of time to see what insects are on the water, you can create something that they're used to. Still, I'd love to see how you do that arm action without rocking the boat."

"You show me how you design your lure," Marvin said, "and I'll show you the wrist swing."

Frank smiled. "*Deal.*"

If anyone had told Frank he was about to go into a room full of black people and, within a short time, he would forget that they were black, he would have thought them a liar. Yet that was exactly what happened. The color of Marvin's skin became about as interesting as the color of his socks. What really grabbed Frank's attention was not what he looked like, but what he said, not *what* he was, but *who* he was. Up until that moment, it had never occurred to Frank that he might have more in common with one black man than he did with many white men.

Carter left them, which was pretty much where they stayed for the rest of the evening. Eventually, along with a few others who had decided to ignore the undeniable fact that she had unplugged the sound system, she had to ask them to leave.

Walking out the front door, Marvin turned to Frank. "5 a.m., Saturday?"

Frank smiled, "I'll have breakfast packed for us, *and* the fish."

After Marvin had said goodbye to Carter and walked off, Frank turned to her. "The worst part of all this, is to see the relationships I could have had."

She took a moment and then said, "It's not too late to be a grandfather to that boy."

Frank's brow creased, "I think it's too late for his father to accept me."

"I don't know," she said, walking him down the stairs, "maybe right now it is." They looked up at a sickle moon, only just visible. She turned to him. "If you're not looking for a new moon, you don't see it, but as long as it keeps growing, you're unlikely to miss it."

"Do you see it?" he asked, looking into her eyes.

She gave him a smile that made his heart quicken. "Yes," she said.

All at once, Frank found himself swirling into the deep black pools at the center of her irises. He took in a breath to steady himself. And then, for the first time, he noticed something else that kept his pulse in a canter—her flawless cocoa skin.

Later that night, Carter was alone in the Point Dume nature preserve. She had her eye locked on the summit high above. Bathed in moonlight, its pointy peak glowed with quiet majesty. She looked down at the long, rolled up bundle in front of her. It was wrapped in a thick Persian carpet, bound with rope. As the mountain got steeper, her progress had slowed to nothing. It would have been fine, if it was just her, but she had to heave up this dead weight. Leveraging her foot on a rock below, she pushed with every ounce of effort she could muster. The bundle began to crossbow, the contents were slipping out.

Looking down at the one side, she gasped. It was Laura Cobb's head. She would have to stuff it back in and keep pushing, but something was slipping out the other side—another body. That was why it was so heavy. As the other head slipped out, and the neck gave way, the face flipped toward her. She screamed. It was her dead mother.

Carter woke up wet with sweat. She shook her head in wonder. Not two hours before, she had gone to bed, unusually content. After giving thanks for what appeared to be a turning point in Frank Brogan's life, she sank into a peaceful slumber, only to be woken to the violence of this. The internal state was an unruly thing, a wild beast that needed constant taming. Carter relaxed herself with some deep breathing, and then she prayed. She prayed for Laura. She prayed for her mother, and she prayed for herself.

The sun shone on a new day. Laura was finding it hard to stop looking at her reflection in the long, silver framed mirror in the Makeover room. She looked at least ten years younger, her hair hung on her shoulders with a full, dark luster. Her face had been made up in the natural way, which left one wondering if she was wearing makeup at all. Her raised posture and long neck stretched out from a pink, silk blouse. Alexia stood behind, admiring her work.

"You are an *artist*," Laura said, continuing to look at her reflection.

"I had great material to work with. But now the real work begins," Alexia said, as she pulled a silver trolley of body products toward her. "Cleanser, toner, moisturizer . . . for when you wake up in the morning and before you go to bed at night. Eye crème will keep those shadows and bags at bay. Coconut body wash, my favorite! Keeps you smelling fresh, but also replenishes the skin. And then, of course, there's the makeup, which you've now learned how to apply; but you've got to set aside the time, at least twenty minutes, and that excludes the cleansing routine. We've figured out your clothing colors, but this is your only outfit, so we've got a big shop to do." She paused, a little breathless. "Men fight wars, women fight body wars, but you—beautiful—are winning. There are going to be real opportunities for you looking like this. No more hardship."

Laura looked down at the makeup trolley, wearily.

Jay and Victoria had walked to the furthest end of the property, reaching the wall that separated them from the Point Dume Nature Preserve. Here the grass was long and uncultivated.

Victoria stopped. "We've been talking for an hour and, well . . ." She pulled out a cigarette and lit it. "I guess that says it all."

He led her a few paces along and pointed to a pair of handcuffs locked around a ring bolted into the wall, one of the cuffs dangling open. "You see these cuffs?"

She looked down at them.

He lifted the free cuff and pointed it toward her. "Would you put it on?"

"You want me to handcuff myself?"

"I'm asking you, but it's your choice."

"What's this, some kind of New Age enlightenment exercise?"

"If you don't want to do it, you don't have to."

Impatient to bring this to an end, she wedged the cigarette between her lips and locked the cuff around her left hand. She took a drag on the cigarette. "Magic, my craving is gone."

"We haven't really been talking for the past hour," Jay said. "*You* have. You've been going on about why you can't give up: because of your parents and your genes, and the nature of addiction and self-medication, and the effect of nicotine on synaptic transmission. You know a lot about why you can't give up. You've locked yourself to the wall of good reasons. Time to set yourself free. You've got the key—it's called *taking responsibility*."

She looked at the handcuffs and smiled. "Okay, thanks for the folksy metaphor, you can uncuff me."

"I forgot," he continued, "there are more bricks in the wall. If you do stop, you'll have to admit that change is possible and that will totally mess up everything you've come to believe—that we are at the mercy of forces beyond our control, that Big Tobacco is the real culprit, that people like us are cynical liars, in it for the money. And what if you're right? Right about all those good reasons? Does that mean you have to chain yourself to them? See, what is indisputable is that you have the key—choice. You *choose* to do this," he motioned at the cigarette, "or you *choose* to stop. You're free. Make a choice. Leave your mother and the boy you tried to impress when you were fourteen and your synaptic transmission out of it."

She shook the cuff. "Can you unlock this, please?"

"I can't do that."

"Why?"

"I don't have the key."

"This is not good." Her voice was clipped now, brittle. "You handcuffed me to a wall."

"No, I didn't. You cuffed yourself."

"You told me to."

"I can't make you do anything. No one can, unless they force you against your free will, and nobody did that. Nobody made you smoke and nobody can make you stop. Except you. As soon as you free yourself from those good reasons. As soon as you stop being a victim."

She sighed petulantly, taking a drag on the cigarette. "Unlock me."

"I'm going back now." Jay turned to go.

"You're going to leave me here?"

He turned back to her, taking a moment to collect his thoughts before he began. "You know, Victoria, you are one of the most head-strong, determined human beings I've ever met. But let's be honest—all those good reasons aside, what you're really a slave to is that dead plant between your fingers. Yes, giving up is tough, but so are you. What happened to your backbone on the single most important issue of your life? I thought you were all about integrity; well, with this you way out of integrity. There are countless people with similar genetic and situational factors who've given up smoking. If you choose not to, that's your business, but stop making excuses. Take responsibility. Stop lying to yourself."

She glared at him and for a moment, he wondered if he'd crossed a line. *No.* He'd already thought it through. This was the method. He had to increase the psychic pain associated with smok-ing. Victoria prided herself on her backbone. That was a core part of her identity. He had to show her that blaming external factors for her smoking addiction was incompatible with backbone, with integrity. If he did it effectively, each time she picked up a cigarette, she would feel a stab at her identity.

"It's time to liberate yourself," he said, turning around. "It's *your* choice. You've got the key."

She shook her hand, rattling the chain pointlessly. "This is going to end badly for you," she hissed.

He turned back to her. "But how's it going to end for you?"

"Unlock me!!"

Jay walked away. He had crossed the line. There was no going back.

5

ALEXIA WAS DOING a final touch-up on Laura's face at the front side entrance of the cinema room, where Laura was about to make her grand entrance. Inside were her grandmother, her parents, her siblings, and even some of her friends from the street. The silence was supercharged, broken only by the occasional whisper. Carter stood at the back of the auditorium. She had calculated that when Laura appeared, her friends and family's jaw-dropping gasp at her change of appearance would help to convince Victoria, who being around to see the incremental change, would have lost sight of the dramatic before and after. It was just that right now, there was no sign of Victoria.

Jay walked in from the back. Carter sidled up to him. "Have you seen Victoria?" she said in an urgent whisper.

"She's cuffed to the wall," he whispered.

"What?"

"I did my 'Wall-of-Good-Reasons' with her."

Carter looked like she'd been slapped. "Oh, no!"

"The key is in the keyhole." He looked up, puzzled. "She just doesn't seem to be figuring that out."

Mickey came through. "Where's Victoria?"

Carter put her head in her hands. "She's cuffed to our perimeter wall."

"What?"

She turned to Jay. "You've restrained her against her will. She could bring a kidnapping charge."

"It was her choice. Besides, she's got the key, not me."

"You've got to go and free her, now!"

"When are we going to start?" It was the man from the street who'd appeared in the video. He was sitting a few rows forward, craning his head back.

"Yeah, he's got to get back to his office—at the *dump*," said his girlfriend, letting out a cackle.

Laura's family looked over at them, dismayed.

"Um, we'll be starting shortly," Carter said, and then whispered angrily to Jay, "Go get her!"

Jay shook his head. "She shackled herself. Only she can un-shackle herself."

From the middle of the auditorium, Laura's brother, dressed in a smart grey suit, stood up and turned to them. "We've been waiting here for nearly an hour, and some of us *do* need to get back to work."

Alexia came in from the back and whispered to Carter, "Laura says she can't do it."

Robert was on his way to the cinema room, when he noticed Laura pacing up and down near the side door leading to the front.

"Getting in a final workout?" he asked, smiling.

She looked up, her face tense with anxiety.

He came closer. "What's the matter?"

She shook her head.

He put his hands on her shoulders and lowered his head to look in her eyes.

"They'll be impressed with this for five minutes," she said, gesturing to her silver evening gown. "That will be it. I haven't changed. I came here thinking I might want to, but really . . . I came here for them. This was my last chance. They're going to disown me."

"Were you happy before?"

"My life is out there on the street. Those are the people who love me, who care about me, who need me. *That's* where I get to make a difference. I know it seems crazy, but I'm not crazy. I just know where I want to be."

"Then there's only one thing you need."

She looked up questioningly.

"The courage to live your own life."

The lights in the cinema room dimmed. A giant-size image of Laura before she had started at Quest, Inc. came on to the screen: Her flabby legs stuck out from a stretched jersey, and oily hair was plastered over her mottled complexion.

Alexia entered from the side of the screen. "Ladies and gentlemen . . ." she stretched out her hand, "Laura Cobb!"

Laura walked in from the other side, looking at least ten years younger than the image on the screen. She wore high heals and a silver evening gown, revealing a fit, toned body. Her hair was tied up in an extravagant coiffed tower of bangs. The small audience gasped in surprise before standing to clap.

Unexpectedly, Laura found herself needing to dab one of her eyes. "Thank you all for coming."

"You are beautiful, my girl, just beautiful!" Laura's mother, wearing a green floral dress, was clasping her hands in delight. Her father nodded slowly, a look of wonder on his face. Laura laughed, dabbing the other eye.

"Are you going to get your office manager's job back?" asked Laura's brother, who stood next to her mother.

"No," Laura said.

"I'm sure she's got something better than that," Laura's sister said.

"Yes, I do," Laura replied.

"What?" her brother asked.

She paused. "Same job I had before—collecting recyclables."

Mickey cut in. "We're still helping Laura find something else."

"Not necessary," she said simply. "I like what I do."

"Where are you going to live?" asked Laura's mother, the light in her eyes fading.

"Where I always have."

Her father stood up. "You're going back to the streets?!"

Alexia raised her voice and smiled broadly. "We're not quite finished . . ."

"Yes, we are," Laura cut in. "I'm going home."

"Home? That's not home," her father said, his lip curled.

"Yes, Dad, my home is out there. That's where my life is. It's not your life, but it is mine. It's where I live and work. It's where I'm needed."

"We love you, Lau!" It was the woman from the streets.

"Where you *work*?" her father said. "You're just a burden to society."

Laura swallowed, trying hard not to take the insult. "I keep eight blocks clean of junk, and get it recycled." She took in a deep breath. "Would it be better if I worked in tobacco, or processed food, or in one of the many companies out there making more stuff that we don't need?"

Her grandmother pursed her lips. "Another missed opportunity."

"Or Dad," Laura continued, "would it be better if I had your job? When we were growing up, I don't think a day went by when you didn't come home complaining about your boss, or your unpaid overtime, or your boredom."

"That job I was complaining about," he said incensed, "put food in your mouth and clothes on your back."

"How could I forget? You reminded us just about every day. Forgive me if I choose not to follow in your footsteps."

"But look how beautiful you look, Lau," her mother said tearfully. "You can't just throw this away!"

Laura smiled at her and then looked down at the elaborate gown. "It's fun being a princess, but . . ." She looked at her mother. "Mom, when you told me you had entered me in this program and I'd been selected, I tried to tell you that it wasn't for me, but then I saw your eyes watering, and I knew how much it meant to you. One by one, you all came to see me. 'Look how lucky you are,' you all said, 'the only one chosen.' So I convinced myself that maybe I would get something out of it, and I have! I really have. I've realized that I've got my life. It's not a life for everyone, but it's *my* life, and the only thing missing is . . . you, being okay with me." Swallowing, "That's the only real thing missing." She caught Robert's eye. "But if I have to," she said, looking back at them, "I'll live without that."

Out in the atrium, Laura's family and friends watched her mother hug her. Her father lingered at the door. From the other corner of the lobby, Carter looked on, biting her lip. Jay stood by her side.

"Maybe you were right, maybe I took it too far with Victoria. I should go see where she is," he whispered.

"I don't really care about Victoria Holt," Carter said. "I care that we failed Laura Cobb."

"We failed her?" Jay asked, surprised.

"Yes. We failed her. We turned her into a beauty pageant queen and sent her back to the streets."

"We're not here to give people a life they don't want."

She turned to him, "Don't tell me she wants to be out there."

"You don't get that?" he said. "All that time I was trying to re-condition myself out of my negativity and doubt about getting her off the streets," he snapped the black band on his wrist, "I was ignoring my intuition that she didn't want to get off the streets. Sometimes, we need to listen to the negatives before trying to silence them."

Carter folded her arms. "I cannot believe anyone *wants* to live on the streets."

"Don't mistake your failure of imagination for her self-deception. I'm proud of the work we've done. Learning to love where you are is worth more than striving to get where you don't want to be."

Carter shook her head. "It's a waste of potential."

"Looking out for people, saving lives is a waste of potential?" Jay was becoming exasperated. "Don't you get it? Quest, Inc. is where we serve. This is our ministry. Out on the streets—that's hers."

Laura walked to her father. After a few moments, she said something. He didn't reply. She was about to turn away, when he did something that surprised even him—he drew her into his arms. His face tightened. It had been six years since he'd held her.

Victoria walked in, flustered and bedraggled. She paused briefly to notice the family scene on her right, before continuing to Jay. She opened his hand and slapped a key in his palm.

"You found your free will?" he asked.

She made for the door.

"Victoria," Carter called. She turned. "Why don't you stay behind and get the full story."

"I'm not writing a story," she replied.

"You're not?"

"No, I think *expose* would be a better word," she said, marching off.

3

The Real Secret

1

NINE O'CLOCK, MONDAY morning. The Quest, Inc. team sat around the Think Tank table. They looked at Carter uneasily.

"Our publicist has got us an interview on *Morning Live,*" Carter began, "Topic: 'Is greatness born?' Two and a half million viewers."

They broke into smiles and votes of congratulation.

"And?" Mickey asked.

"And let's get to work," Carter said, looking down at her slim, black laptop. "Raelene Cleever, high school golfing star. Her dream is to be national champ. She's just entered the professional league, but didn't place in her first game. If she doesn't crack her next match, she'll be out of the league. She says her handicap is her head. She wants some sport psychology—Robert?"

He nodded.

"Oh, and Alexia, she wants to do some work with you."

"Of course," Alexia replied. "How can you expect to win a championship without the right mascara?"

"Leo Zubkin," Carter continued, "great-grandson of Peter Tsarev, the famous Russian author. For the past ten years, he's been working in solitude on his masterpiece. He's now facing difficulties adjusting to literary stardom, thinks he might be heading for a celebrity collapse. Jay?"

"The slings and arrows of fame and fortune," Jay replied. "Sure."

"And finally, Sam Nash, computer programming genius, has been fired."

"They fired the genius?" Mickey asked. "Perhaps his ex-boss should be a client."

"Maybe he was in the wrong place," Carter said, as she stood up. "Do a career assessment. Let's get to it."

They looked at Carter with an unspoken question.

She stepped toward the table. "There hasn't been an article, not even a blog post."

"—Yet," Mickey added.

"The good news is that the campaign is working. We've got clients."

"Sure," he said. "Dead man coaching."

Silence.

"We help people, right?" It was Jay. "That's what we do, we've done it before and we'll do it again. Maybe we're not going to pull it off now—"

"We *are* going to pull it off," Carter cut in, "for no other reason than this: I'm not sending Laura Cobb back to the streets. I won't do it."

"Well," he continued, "maybe we will get her off the streets, and maybe Victoria Holt will decide to pan us anyway. I don't do this for the praise . . . . I mean I like the praise . . . if it comes, but I do this because, it's what I do. It's the way I give back. I guess Victoria Holt does what she does for similar reasons. We can't write that article for her, all we can do is . . . *do what we do*."

After a few moments, they got up to leave. Jay hung behind.

"Thanks for that," Carter said, sitting down.

"I miss you."

She looked up. It was hard for her not to be affected by his words; but fortunately, the old resentment still provided sufficient defense.

"I thought we agreed to keep this door closed," she said.

"I can't really help it."

"Why don't you try one of your thought control techniques?"

"I don't know if I want to." He came closer, prompting her to shift back in her chair.

"You may be better off."

"Is that what you want, for me to forget everything?"

"I have my own thought control techniques."

Jay smiled stoically. "So, have I been weeded out of the garden of your mind?"

"Not at all," she said, looking down at her laptop, "The weeds died a long time ago."

Robert watched Raelene Cleaver smack ball after ball down the driving range. She could have been a model, with her big blue eyes, plump Botticelli lips and long mane of wavy blond hair dropping artfully to the center of her athletic back. She swung the club with a firm, but feminine grace. After hitting a shot straight down the fairway, she turned to him.

"I was born to play this game," she said. "Throughout high school, I never ranked less than two regionally and I was usually one, and now," she gritted her teeth, "second from last! If I don't place in the top four in my next match, I'm going to be kicked out of the league." Her face darkened. "That *cannot* happen." She suddenly smiled cheerfully. "Of course it won't, not with you by my side."

If there was a high school prize for "Most Envied," Raelene would have won it—beautiful, talented, academically and athletically triumphant. Envy would have concealed the obvious hazard of success—keeping its great load up. Robert knew something about that. Once the venerated fell from their pedestals, envy quickly gave way to what the Germans called *schadenfreude*: the secret delight felt at someone else's misfortune. Raelene had felt that toward competitors who had fallen. But now for the first time, detecting in some people's sympathy a runaway sparkle of delight, she saw, to her chagrin, that she had become its object.

"National champ," Robert said, "demands more than high school star."

"I know," she said, "it's all up here." She tapped her head. "I need you to reprogram me."

He looked at her curiously.

"My head's not right."

"Look into my eyes."

Her big blue eyes locked his gaze.

"Do you think you have it in you to be a national champion?"

"I know I do."

"What do you tell yourself while you play?"

"Forget Obama's 'Yes we can,' I say: 'Yes I've won!' That's my mantra, I repeat it endlessly."

"When you lose?"

"I wouldn't want to offend you, Mr. Rivera. I swear a lot. I know that's not ideal, but I quickly recover, reflect on my game, make adjustments, and tell myself, 'Next time, you'll whip them.' I also do a lot of pre-game visualization. I can see myself standing on that podium. I feel the cold metal of the trophy in my hands, as I raise it in the air." She waved to some empty stands behind them. "See the crowds? I can hear them applauding. There are my parents, waving."

She looked at him. "I win before I win." She turned back to the fairway and smacked another ball. "Yes I've won!" she said, as she watched it glide down the fairway. "I know what it is." She turned to him. "Confidence, I lack confidence."

Robert took a step back, "If you were any more confident," he said, squinting into the sun shining behind her, "you'd be God."

While Raelene's confidence was born out of a lifetime of unconditional parental validation, good looks and a spate of early childhood winning, Leo Zubkin's confidence was based on something else entirely—work. Wearing a beige corduroy blazer with leather-patched elbows and sporting a Trotsky goatee, he certainly looked the part. Jay shook his hand warmly.

"Ahh!" Leo pulled his hand away. "Writer's cramp," he said, wincing. "It's a permanent condition."

"I'm so sorry," Jay apologized.

"When you've been writing four hours a day, six days a week for ten years, it's to be expected. I'm still a 'quill and parchment' man. It's the way my grandfather did it. It's how I channel the kindred spirit."

Out of all the possibilities that were scattered before him, early on in his life, Leo had set his heart on just one. With the goal clearly in focus, he had sweated with rare patience and diligence toward its accomplishment. It had not been easy, but he had intuitively understood that organizing his life around a clear goal was a central component in the formula of success. "Goal" was probably not the right word; for Leo, it was an obsession.

Jay led him to a cloud-shaped couch. "Please sit."

Leo had a leather music case under his arm. "Would you like to put that down?" Jay asked.

"Do you ever put down your life?" Leo replied. Jay looked at him, confused.

"This is my book, my masterpiece, my reason for being." He laughed, throwing the bag on to a side table. "Just kidding. It's only paper, right? It's all here"—he touched his heart—"and, of course, there are too many copies to mention." He sat down, pulling the bag closer to him. "Going from hermit to literati isn't easy. I need you to help me make the transition. I don't want to end up like Ernest Hemmingway, a philandering alcoholic who commits suicide."

"Do you have suicidal tendencies?"

"No. But fame can bring out the worst in people. I don't even know what to do with paparazzi. What do you do? Smile sweetly or ignore them?"

"Who is your publisher?"

"You're right. They'll be able to answer that."

"Are they in Los Angeles?"

"I haven't chosen a publisher, yet."

"Oh . . ." Jay shifted in his corner of the couch. "So, that's the manuscript, not the actual book?"

"Exactly, that's why I'm here. I'm about to submit and I need to get it right. This isn't just for any run-of-the-mill pulp fiction outfit. Even many of the highbrow publishers will probably not understand its significance. Do you know how many publishers rejected James Joyce?"

Jay shook his head.

"Twenty-two. So, of course it's possible that my book may get rejected, too. Now, I don't think it's all that likely, but you never know, and then I'm going to need your support, you know, to make sure that I don't waver. I can't allow anything to shake my self-belief. This is just too important. You understand?" There was a note of anxiety in Leo's voice. "I've put too much into this." He let out a breath and sat back. "I have a much more realistic concern."

"Yes," Jay prompted.

"When I finally give this gift to the world, my life will stop being my own. How is that going to affect me psychologically? It was bad enough for my grandfather—he became a recluse, but he only spoke to the zeitgeist; this *shifts* the zeitgeist. That's not immodesty. You see, it's not me writing. I'm just a vessel."

"What's your book about?"

Leo threw his head back with a sigh. "What *isn't* it about? It's universal; it's a monograph on monastic life in pre-revolutionary, rural Russia. It's going to change the way the world sees the world." He looked earnestly at Jay, any shred of doubt now deep down the hull of his titanic ambition. "What's the procedure for dealing with female stalkers?"

Perhaps it was bearing witness to Raelene's desperate clinging to her slipping success, but later that day Robert found himself staring zombie-like into the fridge. He told himself that he was thirsty, that was all. His eyes locked on a bottle of coke. Twenty spoons of sugar and he could drink the whole thing in one minute—he knew that from experience. He would love every full-throated, fizzy rush of it. He unscrewed the cap, letting out a satisfying hiss of carbonated gas. His taste buds pirouetted in time to the uncapped music. He screwed the cap back on, slipped the bottle under his jacket, walked upstairs to his office and locked the door. Sitting at his desk with the bottle in front of him, he wondered what he was going to choose. A few, still, strangely satisfying moments passed. Suddenly, he grabbed the bottle, unscrewed the cap and took a glug, before screwing the cap back on and shoving the bottle back on the table. A few more moments of silent reflection passed. He was surprised to find that the drink wasn't quite as good as he'd expected. It was a little too sweet. Had his taste buds adjusted to lower sugared flavors? Perhaps, and yet still a part of him wanted to drink it. There was some other arrangement happening in the dark recesses of his mind, another deal just outside the light of consciousness that was producing the clamor in his head: *Drink, Drink, Drink!* If only he had an ear to that door, he would have heard this: *You didn't just exchange success for your father's love; you exchanged it for peace. Achievement comes with large demands—the more you have, the more you have to sustain. Look at Raelene Cleever, tormented by her faded glory. Without success, there are no expectations, no pressure and most importantly: No tiene, perder no puede—He who doesn't have is unable to lose. You can have success or you can have peace, so drink.*

Not far away, Victoria Holt was staying at the Malibu Headlands B & B. She was sitting at a small writing desk with leather inlay, an unopened pack of Chesterfield Classic on the far end. She could have published already, but she had put her editor off. This story had the potential to be much bigger than she had initially thought. There was the primary fact that Laura Cobb was now back on the streets, a glaring indictment of Quest, Inc.'s claims. These people had been acknowledged by the President for service to the nation—already a flawed commendation, given their Living Well Campaign had done virtually nothing to turn the tide on obesity, debt and divorce. She had generously given them another chance to prove themselves by transforming people, one-by-one, and they had failed. Didn't that say everything about the fraud on which the personal development industry was based?

But there was something else even more scandalous, something that would take her report way beyond the online pages of *The Huffington Post*—gross hypocrisy. There was the obvious matter of Robert Rivera, the obese health and fitness guru who'd thrown himself off a building. That story had been covered; and, of course, now that Robert was back to his former size, the world would see how long that lasted. But Victoria's journalistic instinct told her there was more. They all promoted this perfect life. No one's life was perfect, including theirs, which meant they were hypocrites. She was sure Mickey had half a dozen skeletons under his bed, or more likely *in* his bed. And what about Carter and Alexia? With the clean-living Jay, she wasn't so sure; but there was bound to be some contradiction with all of them. If she could discover something in each of their lives that smashed what they stood for, she could finally divest the world of their quick-fix transformation myths. If the self-professed gurus couldn't live it themselves, then they were obviously peddling quackery.

Victoria grabbed the box of smokes, ripped the plastic off and pulled out a cigarette. She stared at it, pursing her lips. Something didn't feel right. There was a knock on the door. She shoved the cigarette back into the box and slid it to the end of the table, before getting up to open. Standing there was a skinny man in a blue L.A. Dodgers baseball cap.

"Have you got something for me?" she asked.

"Don't I get invited in for a cup of tea?"

She ignored the question. "Well?"

"Oh, just some photos of Dr. Carter King."

"Come in, come in," Victoria said, unable to control her curiosity.

He pulled a couple of photos out of the inside of his denim jacket.

She grabbed them out of his hand and pulled them up to her face. Her brow furrowed, not quite believing what her eyes were telling her. As it began to dawn, a smile spread across her face.

The following day, having arrived back from a keynote presentation to the National Association of Retirees, Mickey made his way upstairs, talking on his cell phone to his business manager, Simon Lester.

"I don't want to own *half* the Blu Bay development," he said belligerently. "I want to own the *whole* thing! That's the only way we're going to be able to do the redevelopment without a bunch of overfed, geriatric whiners throwing their goddamn walkers in our path . . . Yeah? Well, I'm saying we *deserve* to own it. I have to go. I love you. I know you can do this. Go make it happen."

He hung up and stepped into the unisex bathroom, making his way into the silver metal walled-off area, which had three men's urinals. A middle-aged man in an ill-fitting brown suit stood urinating at the far end. A flap of hair stood up at the back of his head. Mickey zipped up and went to the basin to wash his hands. The man made for the door.

Mickey turned to greet him. "Hi."

Without looking up, he mumbled something inaudible before exiting.

Mickey arrived at his office door to see the man waiting outside. "You must be Sam Nash." He stretched out his hand, before recalling Sam's bypassing of the bathroom basin. Feeling Sam's limp, moist, flesh slither in his palm Mickey was unable to hold back a facial twist of revulsion. "Come in," he said weakly, as he tried to regain his composure.

They sat together on the black and white damask couch in the center of the room. Mickey looked down at his notes. "You graduated top of your class at MIT, and you've been in the same job ever since."

Sam responded in a gravelly monotone, "I invented the program that doubled their revenues. Now that they've got it, they're getting rid of me."

"You were fired?"

"They sent me here as a condition of letting me back. It's a con—they want me out—they just don't want to pay severance."

"Do you want to go back?"

He shrugged.

"What do you want to do?"

"I just want to program. Been doing it since I was sixteen. No one there can do it like me. For them its work, for me it's ... breathing."

"You miss it?"

"They're a bunch of idiots," he said, ignoring the question.

Mickey moved a little closer. "Maybe it's time to look at yourself."

Sam had never been the amiable type, partly because of faint leanings toward autism. He was most at home in his internal world, an impressive structure of computer code that kept him endlessly stimulated. The external world, the world of people, was like a foreign country where he hadn't mastered the language. Facial expression, body language, even words themselves, were often misinterpreted. Not realizing his incompetence, he assumed his understanding was correct: people were generally hostile and nasty. His solution? Attack first.

Sam turned to Mickey, making eye contact for the first time. "Have you looked at *yourself*?" he said. "You look like a pimp!"

Mickey looked at him with pure fury burning in his eyes. As the recipient of the insult, it was an old formula: rage about the injury, rather than curiosity about the attacker's motive. By taking offense (certainly, he could have chosen *not* to take it), he only helped to push the blade deeper into the fragile heart of his own self-esteem. Around that self-esteem, Mickey had spent his life constructing his identity— a bright, bold edifice of social position, opinion and style. Enamored as he was with his creation, he still couldn't help seeing himself

through the eyes of others, even those who he disdained. To deflect
the thrust of Sam's negative review, all he needed to do was step
aside and assess its validity. Found to be true, he could be grateful for
the opportunity to switch to less "pimp-like" attire. Alternatively,
given his dislike of Sam's style, he could interpret Sam's dislike of his
as a compliment. Not having conducted this assessment and not one
to simply toil in self-abasement, Mickey would have to draw his
sword and slash back.

He prodded his lapel. "This is mohair, asshole."

Sam's nostrils flared. "What did you just call me?"

Mickey started mouthing the word again.

Sam's preemptive attack had backfired. Now, defending his in-
jured self-esteem would require nothing less than overwhelming,
crushing force. Before Mickey could repeat himself, he was on the
floor with Sam Nash's contorted face over his, and a much less limp
set of hands wringing his neck.

2

JAY AND CARTER were standing on the landing when they heard the grunting and thumping coming from Mickey's office.

"What's that?" Carter asked.

Jay shook his head.

They ran out to Mickey's office.

"Mickey?!" Jay called out at the door.

More grunting. He opened the door. Mickey was lying over Sam, so that now Sam was on the bottom, his free leg stomping on the floor, like the hindquarter of a trapped animal.

"What are you doing?!" Jay demanded, trying to pull Mickey off.

"He tried to kill me!" Mickey screamed.

"You're going to kill *him*!" Carter shouted back, helping Jay to pull them apart.

Finally separated, the two men remained on the floor, breathing heavily, like two overworked oxen.

"He tried to strangle me," Mickey said, after catching his breath.

"He called me an asshole," Sam replied.

Carter looked at Mickey, flabbergasted.

"He called me a *pimp*," Mickey said sheepishly.

Carter frantically turned to Sam and helped him to his feet. "Mr. Nash, I am *so* sorry about this. We will do *whatever* it takes to make this right," she said, wondering how on earth they could possibly make this right, when he clearly had the power to litigate them to ruin. The negative publicity alone could kill them. She led Sam out of Mickey's office, before turning back to Mickey with a dumbfounded shake of her head.

Alexia ran in to find Mickey red-faced and disheveled. "What's going on?"

"He was just beating up one of our clients," Jay answered.

"The guy tried to strangle me," Mickey said.

"Are you okay?" Alexia asked.

"Yeah," he said, deepening his voice. "I got him off."

"Should we get you to a doctor?"

"Nah." He suddenly doubled back. "Ah! My lower back."

"Come sit down," she said, leading him to the couch.

He hobbled over, his face all manly forbearance.

She put her hand on his back. "Do you want me to rub it?"

Mickey pretended to think about it. "Ah . . . okay."

"Lie down."

He lay face down on the couch, a secret smile lighting his face, as he breathed in her perfume. He widened his eyes at Jay. "Thanks, man. You can go."

Alexia looked at her watch, "What am I thinking?" she said. "I've got a session with Raelene Cleever. Jay, will you do it?"

Mickey's smile faded.

"Sure," Jay said. "Don't know if I'll have the same gentle touch, but I'll do my best."

"Do you want to take your shirt off?" Jay asked Mickey, as Alexia left.

Mickey got up, irritated. "Thanks, I think it's going to be okay."

"Please don't tell them," Sam pleaded. Carter had just closed the door to her office. Sam faced her, his shirt half untucked, a couple of buttons broken loose, his hair squashed up on one side.

"Tell who?"

"My company, 'cuz then I'm *really* dead."

"Right," Carter replied, concealing her relief at this unexpected turn of the tables. "Certainly, we'll keep this confidential."

She led him to two antique chairs against a bookshelf-lined corner wall. They sat down.

"You lose your temper often?" she asked.

"Not when people leave me alone," he mumbled.

"Tell me what brought you here."

He wheezed a world-weary sigh, before beginning his gravelly monologue. "There's this guy in HR, every five minutes, he's calling me." He mimicked a whiney voice. "'I don't know how to pull the spreadsheet, how do I add video on to the intranet, where's the data input button.' The instructions are all in the help section, but of course, who wants to click on 'help' when you can call techno-geek every five minutes? Each time I explain, patiently, step-by-step, point-by-point, the next day, it's like he hasn't listened to a word I've said!" Whiny voice: "'How do I pull the spreadsheet again, where's the data input button?' I cracked. I told him to get a new brain. He turns it into a bloody inquisition, which suits Deon—"

"Deon?" Carter injected.

"Big Cheese, Boss Man. See, now that I've designed the program, he's ready to bring in a low-level junior—who I trained—to take over for me, which is what they wanted all along." He stuck the end of his pinkie into his mouth and chewed on the nail.

"Your boss is giving you a second chance," Carter said.

"Yeah, whatever," he replied, swallowing the bitten nail and pouting his lips.

"You get out of here a changed man," she added, "sounds like you keep your job. Why else would they pay for this?"

"I'm already the best in my field." He threw his hands up in exasperation. "What more do they want?!"

Carter took a few moments to reflect. "You know, Sam," she began, "insurance companies had a real problem figuring out which doctors were likely to get sued for malpractice. You'd think it would be easy, right? Just avoid the one's with the lowest test scores—the ones who are likely to be the most incompetent. Turns out those aren't the ones who are most often sued. Actually, it's those who are arrogant, abrupt, spend the least time with their patients—the unlikable ones. The incompetent ones don't always get a free ride, but if they're amiable, take time with their patients, show they care, even when they mess up, they're not usually sued. I guess if the nice doctor gets it wrong, you tell yourself that everyone makes mistakes. The grouch gets it wrong, you say, I never liked that SOB and I'm going to take him to the cleaners."

"What's this got to do with me?" he asked

"Being a genius isn't enough, Sam. You need to be a *nice* genius."

"This is my personality," he said as he shrugged. "It's who I am."

While Sam Nash saw no reason to change, Raelene Cleever was waiting for someone or something to change her. She stood in front of Alexia, a black and silver golf bag by her side. Raelene wore slim, white pinstriped Bermudas with a black, sleeveless, Ralph Lauren open neck shirt, revealing the pert upper curves of her breasts. She looked like she'd stepped out of a golf estate advertisement.

"Blind them with a bit of bling, huh?" she said, lifting her wrist to reveal her white, diamond bezel Hublot, before doing a ramp model turn. "What do you think, what's missing?"

Alexia shook her head. "You look great."

"When football teams play in black," Raelene began, "they play harder and faster, or maybe the other side is just more intimidated. You're going to help me 'wear-to-win!'"

"Sure, clothing has a subtle impact on performance," Alexia said, "but it looks to me like you're on form."

"You know why they call it a Wonderbra?" she continued. "When she takes off her bra, you wonder where her tits went." She lifted her breasts up. "This is all natural, if anything, I downplay it. To shove it in their face is just . . . slutty. At the same time, maybe I'm not using my God-given gifts?" She lifted them up again. "A bit more?"

"Your look is good."

Raelene toyed with her earlobe, flashing the diamond stud, "One carat, flawless, ice-whites. My dad always says, 'Only the best for the best.' I could have got good zirconias for a fraction of the price, and no one would know the difference, but *I* would." She took a club out of the bag. "When I'm out there, I imagine that I'm queen of the course." She lined up in front of an imaginary ball. "My competitors are my servants. Now, the servants have staged a revolution, I'm going to get back out there and *kill* them, and I need you to give me the armor." She swung the club back, smashing an imaginary ball toward Alexia, who couldn't help flinching.

"I've got the talent," she added. "I know that I do." She walked over to the mirror. "I first picked up a club when I was five, and connected with the ball first shot. It just clicked, you know?" She turned back to Alexia, "Probably like when you first put on makeup. I bet you just knew what you were doing."

Alexia nodded, trying not to look offended.

"And now, I don't know . . ." Raelene's gaze drifted into the middle distance. "Maybe I don't have *enough* talent." She quickly corrected herself, flicking her long blonde hair over her shoulders. "I mean, no, that's not it. Of course I've got the talent, but something is missing. Sorry, I don't know why I'm telling you all this, you're the grooming lady, not a performance coach."

Alexia felt an acute need to slap this woman hard across the face. Of course, Raelene was not wrong about Alexia's designation. That was the problem. While Alexia had seen the power of changing people from the outside in, she still found herself feeling like a glorified beauty therapist. Like it or not, she knew that beauty was a power player in the story of success. The beautiful were paid more, promoted quicker, given more opportunities. They were overrepresented, not just among celebrities, but politicians, too; and in one place where one would think nothing but talent would count—sports figures. Raelene Cleever's looks were not irrelevant to her success. Growing up looking like a Little Miss America finalist, she was more likely to be noticed and selected. Coaches would have been more nurturing and affirming. In the urban jungle, it was survival of the prettiest. It was why Alexia was in business and why she felt faintly disgusted that she was.

Putting the club under her arm, Raelene walked to Alexia and scrutinized her face with a concentrated frown. "Seeing you on TV and meeting you in the flesh, I now totally realize how much is possible with good grooming." She stood back, flashing a big smile. "Well done!" And then, frowning again, she added, "You're not going to chick-spite me?"

Alexia looked confused.

"You know, sabotage me because I'm hot?"

The following day, Jay met Leo in the atrium. As usual, he had his leather manuscript bag tucked under his arm.

"Let's walk in the garden, it's a beautiful day," Jay said, opening his mouth into a wide smile, revealing a large piece of spinach stuck between his front teeth.

Leo smiled and frowned at the same time, unable to hide his discomfort at the site of his coach, this nationally renowned expert, with a bit of half-chewed vegetable clogging a dental fissure. The image brought to mind a happy hobo with a missing tooth.

They walked to the edge of the cliff top garden overlooking the ocean. There were two teakwood, white cushion-covered chairs facing each other.

"Let's sit," Jay suggested.

Leo looked out at the ocean, hoping that somehow by the time he looked back at Jay, the detritus of lunch would be swallowed and they could get on with the session. Turning back tentatively, he flinched. Now, all he could see was spinach. Under different circumstances—say at a vaudeville show—he might have laughed.

"In ten years, you've never given anyone your book to read?" Jay asked. Leo shook his head. "Not even a few pages of an early draft?"

"I didn't want someone who didn't understand the big picture to throw me off course."

"How can you be sure you're getting your message across?"

Leo was finding it hard to concentrate on the discussion. "I've spent ten years on this," he said, "crafting every word to spinach."

Jay looked at him askance.

"I mean . . ." He trailed off.

"Yes?"

"Perfection," Leo said, ". . . crafting every word to *perfection*."

"Can I ask you a question?"

"Certainly."

"Have I got spinach between my teeth?"

"Um, yes," he said, both embarrassed and relieved. "Just a little bit, not a lot. Here," he added, poking his own front tooth to indicate the location.

"Thank you," Jay said, nudging the intruder free with his tongue and swallowing. "I was wondering when you'd let me know." He flashed a joker's smile. "People don't like giving that sort of feedback, and that's why we've got to ask for it."

Leo looked puzzled

"Before you even send it to a publisher, wouldn't it be worthwhile to know if there was any spinach under your arm?" Jay pulled a note of paper from his pocket. "Here are three experts in your field—send them your manuscript. Get some feedback."

Leo took the piece of paper and stared at it; after a few moments, he looked up. "What if it's all spinach?"

At Quest, Inc., everyone seemed to be on a quest. Except Doreen, the receptionist. At this point, her only quest was to make it up Cliffside Drive, the last leg of her lunch break walk. Doreen had lived her life with very little gap between what she had and what she wanted. Instead, she felt a fullness, which prompted her most common, unbidden thought: *I'm such a lucky fish.* It was a relic of childhood, like an old teddy bear that she had never let go. It was this feature of her mental landscape that was responsible for the perennial twinkle in her eye. Yet right now, in place of this thought, something far less familiar had been encroaching—the gap of discontent.

As she looked down at the cushiony bulge under her girdle, she couldn't help wondering if it was time to embark on her own quest. There was her marriage—full of love, but without passion. Her finances were adequate, but that was the problem, at Quest, Inc., adequate wasn't adequate. She felt a tinge of guilt. Did everyone have to climb Mt. Everest? Couldn't she just stand at the bottom and cheer them on?

Looking ahead, she noticed a figure far down the road near the Point Dume Nature Preserve. It looked like a woman dancing, a black woman in a T-shirt and shorts. She seemed to be listening to music, although Doreen couldn't hear anything or see any earphones. She was jutting one hip out after the other, palms raised above her head, jazz-hand style, with the inhibition of the inebriated. The scene, at 1:30 p.m. on a well-to-do Malibu road, was strange enough, but as the woman turned, Doreen sucked in her breath. Hadn't she seen that face earlier that morning? Just without the lewd pout. Taking a few steps further, she raised her hand to her mouth. It was Dr. Carter King.

3

RAELENE WAS IN the Body Temple with Robert, doing bench presses. She heaved up what she expected to be her final rep. "Finished!"

"Two more," Robert said.

She sat up, taking a few moments to catch her breath. "What do you think? I want to win Miss Muscle-Dyke?"

"You need more upper body strength to extend the distance on your drives. Come," he said, "let's move on to lats."

She got up, patting herself down with a white towel, the gold letters of her initials sewn into the corner. "I've gotta go."

"You've got four weeks to competition," Robert said, irritated. "Do you want to raise your game or not?"

She held the towel around her neck. "More than anything."

"Are you going to the range?"

She looked at her watch. "I've got a manicure."

Robert's eyes widened. "Raelene, how many hours are you putting in each day?"

"Two or three, if I get there."

"You don't go every day?"

She took a step toward him. "There's a much bigger problem than my attendance at the range."

"And what's that?"

She sighed, pulling the hair back away from her face. "This is not easy for me," she began. "I need to ask you something, but I need to know that you are going to answer absolutely honestly."

"That's all you're going to get from me," he replied, "honesty."

"Do you think I've got the talent to be number one?"

"Do you have the potential? Absolutely."

"Really?" she persisted.

"Yes."

"Okay," she said, relieved. "Then I know what it is."

"What do you mean?"

"I've watched *The Secret* about a hundred times, I've meditated on the law of attraction, done the visualizations, the affirmations. I didn't go into my last match believing I'd win, I went in *knowing* I'd win. But I didn't just *not* win, I came in *eighth*! It's clear what the problem is: *I'm not doing it right*. Help me put *The Secret* into practice. That's the only way I'm going to become the world's number one female golfer."

Robert looked at her, incredulous.

"Come, out with it," she insisted. "Give me the inner secret of *The Secret* and let me go win some trophies."

Robert shook his head. "I don't think you should play that competition."

"What?"

"You haven't put in the hours."

"So what?" she asked, shrugging her shoulders.

"'So what?'" he repeated, unbelieving.

"Yes, *so what?!*" It was in that moment something snapped in Raelene Cleever. "Do you know what a slog it is out there in the heat and the dust?! You try hitting a little white ball for six hours straight!

Trudging hill after hill, after hill after hill, getting sweaty and dirty and sore! You know what? Sometimes, it just gets on my tits! Boring! Yes, there, I said it." Her cheeks were flushed with the satisfaction of her confession.

He nodded. "So, you want to short-circuit that process with an incantation to the Secret God of Success?" Actually, he could understand, even empathize. If you could pray, instead of practice, why not? There were more times than he would like to admit when he also hated the slog of staying in shape, and a ten-minute daily daydream would be a welcome substitute.

"Are you telling me there's no law of attraction?" she asked, as if he was a heretic disputing the holy gospel.

"I don't know," he said simply. "I do know about the law of action. We need to dream and visualize and believe and maybe pray, because that helps us figure out what we want, focus on where we're going, and motivate ourselves to get there. But above all, we need to *act*. The problem is that you don't want to put in the hours, because you don't really love golf, do you?"

"Of course I do! I *love* to win."

"That's not what I asked you. Everyone loves to win. Do you love to *play*?" He let the question hang. "You want to pick the fruit without planting the trees. You're invested in the outcome, instead of the process. That's why you visualize yourself holding a trophy, instead of hitting the perfect shot. You're attached to winning, not playing, and that's precisely why you won't win."

She flicked her hair back in distaste. "Wow, you really know how to raise a girl's confidence!"

Carter was speaking at a Quest, Inc. parenting seminar at Pepperdine's public conference facility. With views across the Pacific, Malibu University had been voted the most beautiful college campus in the country. Quest, Inc. would need to take their larger seminars into Los Angeles; but for a few hundred people, this was perfect. It also lent their operation a veneer of academic respectability. The university establishment had never been friendly toward the self-help movement. It was considered too light, too easy, too devoid of scientific jargon. The maze-like journey to knowledge was meant to be long and arduous, not something to access in a weekend seminar or a how-to book. Carter called it the "academic masochist's bias," if knowledge wasn't punishingly difficult to access, it couldn't be valuable. Or at least it couldn't be financially valuable to institutions that depended on multiple-year enrollments. Hence, the endless extolment of theory in most academic programs—this was much more time-consuming than any life improving, practical application. The upshot was that you could leave a four-year degree in the social sciences without being any more socially effective. It was why Carter had left academia. Now she was back, borrowing its stamp of legitimacy.

The hall was packed with mothers and fathers, all hungry for the parenting formulas that would give their kids a better chance, the formal education system having resoundingly failed to provide adequate preparation for life's most important task.

Carter had asked Sam Nash to attend this session. He sat at the back in the same disheveled suit he always wore. Carter stood center stage, speaking with an understated charisma, confident in the significance of her message, not needing to infuse it with soaring inflection. Clicking the remote, an image of a painfully shy-looking child came on screen.

She began her closing: "Psychologist Robert O'Connor selected a group of the most socially withdrawn preschool kids he could find. He divided them into two groups. The one group watched a film of a shy child looking on at a group of extraverted children in various social interactions, like chatting or playing together. Gradually, the shy child makes overtures to the group, is accepted, and starts having fun, too. The results were extraordinary. After seeing the film, the shy children immediately became more sociable. Even more astounding, six weeks later, the shy children who had not seen O'Connor's film remained as isolated as ever, while those who had, were now the most sociable in their class. Through role modeling the child in the film, the very fabric of these kids' personalities was transformed. Sometimes, personality looks like stone. Just remember what Michelangelo did with stone."

After Carter had finished signing books and the last of the audience had left, Sam ambled up.

"So, how do I get other people to change their personalities?" he said.

Carter smiled in surprise. "That's what you took out of my presentation?"

"I worked with nasty morons."

"*Worked?*"

"I had a run-in with Deon. He fired me on the spot. So, thanks for nothing."

"You know," Carter said, "you shouldn't waste a good crisis. Maybe this is the moment to start working on yourself."

"I'll see you around . . . *not*."

"Sam," she called after him.

He turned back.

"Finish your sessions with me."

"I don't have a job. How am I supposed to pay your crazy-ass fees? Steal Google headquarters?"

"Your company paid for your program in advance."

He took a moment to think about it. "Call Deon," he said. "He's the one in need of a personality reboot. I've got more important things to do, like finding a job."

Carter watched him turn and go. Another one down. Nobody said helping people change was easy, but was it supposed to be so difficult? She sat down in the front row of the empty auditorium, contemplating the future of a personal transformation agency that wasn't doing much personal transformation. She turned on her phone. It beeped to signal a text message. She opened it.

From your fire, let the flame be lit in each of them. Have a terrific session! Forever in awe of your bold, beautiful blaze. Love, Jay.

Damn him. She had succeeded in extracting him from her head and now he was replanting himself. "Who is the gardener of your mind?" she asked herself aloud. "I am," she replied. "Then weed, weed, weed."

Victoria Holt was sitting in a rocky cove on Point Dume beach. Up ahead, the water rolled in calmly, in sharp contrast to her state of mind. She found herself in a most unexpected dilemma. Ever since Jay's ludicrous exercise, where she'd been coaxed into handcuffing herself to their garden wall, she had been unable to smoke. She still had fierce cravings; but when she reached for a cigarette, Victoria felt like a moron enslaved to a plant. The feeling was such an unpleasant affront to her sense of herself as an empowered individual that it actually became easier *not* to give in to the craving. Also, as she soon realized, while the craving passed, the feeling of being an enslaved moron did not. She wasn't convinced Jay or his silly little game was the cause, but Victoria's ultimate value was truth, and she was not about to lie to herself or anyone else. If she had given up cigarettes, it had coincided with something he had done. But there was something else. She had also documented evidence, full-color photos to be exact, that Dr. Carter King was a binge drinker or drug addict. She got up and started walking back to the car. It was a mess—how would she write an article about an agency that had some, albeit minor, role in ending her nicotine addiction, yet who's director was an addict?

"Yeeeeee!!!"

Jay glided down the road on the back wheel of his orange, hybrid mountain bike; tucked into the straps of his sandals, his white linen flat-fronts flapped in the wind. With a few minutes before his session with Leo Zubkin, he was practicing his wheelies. The front wheel levered down and he came to a halt. His record was eight pedals on one wheel. It was a hazardous business, and he was not unacquainted with the occasional scrape or bruise; but he'd discovered that he felt most alive when life was under threat. This was, perhaps, a wimp's substitute for high-speed super bike racing; but for him, it was enough to summon the adrenaline. And, to be fair, there was always the possibility of cracking the back of his skull open.

Determined to get to the magic number—ten—he had time for one more attempt. With one foot on the ground and one on a pedal, he breathed in deeply, visualizing the motion he would undertake, seeing himself triumphantly completing ten full revolutions. As he felt the mere possibility morph into a foregone reality, he pushed down on the pedal, jerked the handlebars up, and pulled his body back. The front wheel lifted gracefully off the ground. Suspended in the air, the bike became weightless, as if for a few moments he was paragliding instead of cycling. One pedal, two, three, four, five . . . a little wobble. At the first sign of danger, the self-preservation instinct pushed him forward to re-stabilize on two wheels. He had to fight this. Leaning back, he pushed on the pedal and straightened his arms. Six, seven, eight . . . and a half. All at once—it was mercifully quick—

the seat of the bike slipped out from under him, the bike flipped over his head, and he landed on his back, as though he'd suddenly lain down to sleep.

Jay stared up at the sky, perfect Malibu blue. For the first time, he realized what a beautiful day it was. He'd been so close to that ten, felt so sure. Confidence was a lure—it got him up on the bike, helped to keep the fear at bay. The trick was to maintain it. At that moment, as he lay on the ground, he needed to hold that confidence as an antidote to the embarrassment of being seen sprawled across the road. *Cling* to that confidence in the moment of his conquer, so he would reflect on what he needed to do differently and get straight on to his next attempt.

Easing himself up, Jay picked up the bike. He had received a mild wallop, but, a little disappointingly, there were no visible war wounds. He had much improved his falls. If it wasn't time to go in, he would have gotten back on the bike.

Standing, Jay saw someone storming toward him from down the road. It was Leo Zubkin. Shaking some papers he had clenched in his fist, he came to a halt, his face just inches from Jay's. "I got the evaluations on my book back." Jay decided it best to say nothing. Leo caved his head in, as he pulled the pages up to his face with both hands. "'Dear Mr. Zubkin,'" he read, "'congratulations on attempting the formidable challenge of writing a book. What you have is a first draft with probably a few more to go. Don't be discouraged; it takes time, patience and practice to develop an intelligible message. Yours, Sincerely . . .'"

"Well, that's just one opinion," Jay said helpfully.

Leo smiled sourly. "The other one said as a second language English speaker, I should take English classes."

"Nothing wrong with brushing up your language skills."

"English is my mother tongue!" Leo shouted. "The third person won't return my calls."

"Okay . . ." Jay said, thinking hard about what exactly was okay. "Now you know, so what are you going to do about it?"

"What am I going to do about it? This is what I'm going to do about it: I've come to ask you why you told me to send my life's work to three imbeciles? This is not helpful, Dr. Jay, not helpful at all."

"Should we go inside?"

"No, I don't want to go inside. I want a refund."

Jay noticed Victoria Holt approaching from across the road. He put his hand on Leo's shoulder. "Let's go inside."

Leo shrugged it off, "No!"

"Leo, you've worked incredibly hard over the past ten years, but you've never received any feedback. This may be very difficult for you to hear, but have you considered that they may be right?"

Leo's face flushed as if he was about to hit Jay; but instead, he pulled the manuscript out of his leather bag and threw it in the air. The pages seesawed chaotically down to the ground. With that, he got down in the gutter and lay down on his back.

Jay kneeled down beside him. "Leo, what are you doing?"

"I'm lying in the gutter," he said with tears in his eyes, "where I belong. This is my contribution to the world: When the biggest losers look at me, they will feel better about themselves."

"Jay?" a voice called from above. He looked up. It was Victoria Holt. "I seem to have interrupted you raising up a life."

4

CARTER WAS SIPPING pensively from a mug of tea at a black granite counter in Healthelicous, the Quest, Inc. kitchen.

Robert walked in. "Hey," he said.

Carter looked up distractedly. "Hi. There's some green tea in the pot."

"Thanks." He poured himself a cup and pulled up a stool opposite her.

"How is your book going?" she asked.

"Yeah, yeah, good, good."

She was too preoccupied to notice the overstatement.

"What if a leopard doesn't change its spots?" she asked.

"It doesn't."

"Then what are we doing?" She put her mug down with a thud.

"Fortunately, we're not in the leopard transformation business."

She cracked a smile.

"I know the feeling," he said, "Raelene Clever thinks the only thing holding her back from success is a secret spell, which I, the chief wizard, am hiding."

"Is it our fault? Do we make it sound too easy?" Carter's face tightened. "And then when they realize they've actually got to get off their butts and do something, their morale fizzles."

Jay ran in, breathless. "Victoria Holt was here."

"Oh joy," Carter deadpanned, taking another sip of tea, doing her best to avoid getting rattled.

Robert stared at the black marks smearing the back of Jay's white linen outfit. He put his hand on Jay's back. "Zen grunge, nice."

Jay looked over his shoulder at the marks. "Just learning to fall better." Turning back, he added, "Victoria's given up smoking."

"That's fantastic!" Robert said.

Carter looked up from her tea. "What's she doing with her article?"

"She wants to give it a few more months," Jay replied, "to see how things go with our other clients."

"That's sweet," Carter said. "She's put us on probation."

"Yeah, that's the other thing. She walked in on me trying to extract Leo Zubkin from the gutter."

Carter closed her eyes.

Robert stared at her. "This isn't an episode of *The Swan*. Change is an imperfect process. You take a few steps forward, a few back, a few sideways."

". . . And with a bit of help from the top life coaches in the country, you're lying in the gutter," Carter bit her lip.

"I've got to get to a workshop," Robert said, getting up to leave, "but I do know this—when you hit rock bottom, if it doesn't kill you, the only way is up."

Early that evening, Robert, Alexia and Mickey were sitting at a corner table at Lola's, a downtown Malibu pub, having a drink.

Mickey leaned forward animatedly, "... to which he replies, 'Don't tell me—you've eaten my socks!'" They sat silent waiting for him to continue. To his horror, they had no idea he'd just said the punch line. Like a man drifting from shore without a life jacket, he began flapping for a way to draw himself back in. He laughed, hoping that would act as a contagion, like canned laughter on a sitcom; but they only smiled weakly. *Damn them,* he thought, *who do they think I am, Jerry Bloody Seinfeld? Throw a dog a bone!* But Alexia was receding further and further away with every second that he failed to prove his smarts. Mickey wasn't going to sit there watching himself drown in front of her. Taking a sharp breath in and scrunching up his face, he gripped his lower back and pulled himself forward.

Alexia got up. "You all right?"

"My back," he spat out dramatically, "ever since that maniac tried to kill me."

"Still bad?"

Out of danger, Mickey allowed himself to relax a little. "Just a spasm, it should be okay." He made sure the pain in his face was still sufficient for anyone with an ounce of humanity not to still demand a pant splitting pay-off line.

"Sure?"

"Absolutely," he replied with a stoic nod.

She took out her purse. "Well, I need to get going."

Mickey wondered if it wasn't too late for his back to get bad again. "No, no," he said grabbing the bill, deciding instead on a display of generosity, "I've got it."

"Thanks," Alexia said. "See you tomorrow."

"I'm going to make tracks, too," Robert said, getting up, "I'm just going to the restroom."

"So," Jay said to Mickey, the two of them left behind, "I'm not sure I get it. Why did he think she'd eaten his socks?"

Mickey felt the urge to thump his beer mug down on Jay's fingers. "My phone is ringing," he said with sudden resolve.

Jay looked at the silent phone on the table. "No, it's not."

"Yes, yes it is," he said picking it up. "It's on silent."

"Hello," he said into the phone, "yes, how are you?" At that moment the phone rang for real, playing the NFL theme music. Mickey got a fright and dropped it. It tumbled across the bar table. He snatched it and put it to his ear, "Hello?" He put his hand over the receiver and whispered to Jay, "Crazy-assed phone."

Jay mouthed a goodbye and left.

It was Simon Lester, Mickey's business manager. "What is it?" He picked at the label of his beer bottle, as he took in the news. "You telling me that, even with the refinancing, we're still going to have a shortfall on the monthly construction payments?" He shook his head. "What are these monkeys pricing our portfolio for, a post-Christmas sale . . . ? Yeah, yeah, yeah, I know there are always other deals, but God wants us to have *this* deal . . . because, because we're going to do so much damn good, they're going to name a *park* after us! . . . One month?!" He slammed his fist onto the bar counter. "Geriatric gangsters got our balls in a vice! You've got to find a way to bring more money to the table . . . No, we have to do this . . . because, because, *I don't do losing.*"

Out in the parking lot, Alexia noticed a figure lurking in the shadows with what looked like a club. Instinctively, she took a step back. The person moved toward her into the light. It was Raelene Clever holding a golf club.

"I lost," she said. They were alone. "Again!" she added. "Nothing that *any* of you have done has helped in the least! In fact, you made it worse. You shook my confidence, made me feel I wasn't doing enough."

"You *weren't* doing enough." It was Robert, who had just entered the parking lot.

Alexia breathed a small sigh of relief.

"Here is the secret," he said. "Belief minus action equals delusion. You weren't prepared to put in the hours. Here is another secret: Belief plus action equals a fighting chance, not a guarantee, just a fighting chance. You never gave yourself a fighting chance."

She gave him a scowl.

"Let me ask you something, Raelene," he said, unfazed. "If all 25 people in that tournament had *The Secret* giving them absolute confidence, enabling them to believe 100% they would win, who would win?"

"Me!" she screamed, marching toward them gripping the club with both hands as she swung it back. "I have a gift! At age eight, I was smashing girls twice my age!"

Alexia, seeing Raelene about to smash open her head, lifted her hands in front of her face and screamed, "No!"

Raelene, realizing what Alexia was thinking, stopped. "You think I'm going to hit you?! You think I'm crazy?!" She shook her head in disgust. "I'm a young, beautiful woman out alone at night." She looked at the golf club in her hands. "Would I come without protection? You think I hate myself?"

"Right," Alexia said, lowering her hands tentatively.

"Listen to me," she said to Robert. "I was born to play this game."

He nodded, "But do you *live* to play it?"

Carter was working late when the intercom sounded. She walked downstairs and peered into the video surveillance screen. It was Sam Nash. Pressing the remote, the gates swung open. She unlocked the immense wooden front door. He got out of his car and walked to the bottom of the stairs. Looking weary and worn down of his customary defiance, Sam also seemed to be even more disheveled than usual.

"Would you rather I went away?" he asked.

"Why do you ask that?"

"The way you're looking at me."

"I'm smiling at you."

"You're irritated that I'm disturbing you."

"No," Carter said, amazed at his misinterpretation, "I'm *happy* to see you."

He tentatively made his way up the stairs toward her.

"Has it occurred to you," she said, "that you don't always read people correctly? You seem to interpret neutrality or even friendliness as hostility."

He shrugged.

"This is important," she insisted. "Perception creates reality. Come," she said, leading him through the entrance hall to the expansive reception area. They sat on a long, white couch.

"No one wants me," he said simply.

She felt a sudden, unexpected welling of sympathy. It was the bald vulnerability of the statement. She resisted the urge to put her hand on his arm. "How many job interviews have you had?"

"A lot," he said with deliberate inexactness, the armor back.

She got up. "Sam, what do your computer programs do?"

"Huh?" He wasn't expecting to go into an IT discussion.

She asked the question again.

He shrugged. "Organize information more effectively."

"So that?"

"The company saves time and money."

"So that?"

"Profits go up."

"So that?"

"I don't know!" he yelled in frustration. "So we all live happily ever after!"

"Exactly!" Carter smiled. "You get to do what you love, because it makes people better off. That's the only reason anyone employs, dates or befriends anyone. Unfortunately, as Mr. Nasty, you make people worse off and so they're willing to sacrifice the fruits of your genius not to be around you."

"I can't help it," he said. "People just don't like me."

"You don't like them."

He was incredulous. "I'm not going to like someone who doesn't like me."

"Has it ever occurred to you," Carter began slowly, "that they're thinking the same thing?" He looked at the ceiling, as his brain tried to compute this turnaround. "You're so scared of being rejected, you make sure you can't be, by rejecting them first. Then, instead of disappointing you, they fulfill your expectations." She sat down next to him.

"Dave and John are from two different departments within a company; they will be changing positions for a month. Dave describes the people in his department as kind and caring. John warns that his colleagues are mean and nasty. A month later, they meet up to share their reflections. 'I don't know what you were talking about,' Dave says. 'The people in your department are every bit as wonderful as the people in mine.' 'Are you crazy?!' John replies. 'The guys in your department are even meaner than in mine!'" She paused, hoping he would get the insight on his own. Then she added, "How you see people, makes them how they are."

Sam looked down disdainfully at his nails and started chewing one of them. This was not the response she was hoping for. He stuck out the tip of his tongue, ejecting the fragment. It torpedoed toward her crossed leg, landing inches away on the marble floor. This was too much. "You know that's just not socially acceptable!" she snapped.

"What?" he said with genuine blankness.

"Biting your nails and spitting them out."

"Must I be conventional?"

"Unless you see your lack of hygiene as part of your unique individuality! Do you know that you smell?" His eyes widened in an affronted glare. "You don't shower enough," she continued. "You always look like you just rolled out of bed. This is not subversive, it's off-putting."

He folded his arms. "I'm exactly the way my father was. I got this all from him."

"Right, and next you're going to tell me that it's because your mother never breast-fed you. While you're pointing fingers at the arsonist, the house is burning down."

"Look," she said, changing her tone, "Your social habits are like a computer program you've developed to deal with the world, Sam, and maybe you did pick up that program from Pops, but now *you're* running the program. The only difference between you and Mr. Nice is that you're operating on different programs. If you're getting results with Mr. Nasty, fine. If you're not, change it. You're not the program; you're the programmer. Have some fun! Do a little reprogramming. You might like the results."

He looked away. "I don't smell."

Carter began to feel like she was swimming against a tsunami. "Right, and nor does what you leave behind in the toilet. That's why I'm here, I'm the stink detector."

Sam started shaking his head from side to side, as if with each shake he could erase a few more of her words.

"Look, look at me," she said. He looked up. "*Your program isn't working.*" Her words came out staccato steady. "There is a lot that we can do to help you. There is facial expression recognition software to improve your social perception, and there are behavioral transformation tools to improve your social interaction. You can turn your life around. So," she said, taking in a breath, "you're either going to decide that I'm just another bitch who doesn't like you, or maybe, just maybe, I care enough to want to see you put your genius back to work."

The following morning, with one hand on the wheel and one on his ear, Mickey pressed the pedal with the same belligerence as he pressed upon his business manager, Simon Lester. "Nobody's got the vision that we ... Don't, don't ... please stop sounding like my mother ... Correct, because that's your job, find a way to make up the shortfall ... Listen to me, no, listen to me, just *listen* to me for a second!" He inhaled deeply. "I'm sorry I'm shouting here. I promised Robert I would stop shouting. I'm trying not to have a heart attack before I'm 40. Look, you can do this. *We* can do this. Grow or die, yeah? Grow or die. Come, let's show this city what a 21st century property development looks like, okay? Find a way to make up the shortfall, okay? Thank you, thank you. I love you."

Mickey switched off the phone and made for the driveway. There to greet him was the spectacle of Alexia, Jay, and Haydon, their security guard, pressed up against the big, wrought iron security gate. They were trying to push it open. Mickey pressed the green button on his remote control. The gate rumbled ominously. Alexia, assuming that their efforts had paid off, whooped, but the gate only stuttered down to a whimper. They turned to see Mickey getting out of his car.

"We're locked out," Alexia said, bouncing from foot to foot. "Something's wrong with the gate motor. I've got to get inside. I need the restroom."

Sensing an opportunity for a heroic intervention, Mickey marched up to the gate, hunkered down and clutched his fingers in a double open palm. Looking up at Alexia, he said, "Step up."

She looked up at the unscalable height of the gate and then back at him, with the sympathetic look she reserved for the feebleminded.

Carter and Robert, having parked alongside the curb in front of Mickey, walked toward them. And, there they all stood—America's foremost self-help gurus, struck dumb by a faulty gate motor. Next, Leo Zubkin arrived for his session with Jay. For the first time, there was no sign of his leather-bagged manuscript. He looked unsteady, as if he were missing part of a foot.

"Something's wrong with the gate motor," Jay told him. "Maybe we should go to a coffee shop for your session."

"You got the remote?" Leo asked.

"Yes, but it doesn't work." Jay pressed it.

Leo listened as the motor rumbled to life and then stuttered back to infirmity. "The contractor centrifugal switch," he began. "The stationary portion sounds like it's rocking from one side to the other. It needs pressure on the bottom casing." Taking no note of the group's uncomprehending faces, Leo went to the trunk of his car and returned with a long wrench. Stretching his arm through the gate, he smacked the under casing hard.

"Try to open it," he said to Jay.

Once again, there was a brief rumble and then nothing. He smacked it again harder. This time, the gate hummed serenely and opened, much to the awe and exhilaration of those mystified by the magical workings of mechanical things.

"Probably best to replace that part," he said. "I'll do it, if you like."

Alexia kissed Leo on the cheek and ran up the drive to relieve herself, leaving Mickey wondering if he had chosen the wrong profession.

Up in the house, Leo sat in front of Jay on the cloud-shaped couch.

"I had no idea about your mechanical abilities," Jay said.

"Been working with locomotives since I was a kid."

Jay moved in closer. "How are you?"

He shook his head like a man who had lost everything.

Jay pondered for a moment and then began, "I want you to imagine something, okay?"

Leo nodded.

"Imagine that you are granted your dream day, where you can have and do anything, anything you want. What happens, from the moment you wake up to the moment you go to sleep?"

Leo sighed deeply. "I don't know."

"Imagine it," Jay prompted, "as if you're in it right now."

Leo closed his eyes, "I wake up next to Sandy, my wife. She's arranged a high cholesterol breakfast, which I finish up before rolling over and making love to her. She orgasms . . . three times. While she gets the kids ready for school, I read the latest edition of *Popular Mechanics*. The kids jump into bed with me and tell me I'm the greatest father in the known universe. For the rest of the morning . . . let's see . . . I work on my locomotives. Sandy comes back and makes us lunch. In the afternoon, I don't know, I fix a friend's car. That evening," he took in a deep breath, "we go to a dinner, where I receive the Man Booker Prize. The chairman of the committee tells the audience that I am the greatest living author." He opened his eyes. "What's the point of this?"

"Are you aware that in your entire dream day, you never wrote a single word? You want to win a literature prize, but you don't want to write."

Leo looked confused, as he tried to fit the square peg of this new insight into the round hole of his understanding.

"Wouldn't it be better," Jay said, "to devote your life to your passion, instead of your fantasy of what you think you're meant to be?"

Seeing that round peg for what it was, Leo felt a surge of indignation. "You want me to become a mechanic?"

"Is that your passion?"

"That's a hobby!" Leo protested.

"The best jobs always are," Jay replied.

Leo threw his head back in disdain and got up. "You're supposed to be all about embarking on an audacious quest, yet here you are trying to kill my ambition and turn me into a grease monkey!" With that he turned around and stormed out.

Jay slumped back in his chair. *Audacious quest indeed.*

5

TWELVE WEEKS SINCE his arrival at Quest, Inc., Sam Nash, obnoxious, disheveled misanthrope, stared into the calm eyes of a clean-cut, stylishly suited, rather attractive man in a silver framed, full-length mirror. Alexia stood behind him.

He shook his head. "It's not me."

"You like the suit, the shirt?"

He nodded.

"The style of your hair?"

He nodded again. "Just doesn't feel like me."

"What sort of person is the man in the mirror?"

"I don't know," he took a step closer, looking deeper into the brown eyes. "Relaxed, nice to be around."

"Why can't you be him?"

He turned to her, "It's like these techniques Dr. King is teaching me, you know, listening, using people's names, giving compliments. It feels . . . fake."

"When you walked in this morning, greeting me by name and complimenting me on the look of the Makeover room, did you not mean what you said?"

"It's what Dr. King taught me," he replied. "'Compliments build rapport.'"

"So you don't really like this room?"

He looked around. "No, I do."

"Before, you just wouldn't have said anything, because that's not what you'd been taught. Then you discover that maybe there's another way, but it doesn't feel like you. *You.* Who *are* you? We're brought up to find a personality and stick to it—choose a lane, any lane, but if the lane's taking you to hell? I mean, as personalities go, yours was great . . . for a rodeo bull, or as a substitute for water torture." She was on a roll. "You were like a pig at a Bar Mitzvah." She laughed. "Hey, no problem. If you can't be a good example, at least serve as a terrible warning!" He breathed in and out rhythmically. She stopped laughing. "It would be natural to insult me back. Instead, you've chosen something else. What are you telling yourself?"

He shook his head.

"You're telling yourself something now to keep yourself from anger. What is it?"

"'Nobody can make me feel inferior without my permission.'"

"Eleanor Roosevelt. That's one of my favorites. See, self-control is *also* natural. Look in the mirror."

He stared at himself.

"Pretend to be that guy for thirty days and afterwards, anything else will feel fake."

Robert was swimming laps in the crystal blue waters of Quest, Inc.'s outdoor pool. Stretching out his arm to touch the edge, marking another lap, he glimpsed a pair of black high heels. He planted his feet and drew his head up, tracing the tower above him of Victoria Holt. Robert's swim-induced calm splintered. He shifted his goggles up on to his swim cap.

"Do we have an appointment?" he asked.

"Just part of my research," she replied. "Seeing how the transformers stay transformed."

He pulled his goggles back onto his eyes, determined to ignore the field anthropologist, but before he could, she kneeled down and slapped a magazine down in front of him. It was *Playboy*. On the cover, in a bikini, swinging a golf club, was Raelene Cleever.

"Quite a transformation you engineered with her," she said, "from budding sports star to soft porn model."

Robert lifted himself into a sitting position on the edge of the pool, his calves submerged in the water. He looked down at the picture. Raelene's breasts were pushed up unnaturally high, her eyes widened into the camera. She had that excessive pout that suggested a freakish ability to suck onto window panes.

Victoria crouched down and leaned toward him. "Her golf coach says that he can't understand why she's given up, says she had great potential."

"Potential without practice is just potential," he said. "Raelene was more in love with winning than playing." He picked up the magazine and looked closer. "A pretty face and a good body can confer a quick win"—he slapped the magazine back on the ground, picked up his towel and stood up—"whatever that sort of win is worth."

She wasn't going to let him go that easily. "Your score's not looking great," she said, picking up the magazine before standing to meet his eye.

He patted himself down and wrapped the towel around his waist. "We help people figure out what they want and what they're prepared to do to get it. Looks like she figured it out."

"Does it help being inebriated while you do it?"

"Huh?"

She pulled a photo from her back pocket and handed it to him. It was a black woman in the fetal position, asleep on the pavement. Her tattered shorts hiked up, revealing a partially exposed buttock. It took him a moment to figure it out. It was Carter. Robert looked back at her.

"So what do you think?" she said, "Looks like Doctor King could do with . . . *a doctor.*"

Describing his "dream day" to Jay had only deepened Leo's depressive funk. He felt like a religious zealot who'd lost his faith. With nothing yet to replace his amputated identity, he was hobbling badly. He sat on a white plastic garden chair in front of a bonfire he had built on his lawn. Mesmerized by the violent dance of flames, he found himself floating back in time to when he was 14 years old at school in St Petersburg.

It was 1981, and Leo was in his first romantic relationship with Anastasia, a girl so beautiful, bright and good, he knew there could be no other. His boyish fantasies were not of her naked body, but of their growing old together, with a brood of doting grandchildren. Anastasia didn't just love Leo like a girl in love with romance; she revered him. She had read his grandfather's seminal work and convinced Leo that authorial genius ran through his veins. Sometimes, he felt out of her league, as she tried to talk with him on such matters as truth and goodness. Usually patient, she never pushed his reticence. He'd read little of his grandfather's work, and held no opinion on such matters as truth and goodness, other than that Anastasia was both.

One Friday afternoon, he walked behind the school bathrooms and saw Anastasia kissing an older boy. He walked away calmly, his brain plainly deaf to what his eyes had just seen. When his friend reported a similar sighting, Leo knocked him to the ground. When

Anastasia began ignoring him, his brain finally got the news. Emerging from the abyss eight months later, he knew there was only one way to exact revenge—become an even greater writer than his grandfather.

Staring into the fire, Leo picked up the box of manuscripts next to him and put it on his lap, peering at the pile of handwritten pages. It had been ten years, ten years of joyless slog. His only satisfaction had been in the anticipation of fame and adoration; the writing itself was like back office work. Work without love was a throttling of the soul. No wonder nothing good came of those ten years.

Leo heaved up the box with a mixture of strain and disgust, and threw it into the fire, where it briefly stifled the flames, shaking up a sprinkling of sparks and ash. He sat down again, watching his self-immolation. He shuddered briefly, as he felt a set of arms drape around his neck and a warm cheek nestle against his own. It was his wife—Jane.

"Better?" she asked.

He looked at her, and then to his surprise, found himself nodding.

Carter was on the city-loft-lounge set of *Morning Live*. A young, male makeup artist was padding her cheeks with a little sponge to keep the glow at bay. As he stepped aside, Carter found herself looking at Guy Rayburn. It was disconcerting to be thirty seconds away from what was expected to be a riveting conversation between her and a man she'd never met before, and who was now sounding forth animatedly to what appeared to be his imaginary friend. In fact, celebrity presenter and producer, Guy Rayburn, had a discrete earphone and microphone, which enabled him to communicate with the production team in the control box.

"Alright!" Guy yelled. "Have the python lady, but then let her stay for 'Cooking Cordon Bleu on a Fast Food Budget' and let's see if we can get the python to have breakfast."

One may have expected an appearance on national TV to be an exercise in pride; but when one saw the insatiable appetite of this content-guzzling monster—and how it spewed out such wide and wild variety—one quickly realized that one was no more than a quick, forgettable snack on the national menu. Still, being a snack was better than being left on the shelf; and Carter felt a surge of adrenaline, as she was reminded that the success of Quest, Inc. depended on how "appetizing" her six and a half minutes were.

Still talking into the microphone, Guy Rayburn gave Carter a little wave. She waved back, pleased for the acknowledgement, if somewhat unsettled that this would be the extent of it. She calmed her nerves the way she did before a big keynote speech, by telling herself this wasn't about her; it was about the people watching and how their lives could be improved through her message. It wasn't even *her* message. She was just a reporter, sharing proven principles for a successful life. It didn't matter what they thought of her; what mattered was that they heard the message.

"Five, four, three, two . . ." The floor manager had begun the countdown, finishing it off with a wave of his hand.

"Dr. Carter King," Guy Rayburn began, reading from the autocue into the camera, "psychologist and best-selling author, has set up a personal development agency. Want to go from No-League to A-League? Apparently, Quest, Inc. can take you there."

No League to A league. Carter winced internally. That was the other thing about being on TV—you couldn't be sure how they would serve you up.

"Do people change?" It was the first time that morning Guy really looked at Carter. It was the same moment that two and a half million other people did. "Can people change?" he continued, "I mean, if you're born a dog, no amount of coaching is going to turn you into a cat."

"No," she agreed.

"No?" he repeated.

Television was like a time compression machine. One could multiply time by a factor of ten. A conversation that in real life would take half an hour, here would take three minutes. Right now, Carter's clock was spinning mercilessly and she'd said only one word, a negative. On the great attention guzzler, there was time for little more than pre-packaged sound bites, and here she was busy thinking.

"No," she said again, "but you could become a better dog, a nicer dog, a smarter dog."

"What about true greatness. Isn't that something you're born with?"

"You've got to be born to be great," she replied, "but that's pretty much where it ends. Anders Ericsson, professor of psychology at Florida State University, spent 20 years studying exceptional individuals in all fields. His conclusion: nothing shows that innate factors are necessary for expert-level mastery in most fields, other than in certain sports, like basketball, where a baseline height is required. And even there, you get a Spud Webb, who at 5' 7", won an NBA slam dunk contest."

"So, how do you become great?"

"Practice. Deliberate practice. The stars spend at least a third more of their time on the field. They also get and apply feedback."

Guy Rayburn frowned doubtfully. "No matter how much they practice, you can't tell me that everyone's capable of being Einstein?"

"Well, Guy," Carter began, instinctively trying to bridge their divide through the intimacy of his first name—just a couple of chums having a chat. "There are many people with a higher IQ than Einstein who won't achieve anything *close* to what he did, because they didn't discover their passion and clock up the hours."

Guy Rayburn's doubtful frown had become a fixture. "Look at you," he said. "You have a Ph.D., you've been acknowledged by the President of the United States for service to the nation . . . and you say that's got nothing to do with the gifts you were born with?" For the second time in her five-minute allotment, Carter was silent for longer than acceptable on a national TV show.

"Dr. King?" Guy Rayburn prodded, with growing impatience.

"My sister . . ." she began.

"Yes?"

"My sister and I are identical twins. That means we are genetically the same. We don't just look the same, we're physical clones . . ." Again she faltered.

"Yes . . ."

It was as if Carter had been dipping her toe in the water and had now resolved to throw herself in. "If genes were destiny," she said, "my twin sister would be on this show right now with me, having achieved all the same things. But she's not—she's a crack addict, who's probably out on the streets right now hustling for her next fix." Carter breathed in deeply, stifling the upwelling, making sure her words hadn't altered the earth's orbit. "We were brought up in the same home with the same abusive, largely-absent father and social welfare dependent mother. We went to the same dysfunctional schools, and then when I was eight, I went to a Thanksgiving party thrown by a well-off community for disadvantaged kids. That day, I became friends with a boy whose parents were psychologists. I started going around to their home just about every day. They helped me with my homework, gave me books to read, but more than that, they always made me feel like I could be more than a teenage, welfare mother, like all the older girls I knew. They had a name for me, 'Miss Fabulous.' Soon, I began to believe I was pretty fabulous and that one day, like them, I would become a psychologist." She looked to the side regretfully. "My sister, Aaliyah, never had anyone instill that belief." She looked back at Guy. "Now, that belief wasn't a gift I was born with. That was a gift I was given."

There was another brief moment of silence.

"Thank you," Guy Rayburn said with unaffected sincerity, before turning to camera. "Next up, fancy a python as a pet? Don't go away! We've got one coming up right here on *Morning Live*."

Later that day, Carter walked into the atrium. Doreen got up from her receptionist's station, flustered. "I watched the show," she said. "You were brilliant."

"Thank you."

"Dr. King," Doreen continued, "I've seen your sister around here. The resemblance is . . . incredible. I'm sorry, I thought it was you."

"Just let me know if you ever see her again."

"Yes, yes, I will," Doreen replied eagerly, and then added, "Ms. Holt is here to see you."

Carter threw her head back in frustration. "Not now."

Victoria walked in from the open sitting area. "I won't take much of your time."

Carter turned to face her.

"It was a fine performance." Victoria took a step closer. "But you know the obvious question."

Carter did her best to remain calm. "I'm not answering questions right now."

Victoria wasn't fazed. "If you're so good, why can't you help your sister?"

Carter gestured to the door. "I'm going to need you to leave now."

"I'm just doing my job. I want to give you the chance to respond."

Carter turned to Doreen. "Please will you schedule an appointment with Ms. Holt." She made for the stairs.

"We'll see if there's time before going to press," Victoria called after her.

Carter walked upstairs, hoping that Victoria wasn't bluffing, but with mule-like determination not to relent. She entered her office to see Jay reading on one of her antique armchairs. A flash of irritation crossed her face. Was there no peace?

He looked up. "Sorry," he said. "I just didn't want to miss you." Getting up, he added, "I thought we should talk about Aaliyah."

"Yes, it seems that's what everyone wants to talk about. Why Dr. Carter King, Life Coach to the Nation, can't help her own sister."

"Of course we can't be expected to save anyone and everyone," he said, "even if we're related to them. I just think there's still hope."

Carter shook her head, "I have tried and tried and tried and tried. When do I get to stop? I can't . . ." She swallowed hard. "It's too disappointing." She walked to the window. "But when Victoria Holt writes that Dr. Carter King can't help her own family, but she thinks she can help yours. Well, maybe she'll have a point."

Jay took a few steps toward her. "Whose family listens to them? The only way to get your family to do something is to tell them not to."

She smiled.

He took a few steps closer. "I've never heard you talk about my parents like you did on that TV show this morning."

She turned to him, "Your parents took me in as a daughter, they saved my life."

"You were their joy. You really *were* their Miss Fabulous. They would have been so proud of you. I'm sorry they weren't there for Aaliyah."

Carter looked down and shook her head. "I should have done more. I gave up on her. I don't think I ever really believed in Aaliyah, not like your parents believed in me." She looked out the window, so she didn't have to meet his eye with what she was going to say next. "We were Aaliyah and Alisha, the twins, Double-A, two peas in a pod. Not long after your parents started calling me Miss Fabulous, I became class president . . . and at school they started calling me Carter, after President Jimmy Carter. It stuck. I was no longer Alisha—just one of the twins, and I liked it. I got my own identity. I was no longer one of two peas in a pod; I had my own pod. I never stopped loving Aaliyah, but I didn't need her to succeed. Success was mine, it was how I separated myself. Maybe I didn't even want her to succeed."

Jay walked around so that he could face her. "You've done everything you could to help her." He followed her gaze out the window. "My parents should have been there for her, too."

"I could have asked them, but I didn't. Instead, I left her with my crazy mother. When I was at your house, I pulled back my feelings of missing her. There was a ticket out of bedlam and it was mine."

"Maybe you didn't think you *could* ask."

She shook her head.

"You were a little girl. Alisha. Just a little girl. And I loved you."

She turned her head to meet his gaze.

He took a step toward her. "Confession: *I* didn't want anyone else around."

There was a long while where they didn't say anything, where they just let all the old feelings float to the surface.

It was Carter who broke the silence. "And then you *stopped* loving me."

"No." He shook his head. "No, never."

She went back to sit at her desk, collecting herself. "You're right, I stopped loving you. You stopped loving me. It was mutual." And what had risen to the surface, at least for her, just as quickly, sank to the bottom.

He bit his lip, deciding it best to return to his original purpose. "Maybe it's time for me to try with Aaliyah."

"I don't even know where she is now," Carter said in her new tone. "I tried to track her down. She's disappeared again."

"She'll come back, she always does."

"We'll see."

He walked over to her desk. "*Catalyst* would have been a better name for this agency," he said. "That's all we can be for anyone, a bridge between where they are and where they want to be. They've got to walk that bridge." He leaned on her desk. "I just wish you'd walk that bridge to me."

She looked up at him. "Been there, done that."

4
NDE

BLOG
No limitlessness

Victoria Holt
Investigative Journalist

Soon I'll be releasing my feature article on the great self-help guru superhero quest. You'll be getting the good, the bad and the . . . well, wait and see. In the mean time, all this has sparked an old memory. When I was four I watched Superman. Leaving the cinema, I started climbing the third story balcony balustrade, ready to jump. My father pulled me down and told me that I couldn't fly. I cried all the way home. It was the beginning of the end of a child's illusion of omnipotence. Perhaps we never entirely give up on becoming Superman. Is that what makes the "be-all-have-all-BS" of the personal development industry so seductive? But we are limited, and we are going to die—not cheery, but I thought the truth set us free.

Read Post | Comments (946)

1

GEORGE KELLEY SAT up front alone. Staring at him from behind a big, glossy boardroom table were five people. Each one of them was an expert on his life. George could have been dead—this could have been Judgment Day. But he wasn't dead. He was at Quest, Inc., and he was about to find out who he was, so that five of the best personal development experts in the world could help him become who he wanted to be. It was just that, at this point, finding out who he was, felt like waking up to the force of a blunt object to the back of his head. Yet, George Kelley, 56 years old, auto parts dealer and occasional bar brawler, was staring back out at them as if he was listening to the weather report.

"Mr. Kelley, you're about 50 pounds overweight, weight which you carry on your waist, making your heart a ticking time bomb." Robert Rivera was just getting started. "Thirty years of fast food and soda have turned your arteries into toxic waste pipes. I know the feeling," he opened his arms and looked down at his own body. "Sometimes, we forget we have to live in these things. As for exercise, beer relays to the fridge don't count. You may be 56, but our tests show your biological age is at least 66. We've got 12 weeks to turn around forty years of self-mutilation."

George pursed his lips involuntarily.

Next to judge was Alexia Redmond. "I don't know why so many older men think the world would start questioning their sexuality if they used skin care products. We can't really reverse the damage, but we can start to slow it. As for personal grooming, I'm not sure if you've ever done any—perhaps when you needed to impress a woman. Once she became your wife, you slipped on personal hygiene, too." George smirked. Alexia concluded, "We've got a lot of work to do."

Now, it was Mickey Prodi's turn. "George, I'm disappointed. With your own successful dealership, you earn a great income. You should have been a millionaire *years* ago. Instead, take any homeless beggar without a cent in his pocket and he'd be richer than you. Do you see it as an obligation to spend every cent you've got, and then some? If you don't cut down your spending, kill the debt and start investing, you're going to be selling used auto parts until you finally have that heart attack. And if *that* doesn't kill you, you can look forward to a homeless shelter, unless one of the kids can convert the garage into a spare room."

George looked away, feigning disinterest. Maintaining that demeanor was going to be more of a challenge with Dr. Carter King, never one to approach for a good cry and a hug. She looked up from her notes. "You've got the impulse control of a five-year-old. You're spending yourself into homelessness, eating yourself to death, and that's just the half of it. Your sons refuse to have anything to do with you. The only time your wife sees you is when you're slouched in front of the TV, barking orders at her. Speaking of which, did you know you make her life so miserable, her septic ulcers were probably brought on or at least exacerbated by you? If that weren't enough, you have an assault charge against you, laid by none other than your brother. I'm not sure Cain and Able is the best biblical story for you to be trying to emulate." She shook her head. "I'm not optimistic. In

my discussions with you, I noticed very little of the commitment necessary to make such a radical turnaround. I don't want to waste your
time, or ours."

George looked at her sullenly.

"George?" It was Dr. Jay Lazarus. George turned to him.
"You're here. Most people will never take the step that you have.
That's good enough for me." He shot a glance at Carter, before
looking back at George. "It's never too late to be the person you
were meant to be. You've got 12 weeks. Are you ready to be that person?"

When he caught that first glimmer of hope, something happened
to George. Suddenly, he found himself having to hold back the water
behind his eyes. He swallowed and nodded.

"Carter."

Jay had caught her walking into her office. She stopped and
turned. Her dark skin glistened under a white, open neck blouse. For
a moment, he forgot what he wanted to say.

"Did you see that?" he asked, recovering his train of thought.

"What?"

"They're following your tone. All of them. It was an assault. He
nearly aborted."

"Life's too short. We're not here to play the violin while the
Titanic goes down."

"Since when did we become the inquisition?"

"I'm tired of working with the apathetic. It's time they were con-
fronted with the reality in the mirror."

"What about a bit of positive expectation?"

Carter walked to the window. "There was a girl who, along with
the rest of her class, had to say what she wanted to be when she grew
up. She said, 'a scientist.' Her teacher replied sympathetically that she

should try to be more realistic and think of becoming a cook or cleaner instead." She turned back to Jay, "It was a gift—one of the most powerful things anyone ever said to her. Proving that teacher wrong became her inspiration."

"That's a great story, but I think you're leaving out some of the characters. That girl also had two people in her life who made her believe she could be *anything*, if she found something she loved and worked hard enough at it."

Carter continued, "I don't believe George Kelley will respond to a gold star and a pat on the head, but maybe he'll feel angry enough to prove me wrong."

"I get it," Jay said, "define his negative behaviors and then punish them with a slap of shame. If he wants the shame to stop, he's got to stop the behavior. Dr. Phil in a box. Only problem is that unless you're in front of a live studio audience, the easiest way to stop the shame is to run away."

"Has he run away?"

Jay sighed. "Apparently not. Yet."

She sat down behind her desk. "Jay, how are our clients lives better because of you?"

He thought about it. "They're more in touch with themselves, happier, more at peace."

"How do you know that? How do you measure that?" She didn't wait for an answer. "See, I don't care if they hug a tree and discover their inner child. I want to know that they've averted divorce, lost 50 pounds, started a charitable foundation, won the respect of their delinquent kids, found a love-match, dumped their minimum-wage job and started a business that made them rich."

He leaned in toward her. "And if they've got all that and they're still unhappy?"

Carter switched on her computer. "Give them Prozac."

Jay stood there looking at her.

She looked up. "Or is Prozac too pedestrian? Maybe you've got something more experimental in mind?"

A woman, her face strangely yellow, looks ahead, glassy-eyed. Her hands fiddle aimlessly with the hem of her hospital gown. She is stooped and shrunken, her skin lined, her expression defeated. She looks about fifty, a rough, worn out fifty.

Voice

A person may have just two to three drinks a day over ten years to develop cirrhosis of the liver. Ms. Lewis is 28. She developed the disease after just six years of binge drinking. This is what a healthy liver looks like.

An image of a smooth, reddish-brown, fleshy triangle comes onto the screen.

Voice

This is what Ms. Lewis's liver looks like.

The same image dissolves into a grotesquely pock-marked, bloody maroon mess.

Voice

Liver cirrhosis cannot be reversed. Ms. Lewis will die, if she does not get a transplant.

A documentary was being screened in the Quest, Inc. cinema room for an audience of one: Jenna Lowe, nineteen. Her right arm was in a plaster cast up to the elbow. With her other hand, she fiddled with a small, gold hoop, pierced through her belly button. At the back of the room, a woman stared out from the darkness. It was Alexia. The film stopped and the lights came up.

Robert walked into Jenna's field of vision. "At your current rate of consumption, that's what you could be looking forward to within the next five years."

"I'm not an alcoholic," she snapped. A strand of blonde hair fell defiantly across the stitched up cut above her left eye.

Robert moved in closer. "Binge drinking and waking up in a strange man's bed is not a good sign of moderate alcohol use. Nor is writing off three cars in four months."

"I'm okay! Sometimes things get a little out of hand. I'm enjoying my life."

"Why are you here?" Robert was losing patience.

"I got accepted. My fees are paid, right?" A flirtatious smile crawled onto her lips, her ocean blue eyes shone at him. "I'm ready to have you help me turn things around."

Alexia slipped out the back, unseen.

Later that day, Mickey was presenting a seminar at the Marriott's Grande Ballroom in downtown Los Angeles. The auditorium was packed with nearly a thousand people in search of the secret formulas of financial success. As a coaching client, it was mandatory for George to attend this particular seminar. He sat at the back by the door.

"Is money the root of all evil?" Mickey threw out the words brashly. "You tell me. The majority of murderers come from low-income families. The majority of rapists come from low-income families. The majority of all prison inmates in this country earned less than ten thousand dollars a year before they were incarcerated. Is money the root of all evil? No my friends. *Poverty* is the root of all evil. God wants you to be rich!"

Mickey was delivering his "How to Master Your Money and Grow Rich" program. He wore a blood red silk tie, matching suspenders and gold cufflinks. It had occurred to him that standing on stage, one thousand pairs of hungry eyes glued on him, was at least as good as sex, which for Mickey Prodi was quite an observation.

"Change your attitude to money. See this suit?" He opened his arms out wide to the masses, the messiah of financial freedom. "Great tailoring, every bit as good as an Armani, just without the label. 80% of American millionaires shun designer brands, they live in modest homes—they're frugal. They would rather have big bank accounts than big status symbols. When you see somebody who looks like a walking label, see them paying for the privilege of advertising for that company—insane! You also might want to imagine them struggling to pay an overdraft. Some people fake orgasms—more people fake wealth."

The audience laughed, delighted. The secret, he had quickly realized, was to treat it not as a lecture, but as theater. Having *performed* this piece over a hundred times, he was banking on the next question, which today would be shouted out by a middle-aged man in the fourth row. "So, why are you wearing a Rolex?"

Mickey smiled, always making the answer sound like this was the first time he'd heard the question. "When a Timex would perform the same function at a hundredth of the price? Sometimes you have to pay for beauty. Not that I did, it was sponsored. When you're rich and famous and need nothing, you get given stuff—it's a cruel irony. Does that make life unfair? No!" Lifting out his arms again. "*You* can be rich. The first thing you've got to do is . . ." He pulled a ticket out of his suit pocket. "Cameraman, can you please focus in on the lie in my hand." The camera zoomed in, so the audience could see a lottery ticket that he was holding. He tore it up. "Stop handing your financial destiny over to chance. Reclaim your power. Put your financial faith in good hands—your own!"

The audience roared approvingly.

There was a time as a teenager that Mickey had wanted to be a rock star. This, he now knew, was better. He wasn't just blabbering pretty lyrics he was preaching "the Word". Financial advice was to Mickey like the Bible to an evangelist. He hated to see people go to financial hell. He had no delusions of grandeur; they weren't his words. He was just a disciple of financial *uncommon* sense. There may have been audience members who saw his outsized confidence as evidence of an outsized ego; but Mickey never saw himself as exceptional. On the contrary, as someone who had struggled at school, Mickey was secretly convinced he was below average. (Actually, his real problem had been undiagnosed dyslexia.) In his mind, *not* being special was exactly what made the *message* special—it had proven itself on him. His confidence was a function of his conviction.

"Don't forget to sign up for next month's investment seminar. Find out how I built a multi-million dollar property empire in ten years. Until then, follow the gospel of wealth . . ." He put his hand to his ear, so the audience would repeat the mantra they'd been reciting all day.

One thousand exuberant voices shouted in unison: "Cut down spending, get out of debt, save and invest!"

Actually, he reflected, this was better than sex. From up here, he penetrated brains. Not all were ready for fertilization; but those that were, would be delivered to financial salvation. That was what made him want to sing and shout.

Once Mickey had finished signing autographs and the audience had dispersed, George approached him. "We should have been taught that stuff at school," he said.

Mickey was packing up his black leather laptop bag. "The government is too busy trying to turn us into nine-to-five salary men, shackled to a mortgage, spending money we don't have to bring in the taxes they get to squander."

George followed him into the foyer. "What if you needed to make a lot of money quickly?" he asked.

Mickey spoke while taking out his phone and turning it on, "The only people who get rich quick are people who write and sell books called *Get Rich Quick*. The vast majority of self-made millionaires are people who have saved and invested for most of their lives."

"So that counts me out."

"How old are you?" he asked, while dialing his cell phone.

"Fifty-six."

"You've got say, ten years to retirement? You can do it. We'll look at a plan in your coaching session." Mickey put the phone to his ear.

"What if you needed to get rich in six months?" George asked.

Mickey shrugged. "Rob a bank." And then into the phone, "Simon?"

Covering the receiver, he whispered to George, "Excuse me."

As George walked off, Mickey spoke into the phone, "Okay, I got your mail, so let me understand this: Part of our cash component covers the bank deposit for the land. The other part goes to Feinstein, who guarantees us a 25% return paid over twelve months. This covers the construction costs. Question: How does he guarantee 25%? He's got options in Columbian coco fields? Just remember, if it sounds too good to be true, you're about to be screwed by an industrial jackhammer. Do the due diligence. I want this deal, but I'm not running for the train with my pants round my ankles . . . Yeah? Deadline, shmedline! I know good sales B.S. when I see it. It's the way my Nana peddled aprons. 'Offer expires today' gets miraculously resurrected tomorrow . . . Just do the due."

Back at Quest, Inc., Robert was staring into the fridge when Carter walked in. Sensing someone behind him, he closed the door.

"You scared your book might be too much of a success?" she said.

He turned around.

"Is that why you're holding it back?"

"No," his mouth said, while on some other layer of his brain, she had just slotted the final piece of the puzzle into place. He wasn't just scared of success; he was terrified.

"Really?" she persisted, giving time for the completed puzzle picture to emerge into consciousness.

It was preposterous that one could be resistant to what was universally considered the inherently positive state called "success," so it took almost a half a minute of Carter's patient silence for Robert to finally sit down at the table and say, "Success could kill me."

Carter pulled up a seat opposite him. "If your book shoots you to prominence, and you fall again . . ."

"The shame would take me out. I don't think I could live with myself."

"You're a stronger man, you'd get over it."

"But do I want to put myself through that?"

"You may find that you're more motivated to sustain it, given the consequences of failure."

"It's too risky, not just for me, but for the agency."

"Accepting Victoria Holt's challenge was one of the riskiest things I've ever done. Had I calculated that risk a little better, would I still have done it? I don't know. But one thing it has done is pushed us all harder. Risk stretches you."

He looked away for a few moments and then turned back to her. "I need more time."

She nodded. "Okay, just know that success always comes with hazards—there's the pressure to maintain it, sometimes it attracts jealousy, and yes, losing it can be humiliating." She leaned in toward him. "So? *Get over it. Man up.* This isn't about you; it's about them.

Success is just the applause you get when you give people something of value. The world needs your story. Minimize your risk. Start small, present the material in your book in a focus group at Pepperdine."

He gave her a doubtful look.

"You can never eliminate risk. That's the price, not just of success, but of life."

Alexia knocked on Jay's door.

"Come in."

She entered. The room was empty. "Jay?"

"How are you, Alexia?"

"Confused, actually."

"Walk behind the desk."

She did.

"Hello, Alexia."

She looked down, immediately snapping her head back in alarm.

"You okay?" he asked.

"Fine," she lied. "Never been better."

His eyes were closed; his body lay in a simple, pine coffin.

"You won't find anything more relaxing," he said.

"I don't know, maybe base jumping."

"On the annual holiday of atonement, some of the Jewish mystics used to dress up in their burial shrouds and lie in their graves. I thought that might have attracted too much attention, so I just bought this coffin. Without the lid, it's not that claustrophobic."

"That's very reassuring." She sat down on a chair next to him.

He opened his eyes and stared up aimlessly at the ceiling. "It's hard to get too flustered about the small stuff, when you remember how soon you're going to be dust." He took in a deep breath. "Instant cure for self-obsession. In a hundred years—a cosmic nanosecond—I won't even exist in someone's memory. There's something liberating about such complete obliteration. Suddenly, nothing is all that important. You should try it some time. I've got an orthopedic cushion in here, so it's really very comfortable."

Alexia stood up. "While we remain unobliterated, I need to talk to you about one of our clients—Jenna Lowe."

The telephone started ringing. "Would you mind getting that?" Jay asked.

Alexia picked up the receiver. "Dr. Jay Lazarus' office? Dr. Lazarus is . . ." she looked down at the coffin ". . . on *deadline* at the moment. Thank you, I'll tell him." She hung up. "Your four o'clock is waiting for you in the garden," she said, looking out the window. "And right now, she's . . . flying."

Jay climbed out of the coffin and looked out the window. A sprightly lady in her 80's was bouncing gleefully on a trampoline at the far end of the garden.

He turned back to Alexia. "You wanted to talk to me about something?"

"I think she needs you."

He smiled at the spectacle below, before making for the door. "I'm not sure she does."

By the time Jay got outside, Rose Andrews was lying barefoot on the trampoline, staring up at a partly cloudy, blue sky. He slipped off his shoes, hopped up on the trampoline, and sat down cross-legged on a padded corner, facing her.

She sat up and gave him a big smile that sent little wrinkles racing out around her eyes. "I loved *Natural Ecstasy*," she said.

"You read it?" Jay replied, with delighted surprise.

"Wasn't that your intention?"

Jay had never become blasé about people reading his books. It was magical the way a bit of tree pulp could become a remote microscope into his mind, revealing his deepest ideas and concerns to anyone who was interested. *Natural Ecstasy* grappled with creating the drug-induced experience of ecstasy *without* the drug. It had been, for Jay, a long personal journey into religion, mysticism and psychobiology. And this woman sitting before him knew the whole story—knew his most intimate thoughts—without him having to say a word.

"'To live in misery is to spit in God's face,'" she quoted. "'It's like using the Mona Lisa as toilet paper.'"

Jay gave her a puzzled look.

"A line from your book," she said.

That was the other thing; while minds forgot, books never did.

"Yes," he said, recalling, "perhaps a little harsh."

"No, I love that. Look at this beautiful life, Dr. Jay," she gazed out at the ocean. "Misery is the ultimate ingratitude."

"Well, it's an honor to meet the third woman to fly solo across the Atlantic."

"Life is an endless feast," Rose said, her eyes sparkling. "So much to taste, so little time."

"Another line from my book?"

"No, that's my own."

Jay smiled bashfully, and then looked down at a file in his hands. "You're a decorated World War II intelligence agent, the youngest woman to work behind enemy lines, you have a master's in social welfare, four children, nine grandchildren, six great-grandchildren, and you were the founder of Haven for Battered Mothers." He looked up at her. "Perhaps you should be telling me how I can achieve *my* quest. What can we possibly do for you, Mrs. Andrews?"

She flashed him a wry smile. "You think I'm too old to be thinking of a change in direction?"

"No, just too capable to need our assistance."

She stood up. "You help people to achieve their goals. No matter how scary or difficult?"

"Yes," he said, getting up himself.

She took a step toward him. "Whatever the goal is?"

"That's right."

She took in a deep breath. "My goal is to end my life. Will you help me?"

2

AT THE OTHER end of the garden, unseen by Rose and Jay, sat Jenna Lowe. Never had she seen anything quite like it, the ocean stretching out forever. She saw herself sprinting, rapturous, across the dappled surface, her feet, splashing out delicate droplets of water before launching herself on a shaft of sunlight across the horizon into, *where?* She couldn't say. "Wonderland," whatever that looked like. *Launching myself on a shaft of sunlight,* she mused. *That's a cool image. I should write a poem . . . Not.* What did pretty words matter, in the greater scheme of things. Staring ahead, she scratched her plaster cast.

Mickey was taking in the same view, talking on the phone to Simon, immersed in his drama of money and power, when out of the corner of his eye, he spotted the girl, surely not much more than a girl. He found himself gravitating toward her, talking louder, so she could overhear his conversation, tensing his financial muscles: *Look how rich and powerful I am.*

"Yeah . . . ex-head of New York Stock Exchange . . . ? Head of Bank of America? Stop, you're giving me a hard-on. If they're on board with Feinstein, the 25% return is legit. There's our due diligence. And you're sure that will give us the cash flow to cover construction on the whole development? Then what are you waiting for? Sign! Go put your tap shoes on and call me after the standing ovation." He turned off the phone, slipped it in his pocket and walked over to her.

"Some view, huh?" he said.

She looked up at him, shading her eyes from the sun.

"I bought the house before I even went inside. With a view like this," He gestured behind at the property, "that could have been a caravan."

"It's yours?"

He nodded, doing his best not to look smug. "I'm a romantic, and this must be the most romantic spot on the planet." He sat down next to her, trying hard not to worry about pressing his $900 trousers into the grass.

Mickey noticed a stray leaf in her hair and found himself fearlessly raising his hand to remove it; and then, *damn*, his hand shook. As debonair as he was attempting to appear, breaking into the personal space of a beautiful young woman, even after declaring that she was sitting in his kingdom, was clearly more than his nervous system could handle.

"*Mickey,* can I please talk to you?"

They looked up to see Carter.

"Excuse me," he said to Jenna, getting up and walking off with Carter.

"What are you doing?" she asked.

"Checking in with a client."

"You nearly had your hand on her."

"She needed a friend."

"Not *your* kind of friendship."

He sighed impatiently.

"You don't think we're being watched?"

"My conscience is clear."

"Our clients are not fodder for your personal harem. Besides," she said, exasperated, "the girl is not even 20. What is *wrong* with you?"

"I'm losing my patience."

"No!" Carter said, raising her voice and then lowering it to a constricted whisper. "I'm losing *my* patience. Your behavior could sink this agency." She closed her eyes and then opened them, "Please, please, don't jeopardize what we've built. Victoria Holt would just love to get her hands on something like this."

"Let's face it," Mickey replied, "she's already got what she needs to sink us."

Dr. Jay Lazarus and Rose Andrews stood on the less manicured side of the cliff top garden, which dropped down a 200-foot rocky embankment into the ocean.

Jay looked at her confused. "You seem so fulfilled. Why would you want to end your life?"

She turned from the view to look at him. "I'm turning eighty-five next month. At this age, I'm a walking NDE."

"NDE?"

"Near-death experience," she replied. "You know, when you're about to die and you see the light at the end of the tunnel. I *live* in that tunnel."

"So you want to speed things up?"

"Many of the world's leading stem-cell specialists believe that, within this century, we'll be able to regenerate just about any cell in the body." She paused. "Look at me, Dr. Jay. What do you see?"

He gazed into her eyes, eyes sparkling with zest. "A beautiful woman."

"Ravaged by age. With stem-cell technology, I would get new skin, new bones, a new heart, a whole new body! What makes us special is our identity, our memories, and that's all up here." She tapped her head. "If I could preserve my brain, there is a chance, a *good* chance, that one day, when the technology exists, a new body could be grown and I could be brought back to life."

Finally, Jay caught on. "Cryopreservation."

"Exactly! For $80,000 and another $500 a year, I can have my head frozen and preserved until . . ."

"Your resurrection," he filled in.

"Gravity didn't stop us from flying. Why should age stop us from living?" she said, shrugging her shoulders as if she was making the most obvious point in the world.

"So, why not wait until you die naturally?"

The sun sprinkled hundreds of thousands of twinkling specks of light across the ocean. "Look at that." She shook her head, smiling. "I'm in love with life." She turned back to him. "I'm lucky, I don't have a brain disease—that I know of—but increasingly, I can't find the right words for things, I struggle to make decisions, forget names. My awareness is . . . *dimming*. I feel it, I'm gradually losing my mind. My doctor keeps telling me that, for someone my age, I'm doing pretty good. My brain is dying, there's nothing good about that. There's a pill I could take that would kill me without damaging my brain—I would have less than an hour for a cryopreservation team to start the freezing process. All further brain degeneration would stop."

"Mrs. Andrews—"

"And you know who gave me the idea?" she cut in. "You."

"I don't see how that's possible."

"Have you read your promotional pamphlet?" She took it out of her dress pocket and read aloud: "'Most people get born once. At Quest, Inc., you get a second chance.'"

He stared at her.

"What?" she asked, "was I not supposed to take that literally? I want a second chance, not now, but in a hundred years, maybe a thousand years, when being born means you don't have to die."

"You must know that it's illegal to help someone kill themselves."

"I can do this on my own. But I'm scared. I don't want to die, even temporarily."

"You want me to help you deal with your fear?"

She looked away. "One of my dearest friends, Meryl, passed away 12 days ago." She paused. "Let's cut the niceties. Meryl was *obliterated* 12 days ago. Maybe I'm being overly ambitious, but that's a fate I would like you to help me to avoid. Yes, this is going to take more guts than flying solo around the world. And there's something else," she suddenly added chirpily. "Next month, we're having a party for my 85th. I've got friends and family coming from all over the country. I want a makeover. I want to look my best for the last time they see me."

Robert gritted his teeth as he looked down at his watch. It was 15 minutes in, and for the second time, Jenna Lowe hadn't shown up for her session. He could understand a setback. Before his recovery, he'd had an avalanche; but he had never assaulted another person's time, which was what Jenna was doing to him, yet again. He looked out of the window from his upper floor office. On the far end of the cliff top garden, he could just make out Jay and an elderly woman; he scanned across to the other side. There she was! Young Jenna Lowe, sitting on the grass, taking in the view, as if she were on Christmas holiday. This was too much. He stormed downstairs, into the garden.

"Where've you been?" he asked, barely containing his anger.

"My session is in an hour," she said with infuriating certainty.

"Your session started 20 minutes ago."

"Oh." Her monosyllabic response wasn't helping his temper.

"And," he continued, "you missed your last session."

"I was at Burning Man," she said, as if this would elicit from him smiling understanding and perhaps a question or two about the festival's more daring installations. Seeing this was not where the conversation was headed, she added, "I only managed to get a lift back yesterday."

He huffed, and hated the way he sounded huffing. "If you miss one more session, you will have to leave."

"Well, let's just do it now." She got up.

"My life is not structured around your comings and goings, please make note of your sessions correctly. This is your last chance."

Jenna walked into the restroom. A woman was leaning on a basin, staring into a mirror. When Jenna saw that it was Alexia, she turned around to leave. It was too late.

"Jenna," Alexia called. She turned back. "How are things going?"

She sighed. "Can't you see?" her face brightened, "Halleluiah, Jenna has seen the light! I am a new person. Before:" Making a big, mock, bad face, "After!" Making a big, sweet face.

"Please, please don't do this," Alexia implored.

"What? I'm reborn!" Even bigger sweet face.

"Don't!"

Jenna dropped the parody. "You said if I came here, you would pay for my car to be fixed. I'm still waiting."

"I said, once you completed your program."

Jenna's reply sounded like she was talking to a particularly slow child. "And— how— do I— do that— without— a— car?"

"You've had three accidents in four months," Alexia replied. "I'm very concerned about you driving before sorting out your life. What's wrong with the bus?"

"Look, you're not my mother."

Alexia's chest heaved. The sting had found its mark. "No," she conceded, "but I am your godmother, and I'm very worried about you."

"You really don't have to do anything for me. I don't know why you bother. You should just leave me alone, like you always did." She swung open the bathroom door and left.

Alexia ran after her. "Jenna!"

She turned around.

"I'll make a deposit into your account, tonight."

Jenna smiled. "Thank you. I will go through the program. I promise."

Alexia had been raised in a six-bedroom Southern-style mansion on the grounds of the Atlanta Country Club, overlooking the lush 16th and 17th fairway of the capitol's premier golf course. Her father was chief executive of a Fortune 500 company; her mother was even busier in her role as an Atlanta socialite. Alexia's childhood need for love and attention was generally greeted with toys and trinkets and later, hard cash. When she was old enough to know better, she vowed she would not repeat her parents' child-rearing method. And yet, as she left Jenna to go off to her session with Rose, it occurred to her, that was exactly what she had done—neglected her orphan goddaughter, and now sought to buy her compliance with cash. It reminded her that the majority of abusers had themselves been abused. It was a grotesque unmerry-go-round. How could a victim so effortlessly become a culprit? How could she replicate the very behavior that had caused her pain? *Because*, she reflected, *we don't do what our parents say, we do what they do. We learn their behavior like an apprentice, by watching.* But there was a way to break the chain. *Decide.* From the Latin, "to cut off." She had to make a conscious decision to choose something else. She had to cut herself off from her toxic inheritance, cut herself off from what she knew. Slicing off the familiar was hard, but it was absolutely doable. Right now, though, Alexia was praying that just this last time, the old way would work and Jenna would be bought. She believed her goddaughter's life depended on it.

Carter was the last to leave for the day. It was already dark. She locked the door behind her and walked downstairs to her car. Without warning, a voice sound accusingly from ahead of her.

"What's your story?"

Carter stopped. "Excuse me?"

"What's your story?" A figure began to emerge from the shadows. It was George. She looked for Haydon, their guard, but couldn't see him.

George came closer. "That was your presentation at my son's graduation. Occidental College, earlier this year."

Remembering, Carter nodded.

"'At the end of your life, what story will you leave behind?' When you said that I . . . I felt my throat go tight. I thought I was having an asthma attack. For days afterwards, I kept hearing your words: 'At the end of your life, what story will you leave behind?' It was like a bad song that gets stuck in your head. I looked at my kids, my wife, my work, and I saw that, if my life was a story, the happy ending would be my death."

Haydon walked toward them from the gate. "Everything okay, Dr. King?"

"Yes, thank you, Haydon."

She turned back to George. "If you stayed for the end, you would have heard my final words: 'Whatever is happening in your life now, the next chapter is in your hands.'"

"That's why I'm here, but I don't know how much time I've got."

"All the more reason to get started," she said, turning to go.

"Dr. King," he called after her, "something happened to me, something that changed everything. I want to write it, my story, as a way for them to understand."

"To justify your actions?"

He shook his head. "It's too late for that. But maybe my story can do some good, can teach my kids something. I've never really given them anything; I want to give them this. When we first met, you asked me what I wanted—*What do you want, George?*—and I made some dumb-ass comment about a Jack and coke. I want to write my story. Will you help me?"

"Start living a better story, and then we'll help you write it."

"I've lost two pounds, drawn up a spending plan and opened a savings account," he pleaded.

She stepped toward him. "You probably don't know how much I want to just dive in and help you, but sometimes, the best thing I can do is stand on the sidelines. Make some more headway first. You've got time."

If only I had, George reflected.

3

ALEXIA WAS DOING Rose's make-up at the cosmetics counter in the Makeover room.

"We're almost done," she said, leaning over Rose. "I'm just lifting your cheeks." Rose smiled, enjoying the gentle caress of sponge on her face. ". . . Then, we're going to rub it all off and you're going to learn to do it yourself."

Rose opened her eyes and took in the fine features of the woman working on her. "You're beautiful," she said.

Alexia laughed. "Thank you, I don't always feel beautiful. I'm turning 30 next year."

Rose looked confused.

"A woman's reproductive peak is about 22. That's when she's at her most desirable. From then on, its droop, drop and dry up. My mother used to say that if life was fair, as we grew older and wiser, we would become more beautiful. At age 90, we'd be supermodels." Alexia stopped dabbing Rose's cheeks. "When she hit menopause, my father swapped her for a 28 year old. The tyranny of youth and beauty. But we've got ammunition," she said, beating her cosmetics sponge in the air.

"You think you have any chance of looking like you do now in 40 years?"

"I'm not going down without a fight," Alexia said with a joyless laugh.

One final dab on Rose's cheek and Alexia sat back to admire her work. Something was wrong. She pulled out a pair of tweezers. "Last thing . . ." Plucking a stray hair from Rose's eyebrow, she declared, "We're done!" She picked up a mirror and held it up. "What do you think?"

Rose regarded her image and smiled uncertainly.

"What a difference, huh?" Alexia said. "See, this is a war we can win!" She started wiping it off, "Now, I'm going to show you how you can do it yourself."

Rose laughed.

"What?" Alexia asked.

"Age is quietly eating me to death and you're helping me hold back the beast with a cotton swab."

Alexia stopped. "There's always Botox."

"And, there'll always be a twenty-something-year-old who's more beautiful."

Jenna arrived late again for Robert's session. After he refused to see her, she made her way to downtown Malibu, walked into the first bar she could find, and ordered a martini.

"Quest, Inc.'s really working out for you."

She looked to her right. It was George.

"Me, too," he added ironically, taking a sip of his beer. "What were you doing there?"

She wasn't in the mood to talk, or to be picked up by an old man. "I don't know," she said, without looking at him, "wasting my time."

"Sounds like my life." He turned back to his drink.

She sat down.

"What do you do?" he asked.

She didn't even bother rolling her eyes. "I hate that question."

"You don't have to answer it."

"I live life, I party, I have fun. Someone wants me to go to college, so I can be respectable like her, so that she can stop feeling guilty." Jenna's drink arrived. She took a sip and, without turning to him, asked, "Why were you there?"

"Because . . ." he started, "it's only at the end of the day that you realize how much more you could have done with it."

"It's never too late."

"That's a fairy tale," he said, looking away. "At a certain point, it *is* too late."

"Too late for what?"

"Become a husband, a father, get out of debt, lose weight and . . ."

"And?"

". . . tell my story."

"What story?"

He took in a deep breath. "Something happened to me, something that changed everything. It's the only thing I've got to leave behind—that story. I've never told a single soul." He turned to her. "You, what do you want?"

She took off like a cyclist without brakes, "I don't want to go to college, I don't want a nine-to-five job, I don't want to get married and have kids!"

George raised his brow and nodded. "Sounds like you know what you *don't* want. So, what *do* you want?"

Silence.

"I don't know." She shrugged. "Whatever."

He started laughing.

"What?"

"The single most important question of your life and you come up with, '*Whatever.*'"

She took another sip of her drink.

"But I get it," he said, "I would never have used that word, but I get it. My oldest brother was a track god. At 16 he held the fastest 800-meter in the school district. Girls loved him. Boys loved him. He didn't laud it over anyone, you know? As far as he was concerned, it was just this thing that he did, that he loved, that he happened to be good at. Also, Jamie couldn't deal with injustice. If a teacher picked on a weak kid, he would stand up for the kid, even if it meant falling out of favor with the teacher. Oh, and he loved dancing! I know, not something you'd expect from a jock, but put on some music and he would get into the groove like Michael Jackson. And he had the *moves*. The music got into his body, into his soul. And then one day," he swallowed, "he was gone. I got home from school and the police were there. My mom's face was all red and puffy. My dad's eyes were like stone. If you'd asked me to guess what happened, it wouldn't have been on my top ten. He was dead. Impossible, right? How can you be dead, when you were alive at breakfast? How can you be dead, when you were the best thing life had created?" He rested the palm of his hand on top of his glass.

She stared at him. "How'd it happen?"

"He was training early one morning. A drunk driver mounted the sidewalk." He pushed the glass forward. "Nothing seemed important any more, you know? If he could die . . ."

"Then, what's the point of anything," she filled in.

"Right."

She looked out ahead at the shelves of bottled alcohol and then spoke very softly. "The word 'whatever' wasn't in my vocabulary. And then I started using it almost constantly."

"What happened?"

She lifted her plaster casted arm on to the bar with a clunk. "When I was 13, my mom croaked."

"Ow!"

The shriek came from Jay's office.

"You should feel calm, at peace," Jay said, "death is a place of release. No more pumping iron, no more bland protein shakes. No more ego. Surrender."

"Aahhg!" Jay looked down. "What's the matter?"

Robert was lying in Jay's coffin, his face clenched in discomfort. "I think I've got a splinter in my butt."

"Oh, nonsense."

"I'm telling you," Robert groaned.

"Well, get out."

"I can't."

"Why?"

"I'm stuck."

Jay grabbed his hand and pulled. A 200-pound, muscle-packed coffin was no match for his wiry frame. He fell on top of Robert with a howl, producing the spectacle of two men sandwiched intimately in a pine coffin. At this point, like in a bad farce, Alexia walked in.

"Oh, oh, oh," she said, as if by repetition, the image would expose itself as nothing more than a bizarre flight of her imagination.

More sounds emerged from the underworld: "Uuurghhhh! Ahhhh!"

Realizing this was for real, Alexia decided that giving them their privacy would be the best course of action. She turned to leave.

"Alexia!" Jay called, having managed to roll off.

She turned back and, seeing his distress, ran forward.

"Help me get him out," he said, standing up.

She looked down at Robert. "Stuck . . . in limbo?"

"Purgatory," he wheezed.

She and Jay grabbed each of his hands and pulled. He didn't budge. They pulled harder. Finally, with a wood-splitting crack, like Frankenstein waking from the dead, Robert seesawed up.

"Uggh," Robert moaned, reaching for his backside. He pulled out a splinter and shoved it in front of Jay's face. "Are you trying to torture me into enlightenment?"

"Pain is an illusion," Jay said.

Robert turned Jay around, bent him over and stuck the splinter into his butt.

Jay snapped up with a shriek, "Ahhhh!"

"What?" said Robert, "I thought pain was an illusion."

Groaning, Jay turned to them, "You both need to leave. I have a consultation with George Kelley."

"George aborted," Alexia replied.

"What?!"

"He wasn't doing badly," she said, "but Carter was right. He wasn't motivated enough."

"I've got to talk to him," Jay said, still rubbing his backside.

"You know the deal," she reminded him. "If they walk out, it's over. Have you seen Jenna?"

"Carter aborted her," said Robert.

"No!" Alexia cried.

"After missing two sessions, I gave her an ultimatum and she missed a third. Carter felt there was no other option."

"We've got to give her another chance!" Alexia was doing nothing to hide her desperation.

"Did you hear what you just said about George? You said he wasn't motivated enough. Well, neither was Jenna." Robert walked over to her and touched her shoulder. "You can hold out your hand, but you can't make them take it."

Alexia bit her lip. *Or bribe them.*

4

ALEXIA RANG THE bell to Jenna's apartment in one of the seedier parts of Hollywood. Nothing. She called out, "Jenna?" After a few moments she rang again.

Finally, Jenna opened the door in a baggy tracksuit. "Hi."

"Hi," said Alexia, "can I come in?"

"Now's not a good time."

Alexia caught sight of a figure in the room. She craned her head forward. "George?!" She slipped past Jenna, through the doorway.

He was sitting on a beaten-up old wooden chair, one of two at an equally scuffed table.

"Excuse me?!" said Jenna, "I said now was not a good time!"

Alexia shook her head at George. "You're old enough to be her father."

He got up. "We're friends."

"It really isn't any of your business!" said Jenna. "Please leave."

"We're friends," George said again, more firmly.

"Look," Alexia said, turning to Jenna, "I'm sorry."

"For what?"

"For not being there for you."

"You're not my mother."

"No, but your mother was my best friend, and I promised her I would look after you."

"Six-feet under, I doubt she's worrying about it."

"This is about my relationship with *you*."

"This is about you feeling guilty, because I've become a big, fat screw-up."

Alexia shook her head. "I was too busy driving my career, kidding myself that you were okay."

"I'm fine."

"Are you still writing?"

"Is that what you came here to ask me?"

"I'm here . . ." Alexia said, thinking about it, "because there's this beautiful, smart, wild and wonderful woman who came into my life, and not a week goes by that I don't read her poetry, enchanted. I just want her to live a long, healthy, fulfilled life. Because the world would be a poorer place without her." She held her gaze and then turned to the door.

"Alexia?" Jenna called.

She turned back.

"I tried, I really did. I mean, maybe not hard enough, but I'm okay. Thanks for paying for my car."

Jenna's words reminded Alexia how little influence she had over her goddaughter. So, as much as she wanted to keep banging on, she took the least bad option: she turned and left.

Jenna shut the door and walked back into the room.

"Once the party's ended," George began, "the sex is over and you've pissed out the alcohol, are you still *okay*?"

Jenna opened her mouth to respond, but didn't. Instead, she walked over to a tattered, grey couch placed haphazardly in front of her mattress and took out a cigarette.

"Tell me about your mother?" George asked.

She lit it. "What are you, a shrink?"

"You don't have to, if you don't want to."

She puffed a few times on the cigarette, producing a cloud of smoke that enveloped her face. Then, she squashed it out into a tea-cup on the armrest and sat back, staring out ahead. "You could talk to her about anything," she began, "that was my mother. There was this trust. She knew how to listen, you know? Not like some mothers, butting in with a whole bunch of judgment and advice that their daughters weren't going to take anyway. No, she would just listen, and then ask these great questions, and you'd figure it out yourself. By the end of that conversation, you knew what to do, not because she'd told you, but because she'd helped you dig out the answers on your own. You walked away feeling smarter. Not a day goes by where I don't . . ."—she put the heel of her hand to her mouth—". . . just want to hear her voice." She took her hand away. "So," she said, de-termined not to cry, "when you're getting your first period, while a woman like that is getting eaten inside out by stage IV cervical can-cer, it sucks." She took in a deep, steadying breath. "But shit hap-pens. It's okay."

He got up and sat next to her. "No, it's not okay."

With his eyes focused on her, she couldn't hide, even from her-self. Her bottom lip started to quiver, her face crumpled and then the words tumbled out on a river. "They kept telling me it was going to be all right . . . you know? *Mom's going to beat this thing . . . she'll be the last one standing . . . she's a fighter . . . don't worry!* And then she was dead. And I'd missed my chance. I hadn't said a thing to her that meant anything." She wiped her eyes with the back of her hand. "Maybe I knew they were lying, maybe I just didn't want to give up hope." She shook her head. "But then it was too late."

There was a time when George would have bolted from emotion like this. "Death," he said, as she leaned her wet face against his arm, "is just a moment. Throughout your childhood, I'm sure you said many things that meant a lot to her."

"Maybe," Jenna said, pulling away, wiping her cheek with her plaster casted arm. "Whatever."

He smiled. "You and 'whatever' still buddies?"

"Apparently," she said, picking out the cigarette she'd squashed into the ashtray and straightening it out.

"So you write?" he asked.

She shook her head, putting the cigarette in her mouth. "Not anymore." She relit it. "What do pretty words matter when the Big Bastard is around the corner."

"The Big Bastard?"

"Death. Why build a house when you know a tornado is coming?"

He nodded. It was all falling into place. "So drive drunk and drugged, screw whoever, and you might just kill yourself before that tornado comes. Save yourself some disappointment."

No one had ever quite hit the nail on the head like this auto parts dealer from Burbank. The cigarette burned away between her fingers, as she stared ahead.

"It does suck," he continued, "that we get old and die or don't get old and die. But that's why we build houses and write, and look out for each other. That's how we stand up to death, you know? By making the most of what we've got and leaving the place maybe a bit better than we found it." He moved in closer to her. "So help me leave something behind. Help me write my story."

She looked at him, doubtfully.

"The way I see it, Jenna, you need my story like a woman sleeping in a burning house needs a fire alarm. I'm you. And that's scarier than you think."

The following day, Carter sat looking over at Jay on the other side of her desk. He was talking about something or other. Watching his lips dance over the words, she saw that they had lost none of their old form. And then, in what she would later describe as a cerebral malfunction, she saw herself pull her chair back, walk over to the other side of the desk, sit on his lap, put her arms around his neck, and kiss his open mouth. How could she have forgotten his skin against her own? Like smoothly sanded wood.

"So what do you think?" he said.

They were still on opposite sides of the desk. Except the monologue was now supposed to become a dialogue.

"Um ... ." She had nothing to go on. Nothing.

"Maybe you could pay me the compliment of *pretending* to listen."

Carter looked up searchingly and was rewarded with the sight of Alexia hovering in the doorway. "Come in," she said.

Jay turned to the door.

"I can come back later," Alexia replied.

"No, no, we were waiting for you."

"I was just chatting to myself," Jay said pleasantly.

Alexia walked in, closing the door behind her. She let out a frustrated sigh. "We're supposed to be the best development agency in the country. There must be some *technique* that we're missing here."

"How many life coaches does it take to change a light bulb?" Carter asked, and then answered herself. "One, but the light bulb has to *want* to change. That's the technique; they've got to *want* it. And that's *exactly* why I was skeptical about taking on George Kelley. I don't think there's a person in this agency who desires change more than I do, but this is the last time we are going to take anyone on board who we're not *convinced* is committed to their own transformation." She looked away, "It's too demoralizing."

"Part of our job may be to help them make that commitment, to help them see that change is possible," Jay said.

There was a knock on the door. "Come in," said Carter.

George entered. "Hello. Sorry, I'll come back."

"Come in," Carter said.

He looked at Jay and Alexia, and then walked forward to Carter. "I want to come back. I want to make this work," he said.

She gave him a skeptical look. "You've missed sessions."

"I . . . haven't been well, but I'm ready, ready to double my efforts."

"Why?"

"Why?" he repeated.

"*Why* are you ready to double your efforts?"

"Because," he said, looking at Alexia, "I want to know what it's like to have somebody give a damn."

"You can't do this for anyone else but you," Carter said.

He nodded.

"If you miss any more sessions without notifying us, you will be released, permanently."

"Can I set up a session with you to start my story?"

"I need to see that you're going to follow through on your commitment."

He pursed his lips.

"George," said Jay.

He looked at him.

"You're going to make it."

Heading for the door, George passed Alexia and whispered, "Sorry."

Jay and Rose stood in their usual place, watching the sun dipping into the dappled ocean. Jay looked at her, wondering what exactly it was that made her so beautiful.

"I'm not going to do it," she said.

"You're not?" Jay said, without attempting to conceal his relief.

"I'm not doing the cosmetic makeover."

"Oh."

"See this bag?" She lifted the leather bag slung over her shoulder. "I've had it since I was thirteen." She fingered a tattered corner of the flap. "Bradford tried to eat it. Our dog. 1952. I remember, because it was the year my first daughter was born. It's old-fashioned, discolored, lined. It's history, splendid history." She laughed.

Delight, that was what made her so beautiful, he now realized. Her pervasive delight.

"When all my friends and family come and see me tomorrow, for the last time, they will see me as I am, history imprinted on my face."

"'For the last time?'"

"The moment I'm declared legally dead," she began, "a cryonics team starts to get my circulation going with a heart-lung machine. They cool my body down to 50°F. My blood is washed out and replaced with organ preservation solution. That's when I get driven to the cryonics center for further treatment and then decapitation. My head is embalmed, isn't that lovely? Like a modern day Egyptian burial ritual, embalmed upside down in a thermos bottle of liquid nitrogen." She made it sound like her holiday itinerary. "Most people die too unexpectedly or their brains are too ravaged by disease to get a decent shot. *I will survive.*"

"No, no," said Jay, "you will die. You will take your life on the improbability that you will one day rise from the dead. Instead, you will just die sooner."

Her face dropped like she'd received a blow.

She looked up at him, her blue eyes shiny and moist. "How can it just end?"

And that's when he understood.

It was Saturday. Sunshine flooded through the thin, white curtains of Jenna's apartment, presenting the aftermath of a long night: an empty tequila bottle, a glass ashtray overflowing with cigarette butts, and a rolled up bank note and credit card. Jenna lay face down on a large mattress on the floor, her blond, straggly hair sticking out from under a blue-grey duvet. A loud thumping sounded through the door.

A good-looking, young man stuck his sleepy head out from under the duvet next to her. He squinted into the light. "There's someone at the door."

Again, the door banged.

A pretty, young, dark-haired woman emerged from beneath the duvet on the other side of Jenna. She scrunched up her face. "Jeez," she said, "it sounds like Armageddon."

"Maybe you should get it," the man said.

Jenna looked at the two, not entirely familiar, faces on either side of her, and then underneath the duvet at their naked bodies. She scrambled over the man to get to the bathroom, reappearing in a terrycloth robe. The door banged again.

"Get dressed!" she said to her two bedfellows, gathering their clothes and throwing them on the bed.

"Jenna!" a deep, muffled voice sounded from behind the door.

"Who is it?" the naked girl asked, a tremor in her voice.

"Hurry!" Jenna screamed.

"I don't want any trouble." The young man started eying the window for a possible escape route.

Jenna opened the door.

"Wait!" the man yelled, only half-dressed.

"Sorry, sorry," she said to her visitor, pulling her hair out of her pale face, "I overslept."

George walked in and surveyed the room.

"Hi there!" the young woman chirped, with improbable enthusiasm.

"This is George," Jenna said, "George this is . . ." She searched her memory for their names before giving up. "They were just leaving." She ushered them to the door.

"Nice to meet you!" the woman said, sliding by Jenna and out the door.

Zipping up his trousers, the man slipped out, too, leaving as much distance between him and George as possible. Jenna closed the door.

"Big night," George said.

Jenna walked to the mattress, sat down and put her head in her hands.

George sat down on the only chair in the room. "So, this is the life?"

"Look, if you're going to . . ." Jenna looked up at him. "George?"

"Yes."

"Stand up."

He stood, puzzled.

"My God, you look . . . good . . . *really* good."

He was wearing low-slung faded jeans and sneakers, a white t-shirt and baseball cap, and he was about two-thirds his former size. The bulk that did remain was firm.

"I wish I could say the same about you," he replied.

"When did I last see you?"

"I'm not sure."

"Wow," she said, getting up to make some coffee in the small, bare-bones kitchen.

"We've been talking on the phone, mainly," he added.

"How did you do it?" She rinsed two mugs.

"It's like overhauling a car. You roll up your sleeves and do it, one bit at a time. I just needed some instruction."

She put on the kettle and spooned instant coffee into the mugs. She looked back at him. "Incredible!"

"So, can we start?" he asked.

"Start?"

"My story."

"Oh, God, sorry, yes, you're going to tell me what happened." She rubbed a temple to ease a hangover headache. "You know, Alexia got it out of proportion. My writing is . . . pretty brilliant, actually." She flashed him a cheeky smile.

"I'm just hoping you've still got it in you," George said, "because if I have to wait for Dr. King to help me, I'm going to be lying in an urn in my son's garage."

She put the coffee on the table.

He took a blank pad and a pen out of his satchel and placed it in front of her. "If anything happens to me, give it to my wife and sons."

"Look at you. You're going to live forever."

"In case I don't."

She steadied the pen on the page.

"Can you write with that thing?" he said, referring to the plaster cast on her arm.

"I've had it on so long, I barely notice it," she replied, yawning.

He took in a deep breath. "I can't believe I'm actually going to tell someone. Okay . . ."

She put the pen down.

"Aren't you writing?" he asked.

"Actually, let me first get the gist of it. We've got time. At this point, I just want to get a general overview."

George wasn't happy about this, but began anyway. He had finished school, not knowing what he wanted to do; so he followed his father's footsteps into the motor industry. He married his sister's best friend, because she was, as he put it, 'ready and willing.' He hated his job, but stuck it out for nearly 20 years. His life reminded him of those draw-by-numbers pictures. He had joined the dots (not very well), without really thinking about whether this was the picture he wanted. Then, he started an auto parts dealership. This was a little better, largely because he was running his own business and had a little more money, even if he spent most of it on booze and women. He had grown to accept that his wife and kids—here he hesitated— hated him. He often thought that God had made a mistake, that *he* should have died, not his brother.

"If I'm honest," George said, "the thing I enjoyed most was a good bar fight. Maybe because every time I hit a man, I got to take revenge on my disappointment with life. Jenna?"

She had nodded off. Okay, he had to admit it, that was hardly the hold-your-breath stuff of a Hollywood blockbuster; but he hadn't got to the "turning point," that critical juncture where everything changed, where the man after was no longer the man before. And to think it all happened just six months earlier, with a little bit of news. Amazing how a few words could change everything. He needed his boys to know; not so they would forgive him—he couldn't expect that—but so they would at least see he knew what a terrible mistake he had made. His life was to serve, not as a model, but as a warning. This was all he had to give them. Maybe if his father had told him such a story, his life would have turned out differently.

Jenna was snoring lightly. He walked over and looked at her. His head was sore, very sore. He cursed himself for waiting too long. He pulled a blanket over her and left.

Jay had a worried look on his face. He looked down at the file on his desk; the name "Rose Andrews" stared back at him. Opening the file, he looked at her address: *206 Oak Avenue, The Colony.* He pulled out a telephone directory, found the number he was looking for, and dialed.

A woman answered, "Malibu Police Department, good day."

"Ah, hello. There's someone over in the Colony who I think may try to kill herself tonight. Would it be possible to send someone over?"

"Is she depressed?"

"Ah, no."

"How do you know she wants to kill herself?"

"She told me."

"What was that address?"

"206 Oak Avenue."

"There is no Oak Avenue in the Colony," the woman said.

"There isn't?"

"No."

He put down the phone and searched frantically in her file for her number. He dialed.

A man answered, "Hello."

"Hello," Jay replied, his voice tense, "can I speak to Rose Andrews?"

"You've got the wrong number."

Rose had covered all her bases; she'd falsified her contact details. Jay put down the phone, the blood slowly fading from his face.

Later that night, in a red, chiffon party dress, Rose walked barefoot into her lavish kitchen. A maid in a traditional white blouse and black pinafore dress was wrapping up leftover food in tin foil. Empty champagne bottles stood stacked up against the wall.

"You must take all that food, Maria."

She looked up at Rose. "There's so much here, Mrs. Andrews."

Rose walked up to her. "I'd like you to sleep in my room tonight."

Maria frowned. "Aren't you feeling well?"

"No, I'm not."

"Oh, Mrs. Andrews," her voice cracked.

"You've got the number?" Rose's voice was steady.

"Yes."

"You keep watch over me. The moment I start coughing in my sleep," she said, "you just call that number."

"You're going to be fine," Maria said, resolved that she would be.

"We put on quite a party, didn't we?"

"You were the belle of the ball, ma'am."

Rose smiled and went upstairs.

5

MICKEY LAY BACK on the bench, pushing his final few reps. Robert stood over him, his fingers lightly under the bar, ready to provide support in case of muscle failure on the homestretch.

"Ahhhhg!" Mickey grunted, as Robert kept count.

"Eight."

"Ahhhhg!"

"Nine."

"Ahhhhg!"

"One more."

"Ahhhhhhhhhhhhg!"

Robert lifted the bar onto the metal stand, which let out a resounding clang.

Mickey sat up and turned to face him. He took a few moments to catch his breath. "I'm in love with Alexia and I don't know what to do about it."

Robert looked at him skeptically.

"What?" Mickey asked.

"We have to get ready. We have a partner's meeting."

"That's how you support me through this torture?"

"You fall in lust on a biweekly basis, I think you'll survive."

"This is different. I can't get her out of my head and I can't seem to do anything about it. Every time I see her, I feel like I'm 12 again. I can barely string a sentence together."

"What makes her different from all the others?"

"I don't know." He thought about it. "She's like, a person."

"'She's like, *a person*?'"

"She's not just hot, she's not even *that* hot, but she does stuff, you know? Look at the great work she does, the books she's written. She can . . . think."

"That's never been a priority for you before?"

He thought about it. "No."

"Wow."

"I think I may have found my true love."

"How well do you even know Alexia?"

He shrugged. "That's irrelevant. I can feel it."

"In your pants?"

"Listen, are you going to help me or not?"

"What do you want me to do?"

"I don't know. Just coach me through this . . . so I don't look like such an idiot." He stood up. "I can't help feeling she's *the one*, you know, that I've got to be with her . . . not for a night, *forever*. Like this is the person I have to die with. I know, I know it's crazy. I don't even believe in that soul mate baloney. It's just how it feels."

"Okay, I'm here for you. We'll talk it through. But, we've got our meeting in ten minutes."

Mickey stuck his nose into his armpit. "I'm okay. You go shower. I'll stretch down now and shower later."

"That's sure to charm her," Robert replied.

"Hey, don't underestimate these pheromones," he said, pointing at his armpit.

After Robert's shower, he caught Alexia coming up the stairs. She looked like she'd been crying.

"What's wrong?" he asked.

"I can't find Jenna. She's not answering her phone and she's not at her apartment. I've tried the whole weekend . . ." She was struggling to hold back the tears.

"Hey, she's probably away with friends," Robert said, putting a hand on her arm.

"I've got a horrible feeling about this," she said, shaking her head.

Robert cocked his head consolingly. "You told me this is what she does. This is not someone who keeps regular hours, right? I'm sure she's fine."

Alexia sighed, "I don't know, I hope you're right." She looked up at him. "How are you?"

"Fine."

"Really?"

"We need to get to this meeting."

"I'll join you in a minute. I'm just going to powder my nose."

"Not necessary," he said, smiling at her.

She leaned in and whispered in his ear, "You're so lovely," and walked off.

He stood still, wondering what had just happened.

Carter, Mickey and Jay sat around the Think Tank table. Robert walked in with a waft of just-showered freshness, and took a chair.

"Alexia will be here in a minute," he said.

Mickey was munching on M&M's. He pushed the bowl over to Robert, who looked down at the multi-color galaxy of candy and chocolate-coated nuts.

"No, thanks," he said.

"Go on."

"No!" Robert snapped.

They all turned to him.

". . . Thanks," he added. "I've eaten."

"Sorry I'm late." Alexia said, slipping in and taking a seat.

"Congratulations on the work you all did with George Kelley," Carter began. "I am happy to say that I got it wrong. He lost nearly 40 pounds and cleared his short-term debt. I can't claim a shred of his success for myself—it is all due to him and all of you. I do, however, have some very sad news. Every day we invest our hopes and expertise to uplift the lives of others, and so when one of them dies, we need to remember that, ultimately, we are not in control."

Jay knew it was coming he just didn't expect to hear it now. "Who?" he asked, knowing full well.

"No!" Alexia had gone pale, thinking of another Quest, Inc. client.

"I'm afraid," Carter continued, "that I've just been informed George Kelley died yesterday."

Alexia and Jay went from alarm to confusion.

"Did anyone know he was terminally ill?" Carter asked. They shook their heads. "Shortly before coming here, he was informed he had an inoperable brain tumor. It had very little impact on his general functioning, but he'd been given six months to live. Two days ago, he had a massive stroke and died. It seems he had employed us, or rather *you,* as his redemption squad. And now the story he was so desperate to leave behind," she pursed her lips, "is lost. I made a mistake with George. I had forgotten why the time to act is *today.*"

The sun shone through the stained glass windows of the chapel. Three people sat up front, and no more than three more were scattered throughout the hall. One of them was Jenna. She looked like she hadn't slept; there were dark rings under her eyes. The priest stood at the head of the coffin and said a final prayer. He held out his hand toward Keith, the older of George's two sons, who took his position behind the lectern.

Clearing his throat, Keith began, "Funerals are the time when we say nice things about the dead, but I'm not telling lies. George Kelley failed as a father and husband. He failed as a human being. Let's hope that his memory fades quickly, along with the wounds that he left behind." He walked back to his chair.

Stunned, the priest hastily ended the service.

The two sons and their mother exited the church and walked toward the parking lot.

Jenna approached them from behind. "Excuse me," she said. They stopped and turned to her. "I knew your father."

"I'm sorry about that," Keith replied.

Jenna continued, "We were both trying to turn our lives around. We became friends. George deeply regretted the life he had led. He was trying to make it right."

"Who are you?" he asked, eyes pinched suspiciously.

"A friend," she replied. "There was a lot he wanted you to know." Jenna moved closer. "He told me his story. I finished writing it a couple of hours ago." She held up a manuscript. "Here it is."

Keith looked at the papers in her hand and then up at her face. "You can keep it," he said. "We're not interested."

His brother and mother looked on.

"He knew he had done you wrong," Jenna persisted. "And he knew this wouldn't make it better. But if you read it, you'll see how sorry he was, and more than that, you'll see, despite his failings, your father left behind an important story."

"Yes, he did leave behind one hell of a story," Keith said, losing his temper. "A mistress, young enough to be his daughter, has the nerve to show up at his funeral to hand us his ramblings."

"Look," she said, with new resolution, "take it or don't take it, but I was *not* your father's mistress. We were friends, *period*."

The three of them stood looking at her as she held out the pages.

"I'm not interested," Keith finally said, turning around and walking off to the car.

Chad, the younger brother, and his mother, looking distressed and curious, stood still. Finally, Chad reached out for the pages before he and his mother turned to follow Keith to the car.

Jenna turned around to see Alexia, who up until that moment had been keeping a discreet distance.

"Must have been quite a story," Alexia said.

Jenna nodded.

"Hey, your cast is off."

Jenna looked down at her arm, white from sun deprivation. "Yeah, I got so used to it broken, it feels kind of weird being fixed up."

"Tell me about George."

Jenna took in the fresh smell of wildflowers drifting over from the graveyard. George had instructed her to give the story to his family, but he hadn't specifically said she couldn't share it with anyone else.

"George discovers he's going to die," she began, "and he gets inspired to live. He figures this is it. 'I'll make my last gasp count.' Maybe exercise and eating right will turn the tide on his destiny, but he knows that's unlikely. He just wants to feel what it's like to *drive* his life, like getting a Ferrari for a first and last spin—his metaphor. The story of this realization is his only legacy. If he can't serve as a positive role model to his sons, he'll serve as a horrible warning. His last words: 'Don't wait to drive your life, because it's not long before they take away the keys.'"

Alexia nodded.

"I was so busy throwing away my own life, he almost never got to tell me. I went to see him two days before he died. It felt like his story was written for me. I don't want to die without leaving something behind. I've signed up for a writing program."

"That's great!" Alexia said. "I'll pay for it."

"No. No, thank you. I'm going to get a job, and pay my way."

She should have been happy that Jenna was taking responsibility; but cash offerings were just about Alexia's only connection with her goddaughter and she wasn't sure how she felt about that being taken away.

"I'm glad Quest, Inc. helped," she said.

Jenna looked uncertain. "Well, I wouldn't have met George, so I suppose in a way it did." She turned to go.

"Jenna."

She turned back.

"I want you in my life."

Silence.

"What?" Alexia asked.

"Nothing."

"Life is too short, right? Say what you want to say to me."

"Why did you tell me . . . ?" She halted.

"What?"

"Why did you tell me Mom was going to be okay, that she was going to make it?"

Alexia put her hand to her mouth. "Oh, Jenna."

"Why? Why did you tell me not to worry?"

Alexia walked toward her, arms outstretched, shaking her head. "I'm so sorry."

Jenna pushed her hand away. "No! Tell me why. Why didn't you give me the chance to say goodbye?"

"Oh, God," Alexia said, taking a step back, "I'm *so* sorry."

"Why?" Jenna said, with the full weight of a long delayed accusation.

Alexia's shoulders dropped. "I wasn't lying to you. I was lying to myself. I couldn't face it. It was easier to pretend. I loved your mother. I don't think you know how much I loved your mother. I was reading all these cancer survivor books and I convinced myself that a miracle was possible, right until the very end. I thought if I acknowledged the possibility of her death, I might be contributing to it. I know, stupid, superstitious B.S., but until the very moment the doctor called to tell me she had died, I had convinced myself that she wasn't going to. When it happened, I was shell-shocked. Every time I saw you, I saw her." She took a step closer. "I see her now, your beautiful, beautiful mother. You don't know how much you look like her. Back then I struggled to be with you. It meant facing my loss, it meant facing my own mortality. I was weak. I'm so, so sorry."

Jenna nodded. "I understand. *Now*, I understand. I guess we should have had this discussion a long time ago. I didn't deal with it so well myself." She took a step toward Alexia. "You know you can still talk to her."

Alexia looked puzzled.

"It was something George taught me. I ask her questions and I think about how she would answer. With her, of course, the answer was usually just another question." She chuckled. "But it works, and sometimes I can even hear her voice. If you look, you'll find her. Death isn't as final as I thought."

Alexia nodded. "I'll try it."

Jenna took out her car keys, and kissed Alexia on her cheek, whispering in her ear, "Mom loved you, too." With that she walked away.

Once she was at a safe distance, Alexia sobbed for her dead friend, like she had never sobbed before.

Dr. Jay Lazarus and Rose Andrews stood in their usual place, looking out on the ocean.

She turned to him, "You failed me."

He frowned.

"I'm a coward," she said. "You were supposed to help me build the courage to take the leap."

"To help you sacrifice the rest of your life, potentially years of your life, on the infinitesimally slim possibility of eternity?"

"Most people believed the Wright brothers' chance of flying a heavier-than-air machine was infinitesimally slim. The *New York Times* said that if it was possible, and it was a big *if*, it would take, quote, 'ten million years.' Where would we be without pioneers? Look at you and the work you've done exploring ecstasy, crossing the internal frontier into deeper states of bliss. That's my problem. I never quite had it in me to go first. I was the third woman to fly solo across the Atlantic, the fourth to go around the world. I love life too much to be in the first batch to attempt death and resurrection."

"That's why you didn't do it?"

"Probably," she said. "But there was something else. The party was beautiful. Everyone was there, all my children, grandchildren, friends. Some of them gave little speeches about me—I've lived quite a life, Dr. Jay. We laughed. Did we laugh! And at one point, I had a good, joyful, cleansing cry. We even waltzed! My grandson and I. He looks exactly like Donny did at that age. Donny and I loved to waltz. And then they all left, my birthday was over, and I knew I would never have a birthday quite like that again. Even if I live another few years, many of my older friends will not. Some of my grandchildren will be away at college. It was past 12 o'clock and my birthday was gone, dead.

"I lay in bed thinking, and then it occurred to me that it wasn't any less special. Do you understand? The birthday didn't have to continue for eternity to have purpose, to mean something. It could end, a cosmic blink of the eye, all the sweeter for its brevity."

Jay nodded.

"When I was about three years old," she continued, "my older sister and I were talking about something. I don't remember what, but I remember these words of hers like it was yesterday. She said: 'When we die . . .'

"I immediately ran to my father and said, 'Daddy, daddy, I'm not going to die, am I?'

"He looked down at me and replied, 'Girl, we all die.' My dad had a great way with kids," she laughed.

"'Although,' he added, 'you won't die for a long, long time.' 'But,' I replied, 'one day?' Yes,' he said. That day, I cried until I was too exhausted to cry anymore. I was inconsolable. But I think that day something else happened. Death became my friend, getting me up in the morning, never letting me become complacent. This is one friend that doesn't allow you to put off until tomorrow what you need to do today."

They sat down on a wooden bench overlooking the ocean.

"When you first came here," Jay said, "you called yourself an NDE, a walking near-death experience. We're all NDEs, Mrs. Andrews. Life is a near-death experience. Except, those who know it make sure they live the kind of life that you have."

"It's just," Rose began, "when you adore life as much as I do and it starts to withdraw from you, as it has from me, it's like you're about to be dumped by a lover, and this is one lover that you truly can't live without. I felt desperate, jilted, ready to do anything to keep my love, my everything. Not very gracious, I know."

"But completely understandable."

She turned to him. "About a year ago, Meryl, one of my dearest friends, was diagnosed with terminal cancer. I braced myself for a very tough conversation. This was one time I wouldn't be able to say: 'Don't worry, dear, everything is going to be alright.' Instead, I did the usual handwringing. 'I'm so sorry. Have you had a second opinion? Is there anything I can do?' You know what she said to me?"

Jay shook his head.

"'Never mind, darling. All good things come to an end.' I sort of ignored it at the time. I was so caught up in my own fears of mortality, but now it seems like the most beautiful, gracious way to greet death—*all good things come to an end*. She could've looked bitterly at the absence of a future, but she chose to look gratefully at the richness of her past."

Jay nodded. "Or," he added, "you can simply savor the magnificence of the here and now."

She gave him a wry smile. "Are you trying to make me feel better for throwing away my immortality?"

"There's always the afterlife."

"Who wants to be a ghost?" She looked over the rocky cliff. The light of the setting sun fanned across the ocean in a shimmer of twinkling starlets. "Besides," she said, "one life is miracle enough."

Without telling Carter, Robert had taken her advice. Eighteen people, mostly friends and some supportive ex-clients, had been handpicked to participate in his first public seminar: "Falling Up: Turning Setbacks into Stepping Stones on the Road to Wellness." He had hired a small tutorial room tucked away in the Drescher Graduate Campus at Pepperdine University. The participants were sitting horseshoe-style, with Robert standing up front. The seminar was drawing to a close and so far it had gone well. An old college friend's wife, who Robert had not met before, raised her hand to speak. She had an attractive, intelligent face on a body that was about 35 pounds overweight.

"My weight bounces up and down," she said. "What makes you so sure that yours won't?"

She had given him the opening he hadn't managed to create for himself. His pulse quickened, as he shook his head.

"I'm *not* sure." He let the words hang. "Mostly because I'm still having a love affair with the fridge." He felt unexpectedly relieved that it was done.

After a short silence, he continued. "When my colleagues helped me uncover my self-sabotage, I made some tough decisions. I gave up my father's love, which wasn't real love anyway. And by doing this session, I'm manning up to my fear of failure. The mistake is in thinking that knowing the cause, or even dealing with the cause, is the cure. In my case, at least, the effect remained. I had learned to face stress with sugar and fat. Overeating is still my conditioned response to negative emotional states. I'm slowly substituting other forms of stress relief—working out, blissful meditation, low calorie food—but do I still slip up? Yes. But now, instead of pretending I don't, which only adds more stress, increasing the chances of relapse, I'm coming clean with you. I fight this battle every day. I know I'm supposed to stand in front of you as the guru, the do-it-right-every-time-know-it-all. But that would be a lie. *Nobody* does it right every time; *nobody* knows it all. It's time to kill the guru. I'm on this journey, just like you. The only difference between us is that I may have just dedicated a little more time to finding the answers."

The group sat silently, taking it in.

Finally, the same lady spoke. "If your success isn't certain," she said, "what chance is there for the rest of us?"

She had expressed one of his key concerns. If the teacher revealed his vulnerability, would it not break the student's confidence, both in the teacher and himself? He had no other option; he had given up pretending.

"Look," he said, "I may be a more effective coach than I am a player. You may have a better chance than me. But all of us, even the very *best* of us, are fallible. Here's the bad news: according to the latest edition of *Psychology Today*, the majority of addicts, whether it's overeating, nicotine, alcohol, gambling or cocaine, will relapse within a year. Here's the good news: the majority will be clean five years later. In most cases, relapse is just that, a relapse on the road to recovery. Use relapse as a learning opportunity. Ask yourself, what happened? What can I do to avoid slipping up again? We may not win every battle, but we can win the war. Ultimate victory lies in destroying that conditioned response. After intensive research, I now believe I have the weapons to do that. Next month, I'd like to share that arsenal with you—after I've finished testing it on myself."

It was unclear to Robert whether his audience was willing to replace a dethroned guru with a simple teacher who didn't always get it right. The plan was to hand out evaluation forms to find out. The problem was, as he turned to his right to pick them up, he saw that someone had slipped into the room. The sight sent such a tornado of emotion rushing through him, that with his train of thought smashed, he simply turned back to the audience to inform them the session was over.

All the while, in his peripheral vision, he saw his wife, Roxanne Stewart.

"Don't break my heart, don't do it."

Mickey was taking a call, as he sat on the toilet. He had seen it was Simon, who had long developed immunity to Mickey's bodily functions. Besides, this couldn't wait. Simon was about to tell him whether or not their proposal for the Blu Bay property development had been successful.

"Go on . . . tell me." Mickey sat back against the cistern. He shut his eyes, letting the news penetrate the pleasure center of his brain. "Yes!" He got up, punching his first in the air with his pants around his ankles. "You little genius, you little *genius!*" He sat down. "Blu Bay here we come. You know what this means? We can replicate this a dozen times . . . I know, I know, I'll have to tell them—'Bye-bye, Quest, Inc.'"

It was the Friday before the start of a long weekend. Carter was in the Think Tank, at the head of the boardroom table. She stared ahead, her laptop closed, a blue file next to it. Victoria was due shortly. This would be Quest, Inc.'s last opportunity to present their case before Victoria published. Carter had assembled the facts in her head at least a dozen times. She knew it would be a mistake to candy coat anything. There would be no Powerpoint, no PR spiel, no spin; just an honest reckoning of the facts. If Victoria wanted the naked truth, Carter would strip it down for her.

Jay stood outside, his hand on the door handle. He had something to say to Carter, but hesitation paralyzed the small muscles in his fingers. Jay knew that the mating dance required a subtle sequence of approach and retreat. A full frontal declaration killed the seduction of uncertainty. Yet, right now, he was sure nothing less was required. He knocked.

Carter stood up. "Come in."

He walked in, closing the door behind him. "Look," his voice was urgent, "I don't want to wake up one day in an old people's home with a half-ton of regret and no prostate. I've got to know that I tried. So here it is: I screwed up. I should never have left. I thought life was a journey that I had to take alone. I was wrong. I want you back. If you're not prepared to try again, I'll accept your decision, but I don't want you to have any confusion about how I feel: I want you in my life, Carter."

"I know."

"You know?"

". . . How you feel."

"So?" His heart beat like horses' hooves.

Very slowly, she turned her head once, from side to side. The regal subtlety of the gesture was reminiscent of a medieval queen signaling the death penalty.

He nodded. It was awful, but at least he knew he had given it a shot. He wouldn't be on his deathbed wondering about that.

Carter should have sat down, but she didn't. Instead, she continued staring at him. That's when Jay realized her mind was made up— her heart wasn't.

As he took a step toward her, the door opened. It was Alexia and Robert.

"Come in!" Carter called, trying to sound natural.

"Victoria is here," Robert replied, ushering her in. He and Alexia had the same feeling; they were delivering their executioner.

"Oh . . . kay." Carter patted the back of her hair.

Victoria was at least ten minutes early. Carter had planned to have a short meeting with the team before she arrived. Now, candor really was the only option.

"I don't have very long," Victoria said.

"We do appreciate you agreeing to meet with us before you publish. Please take a seat."

Reluctantly, she did. The rest of the team followed, except Mickey, who had not arrived.

"I really don't think there's anything you can add, at this point," Victoria said.

"Well," Carter replied, "I'm not sure you're fully aware of everything that's happened over the months that you've been, ah . . ." She tried to find a word that was less associated with the criminal-justice system, but couldn't think of one, ". . . *investigating* us. We just wanted to give you an overview of everyone's progress."

Victoria deigned her with a nod.

Carter took in a deep breath. This was Judgment Day. She opened the blue file. "Sam Nash," she began, "has not just been re-cruited back into his old company, he's tipped for promotion. You can talk to his boss. In fact, I've got his contact details for you here." She paged through to a letter. "This is from Leo Zubkin. He's work-ing as a mechanic, and it's just to thank us for, as he puts it . . ." she looked down at the page "'. . . helping me find my calling.'" Looking back up. "He says he's happier than he's ever been. Frank Brogan has reconciled with his daughter, regularly sees his grandson and has a multiracial group of friends. He's also sent us a testimonial."

Arms folded, Victoria opened her mouth. Carter put up her hand. "I know, I know, what about the others, right? I am" —she struggled to say the word— "*disappointed* that Laura Cobb is back on the streets. She has more contact with her family, she claims she's better off for her time with us, but yes, she's on the streets and that is a disappointment to me. Had we properly interviewed her up front, we would have realized that she had little desire to change."

"That's where we differ." Jay cut in, "I believe we helped recon-cile Laura to her mission."

Robert nodded, "I'd have to agree with that."

"Well, as you can see," Carter said, "we don't always share the same view. You, of course, will make up your own mind." She glanced down at her notes. "Raelene Cleaver had the ability to be a major force in international golf, and she's given up the game to be-come"—her lip curled—"a glamour model. That upsets me too, but I think being here helped her clarify what she wanted, and what she was prepared to do to get it."

"We're not here to dictate their quest," Jay added, "just help guide them on it."

Victoria looked straight ahead, revealing nothing.

"Jenna Lowe," Carter continued, "I don't know, maybe something has sprouted, it's too early to tell if the roots will take hold."

"It's taken hold," Alexia said, "I'm not sure how much it had to do with us, but she's a different person. I should know. Jenna is my goddaughter."

Before Carter could register her surprise, the door opened and Mickey stepped in. He looked around the room, somewhat depleted after a hard night of partying; but also emboldened by his recent property development victory.

"Victoria? How delightful. Are you joining our little family?"

"Sit down," Carter said.

Mickey complied, extending the disruption with the scrape of his chair. Like a kid who was about to drop out of school, he felt a reckless lack of need for good behavior. The news would be broken straight after this meeting. It wouldn't be easy; he loved them, but there were bigger fish to fry. His days of tap dancing for the likes of Victoria Holt were over. He looked over at Alexia and felt his heart straining at his ribcage. Leaving would either force her to see what she was missing or force him to forget. His decision was being reinforced from every direction.

While Mickey gazed at Alexia, Alexia gazed at Robert. Robert was thinking of something else—what would happen later, when he met his wife for dinner.

Carter turned to Victoria. "You want to know about my sister." She inhaled deeply. "For many years, I kept trying to help her. Nothing I've ever done has worked. She's still an addict, she's still on the streets." Carter gave a resigned shrug. "Change is a door that opens from the inside. She hasn't found that door yet." She slid the blue file to Robert, who placed it in front of Victoria.

There was a hard edge of silence, as Victoria took her time to respond.

Finally, she began. "Your sister may not want to change, but what about the people who do, but don't manage to? Personal transformation is perhaps not as cut-and-dry as you would have the world believe."

Carter thought about it. "Sometimes, I feel that life is a piece of clay, a thing you can mold to your heart's desire. At other times, it feels more like a fish—slippery, unfathomable, a thing you have to lure and coax. But even if it is more of a fish, you still need to go for it, know what you want to do with it. We help people fish for their lives; we just can't always say what they're going to catch."

"I had a cigarette," Victoria said.

There was a collective deflation. The one thing they had counted on was Victoria Holt's personal triumph over nicotine. If that was lost, everything was.

"Just one," she said, looking at Jay, "a few weeks ago. I couldn't finish it. Felt like a slave, like I'd given up on myself, sacrificed my free will. That's what it is, right? At the end of the day: personal choice. There's no such thing as change without choice. What this agency reminded me is who's in charge, and it's not any of you, it's me. It's gone beyond smoking. I've been making some other changes too. I must tell you," she said, looking around the table, "I certainly didn't arrive here expecting to get anything out of it personally. If you want to know the truth, I came here to expose this industry's exaggerated promises and hypocrisy."

"*Hypokrites,*" Jay said, "was a stage actor in ancient Greece: one who pretends to be something he's not. None of us are pretending. Do we get it wrong in our own lives? *Spectacularly,* but an alcoholic can sincerely preach the importance of abstinence and still fall off the wagon."

"There was a time when I thought I had to pretend," Robert said. "That was a mistake. My fallibility is now part of my teaching."

Victoria took another long pause. "The promise of a 'quick easy fix' is not just a lie, it sows the seeds of disappointment and self-defeat. It corrupts the value of what you do. Because, yes, there is something in what you do."

Carter knew this was as close as Victoria Holt was ever going to come to praise, and so this little scrap was literally the answer to her prayers.

"Now," Victoria said, "if you think I'm going to write a song of praise to the five of you, you're mistaken; but I will acknowledge where acknowledgement is due."

"That's all we were hoping for," Carter replied.

"Good," she said, getting up. "Then I should be getting on with it. My editor wants this out early next week."

Against all the odds, it looked like Quest, Inc. was actually going to get a positive review in one of the world's biggest publications. The relief in the room was palpable. They led Victoria out. Carter stayed behind, a smile spreading on her face, as she gave a private prayer of thanks. Jay returned, closing the door behind him. They looked at each other. There were those damn blue eyes of his that made Carter want to dive in and take a swim. High on the wave of their victory, her prudence receded. Elation hid the cost of daring. In lockstep, they closed in on each other.

As Jay kissed Carter, he was acutely attuned to the symphony of sensation in his mouth, the smooth confluence of pressure, moisture and temperature. Pleasing as the physics of it was, there was a transcendent element. He was kissing *Carter*. Beautiful *Carter*. Regal, lovely, wise, resplendent *Carter*. If the face was the window to the soul, right then their souls were playing, (he felt a rise of laughter), dancing, and then, as his heart fluttered, gliding on the wings of one another.

And then the door opened and the lovebirds fell out of the sky. They turned to see two policemen—and for a surreal, retrogressive moment, Jay and Carter had the same thought, that they were breaking some antiquated state morality law.

Carter was the first to summon the faculty of language. "What's going on?"

Robert, Alexia and Mickey were trailing helplessly behind.

"Sir," the first policeman said, "are you Dr. Jay Lazarus?"

"I am," Jay replied.

"We have a warrant for your arrest."

Jay nodded, as if this was less of a surprise than kissing Carter.

As the other officer began to cuff him and read his Miranda rights, Carter didn't just look like she'd crashed down to the ground; but rather, she'd been sucked through to the burning core of the earth. "What the hell is going on?!"

"Officer?" Jay asked, not wanting to implicate himself.

"We have evidence that you have been, and may still be in possession of the illegal drug MDMA, otherwise known as Ecstasy."

Carter cupped her hand over her nose and mouth, as she saw everything they had built come crashing down. Robert had risen and now Jay would fall, and with it all their fortunes. Later that night, another metaphor for life would strike her: a yo-yo. At this point, her focus was on Jay's face, which had taken on the reflection of a strobe light. Victoria Holt had followed the others back in; it was the flaring of her camera flash.

To read the first pages of the 2nd book
in the Quest, Inc. series, please go to

www.questincseries.com

Acknowledgements

According to Joseph Campbell, at the center of all mythology is the hero's quest. Along his journey, the hero meets with mentors to get advice or training for the adventure ahead. I certainly don't consider myself a hero, but I do feel as though I've just completed a quest, and I could not have done it without all my gracious mentors and service providers.

Thank you to: Colin Lumb, for seeing the vision from the beginning and bolstering my self-belief with endless love and enthusiasm; my story coach, Donovan Marsh, one of the world's top up-and-coming filmmakers—this is a much better book because of you; my various editors along the way, Allison Itterly, Willy Mathes, Karen Lieberman and Debbie Klein; Brendan Pollecutt, for multiple reads, insightful comments and helping to keep things American; Cindy Diamond, for shooting straight from the hip and often hitting the bull's eye; Rick Alan, for the wisdom of active listening over advising; cover designers, Karrie Ross and Claire van Niekerk; cover photographer, Cameron Whitman; and headshot photographer, Ashley Taylor.

For reading and evaluating: Nicole Abel, Tamara Botha, Lee Cohen, Peter Darroll, Jacques de Villiers, Catherine Daymond, Sean Dippnall, Ellen Durrant, Nimrod Geva, Cassandra Hove, Scott Irving, Zev Krengel, Leeron Mazor, Joshua Lindberg, Gareth Mcneill, Athenea Mills, Ray Mirvis, Jane O'Brien, Lekita Pretorius, Sue Rosen, Steven Scheer, Martha Scott and Larissa Smit.

I am used to writing non-fiction where quotes are clearly attributed and references provided. That would not be appropriate for fiction. Still, the works of many writers, psychologists and figures from the self-help movement have influenced this book. I want to acknowledge Bob Burg, Robert Cialdini, Alain De Botton, Anders

Ericsson, Sigmund Freud, Malcolm Gladwell, Daniel Goleman, John, C. Maxwell, Raj Persaud, Bill Phillips, Anthony Robbins and Martin Seligman.

The world of publishing is undergoing a revolution—a big thank you to Steven Jackson, Steve Himes and all the good people at Telemachus Press for helping me unlock this brave new world.

Finally, "build it and they will come" is a lie. Build it and market it until you're blue in the face, and they *may* come. A special thank you to Niel Malan for your marketing genius. Thank you also to Michael Jackson, John Kremer, John Locke, Dan Poynter and D.D. Scott. Now, let's hope they come!